# THE LOST PORTRAIT

## *an art crime mystery*

# AK WELLER

**Westley Enterprises Publishing**
Helena, Montana
www.westleyenterprises.com

ISBN 979-8-9916308-5-6 (Paperback)
ISBN 979-8-9916308-0-1 (eBook)

*for John.*

# ALSO BY AK WELLER

*Enemy Closer*
*House on Fire*
*Bigger Fish*
*No Port in a Storm*

# CONTENTS

# REFERENCED WORKS

*In Order of Appearance*

In order not to run afoul of U.S. and international copyright laws, the following artworks have not been reproduced here. Visit akweller.com/gallery to see public domain photographs of the artworks where available, and links to any photographs that aren't in the public domain.


Turner, Joseph Mallord William. *Glaucus and Scylla.* 1841, Kimbell Art Museum, Fort Worth.

Caillebotte, Gustave. *On the Pont de l'Europe.* 1876-1877, Kimbell Art Museum, Fort Worth.

Caravaggio (Michelangelo Merisi). *The Cardsharps.* c. 1595. Kimbell Art Museum, Fort Worth.

Caillebotte, Gustave. *Landscape with Haystacks (Paysage aux meules de paille).* c. 1874. Private Collection.

Caillebotte, Gustave. *Man at the Window (Jeune homme a sa fenêtre).* 1875. Getty Center, Los Angeles.

Caillebotte, Gustave. *The Parquet Planers (Les raboteurs de parquet).* 1875. Private Collection.

Stillman, Marie Spartali. *Mariana.* c. 1867-1869. Private Collection.

Vermeer, Johannes. *The Concert.* c. 1664. Whereabouts unknown since the Isabella Stewart Gardner Museum theft in 1990.

Christenson, Mikel. *Reproduction of Caillebotte's On the Pont de l'Europe.* 2024-2025. Private Collection.


Eva Riordan is an entirely fictional artist. References to works by the American artist Andrew Wyeth (1917-2009) are also entirely fictional, as are allusions to his relationship with Eva Riordan.

# *The Lost Portrait*

I WAS HALF ASLEEP, visions of recumbent nudes on desert backdrops filling my mind, when my stomach leapt into my throat. A hand covered mine and squeezed with violent urgency. I opened my eyes, but the woman sitting next to me had already moved her shaking hand back into her lap, where it twisted together with her other hand and the lumpy, gray scarf she clutched.

Her profile was sharp, alabaster perfection against the darkness all around us. Most of the other passengers had turned off their reading lights and were trying to sleep through the turbulent last leg of our flight, but my neighbor was wide awake. I wondered if the light directed at her face was making her uncomfortable, or if her wide, staring eyes saw anything at all.

As the plane gave another lurch, a squeak popped out of her mouth and seemed to hang in the air for a moment. She forced a slow breath in, then out, and turned to me.

"Sorry," she breathed.

That hunted animal look in her eyes, which were beginning

to tear up, made my heart hurt for her. I reached over and took her hand, asking, "Does it help?"

"A little, yeah," she answered. She hung her head and took a few more breaths.

"What's your name?" I asked.

"Maddie."

"I'm Claire."

The plane began to lose altitude again, more gently this time. The ding of the Fasten Seatbelts light preceded the captain's voice coolly informing us that we were beginning our final decent into DFW Airport. It was sixty-eight degrees on the ground, with a light rain and five mile-per-hour winds from the southeast. He warned us the landing would be quick and a little bumpy, and I wished he hadn't. Maddie's hand twitched in mine, and I squeezed it a little harder.

I asked, "Do you want a hear a story? It might be boring, but we'll be on the ground by the end."

"Okay."

She closed her eyes, almost like she hoped my story would lull her to sleep. I guessed she was about twenty years old—probably a college student. This could be her first time on a plane, and maybe it would be her last. She was almost young enough to be my daughter, a thought that painfully blanked out my mind for a moment. I had to focus to remember the promised story.

Lowering my voice to exclude eavesdroppers, I began, "When I was eight years old, my aunt Eva shared a secret with me that she never told anyone else. Aunt Eva lived in a big, empty old house in Pasadena. She took me down to the basement and unlocked a door, and inside was a safe as tall as she was."

I paused. Could I make the story more thrilling? I had a few respectable talents, but storytelling wasn't one of them. I decided to stick with the facts.

"She unlocked the safe and before she opened it, she made me promise I'd never tell anyone what was inside. Then she warned me it was a grown up thing that I might not like as much as she did, but she loved it more than anything else she owned, and she wanted me to have it after she died.

"She opened the door and took out a painting. It was about eighteen inches long and twelve tall, not very big. There wasn't even a frame on it. 'Claire,' she said, 'Do you know who Andrew Wyeth is?' I told her I did. She was the one who taught me about him. She turned the painting around and told me Andrew Wyeth painted it. It was a naked woman lying in the desert. It was my aunt Eva, but younger, her hair long and dark. She only showed it to me for a second. I think she was embarrassed. She put the painting back in the safe, closed it, and led me out of the room.

"'Someday I'll tell you about the day he painted it,' she said. But she never did tell me, because I went home the next day and the day after that, she died. When I asked people about the painting in her safe and what would happen to it, no one knew what I was talking about. I was just a kid, and no one really listened to me. It didn't help that I couldn't tell them what the painting looked like or who painted it, because Aunt Eva made me promise not to tell.

"That was thirty years ago, and I've been looking for that painting ever since. That's why I was in Chicago. I thought I'd found it, but it turned out to be another dead end. I can't even prove Andrew Wyeth and Eva Riordan ever met, or that the painting ever existed. But I'm not going to give up."

As I spoke the last few words, a bit more impassioned and loud than I meant to be, the landing gear made contact with the ground and we bumped and shuddered to a near stop on the dark, wet runway. We began to taxi in an unhurried path toward our arrival gate, and Maddie's hand in mine relaxed so much I wondered if she had fallen asleep. I looked at her and saw her eyes were still wide, but not with fear.

"Your aunt was Eva Riordan?" she whispered.

"Yes. My great aunt, actually. You've heard of her?"

"We just learned about her in class."

"Well here's something you can tell your professor and your classmates if you want to impress them: Aunt Eva never painted anything if she didn't dream it first. A lot of people think the Rouen Cathedral was painted *plein air*, but Aunt Eva never stepped foot in France."

"Why not?" Maddie asked.

I realized I was still holding her hand, a gesture which now felt awkward and forced. Smoothly releasing it under the guise of pulling on my jacket, I said, "She was afraid to fly."

Maddie smiled, perhaps pleased that she and the famous artist had something in common. She asked, "Can I tell my professor about the painting?"

I wanted to say no, but the word wouldn't come out. "If you want to. She probably won't believe you, though."

Our plane arrived at the gate and stopped at last. Maddie and I chatted a bit more while the passengers shuffled off the plane, then parted ways just outside the secure area of the airport. I pretended to need the bathroom so she wouldn't have to walk all the way to the arrivals curb with me.

At half past three in the morning, DFW Airport was as deserted and quiet as I'd ever known it. I had the women's restroom to myself, so I decided to take a moment and clean myself up. A last minute stop at the Art Institute of Chicago had cost me a missed flight, and my mad, unsuccessful dash through O'Hare to catch the plane had left me sweaty and disheveled. A wiser woman might have used the four-hour wait for the next flight, the red-eye, to wash her face and brush her hair, but I'd opted for an uncomfortable nap instead.

Thanks to that decision, and perhaps also to the nearly forty years I'd spent on this earth, the reflection in the mirror was very little to my liking. There were bags under my eyes, and my hair was so tangled I didn't even try to brush it. I'd baby it when I got home. For now I pulled my waist-length, copper locks into a messy ponytail and called it good. After I splashed some cold water on my face, patted it dry with paper towels, and smeared on some moisturizer, I felt a tiny bit better. I slapped on some deodorant and brushed my teeth, and then I was ready to face the outside world; but I wasn't ready to go home.

I had been so certain this time. The self-styled rare art dealer in Chicago—a charlatan, it turned out—had told me the piece in his client's private collection was a nude painted by Andrew Wyeth when he was on vacation in Santa Fe, New Mexico in 1961. The dimensions were right, and the subject was a white woman with long, dark hair. I'd flown to Chicago at once, giddy with anticipation.

Well, the "rare art dealer" hadn't been entirely truthful or entirely false. His client did indeed own a painting of a nude in the desert, but it wasn't my aunt, and it *definitely* wasn't a Wyeth. No one could have mistaken those bold, almost childish brushstrokes and garish primary colors for the work of Andrew Wyeth's hand. His paintings had a subtle, desaturated quiet about them, that sandpapery texture of a million crisscrossing strokes of his brush, and a depth that photographs couldn't capture.

Now I felt foolish, gullible, and angry. Why hadn't I asked to see a photograph of the painting before I jumped on an airplane? I was just a silly woman with more money than sense who needed to get a real life before she wasted her inheritance on last-minute travel arrangements and pricy dinners for reticent art world insiders.

I left the bathroom and headed for the parking garage, still lost in self-deprecating thoughts. Ren would agree with me—foolish, gullible, et cetera—if he ever found the fortitude to tell me the truth. Instead he'd happily handed over the funds I'd needed, told me to enjoy my "trip to Florence," and asked me to let him know when I was safely home again.

I needed to hire a meaner financial manager. A real ball-buster, like his father had been.

For a moment I was so angry that I stopped, sat down, yanked out my phone, and hacked out a text to Ren.

"I'm back. You shouldn't have let me go. What a waste of time. Thanks a lot."

Leaving the nastygram unsent, I finished the trek to the parking garage and found Lucius sitting right where I'd left him. The sight of my car—another expense Ren should have talked me out of—made my pulse slow, then pick up again as excitement replaced anger.

No one really *needed* a Dodge Challenger Hellcat. It was too fast and noisy for a normal person, and no use at all to a serious auto connoisseur. But I was just the sort of person Dodge had in mind when they designed it. I liked my cars fast and noisy, and I had the resources to snap up a fetish auto the moment I found a used, blue one for sale.

Someone had left a two-inch, black mark on the driver's side door. I carefully scratched it off with a thumbnail, realizing only after I'd been clucking over the spot for a whole minute that I was alone in a parking garage in the wee hours of the morning. I hurried to climb inside, throw my carryon in the passenger seat, and lock the doors behind me.

I barely remembered the drive from DFW Airport to downtown Fort Worth. I was probably too tired to be driving at all, and it didn't help that I was lost in thought again the moment Lucius' supercharged engine roared to life. I managed to find my way safely to my apartment's parking garage, where I left Lucius and my carryon and headed not upstairs, but out onto the street.

The May night was almost cold by my standards, but at least the drizzle had let up, and it wasn't nearly as windy as Chicago had been. The bars were all closed, and the early bird diners wouldn't be open for another hour, so I just walked. Downtown Fort Worth felt safe and familiar, but a tug from my conscience made me pull out my phone again.

I edited my earlier text to Ren to say, "I'm back. It was a bust. Too wired to go home."

I hit Send, and he replied within seconds.

"Go to bed."

"Why?"

"Remember what we talked about? How you're not safe just because you're not scared? This is one of those times."

"You're such a mother hen."

I couldn't help but smile at his response. "I can cluck all night."

"Fine. I give up. Good night."

Having given in, I couldn't justify doing anything but turning around and heading back to my apartment. The ten-minute walk made me so tired I was glad to see the front door to my apartment complex and the promise of a warm bed within.

A man was sleeping under a tarp in the meager shelter of the concrete steps leading from the street to the posh apartment's secure front door. As I passed him, a hand darted out toward my ankle and I skipped away, adrenaline shooting through me like fire. I scurried up the stairs, let myself inside, and peered through the glass at the man, who was now sitting up and gazing blankly across the darkened street.

Maybe Ren was right, and downtown wasn't as safe as I imagined. Or maybe the man thought I was someone or something else and hadn't meant to scare me. I watched him until he lay back down, then fetched my carryon from my car and took the garage elevator to the twenty-first floor.

I let myself into my apartment, savoring the cave-like echo of my door closing. I poured myself a generous glass of wine and walked out onto my balcony to watch the sun rise over the Fort Worth skyline. Since dawn was still an hour or more in the future, I had plenty of time to savor my pinot noir and collect my thoughts.

By my count, this ill-fated trip to Chicago was my eighty-second "trip to Florence" in search of Aunt Eva's lost masterpiece. The first had been twenty years ago, when I was eighteen. That averaged out to roughly two trips a year, though they'd become more frequent in the last five years or so.

I didn't need Ren to tell me I was wasting my time and resources. I already knew it. But what else could I do? I'd been all over the world chasing down a painting I was beginning to doubt really existed, a painting I'd once been certain would be hanging safe and sound in pride of place in my art gallery by the time I was forty.

As the wine hit my empty stomach, I remembered holding Maddie's hand and how frightened and helpless she'd been. It felt good to have helped get her through those last few minutes of the flight, but I should have noticed her distress sooner and done more. I was too wrapped up in my own stupid mission.

I didn't need more money, more time, or more leads. What I needed was help, and not the sort I could get from Ren or from private investigators, art dealers, and internet sleuths. After thirty years, I could no longer deny the reality that whoever had the Wyeth knew they had no right to it. It would never see the light of day through my efforts alone. I needed someone a little more… flexible.

I WOKE UP IN BED with no memory of getting there. A cheerful whistle, like a catcall, came from my nightstand. I found my phone plugged in and saw not one but three texts from Ren. I assumed the third had woken me, since all else was quiet and serene in my bedroom.

"Meet for lunch?" the first message had invited just after 10:00 a.m.

Then, "Nvm, I have a meeting."

"Text me when you wake up." This last had arrived a few seconds ago.

It was 12:16 now. Vague memories filtered into my brain: watching the sun rise, finishing the bottle of pinot noir, and halfheartedly pulling my blackout curtains closed against the incoming day. That red-eye had really screwed up my internal clock.

"I'm awake. On the night shift tonight. Let's have dinner," I replied. He sent a thumbs up, and I replaced the phone on my nightstand and considered falling back asleep.

Enough sunlight made it through my curtains that I had to roll away from the windows to block it out. I was thirsty, but not thirsty enough to get up. My legs felt heavy, like they were still asleep, and a pleasant emptiness in my stomach made me dream of scrambled eggs and little chunks of perfectly ripe avocado. I must have turned on my diffuser before I went to bed, because my room smelled of lingering peppermint and lavender.

I could feel myself slipping into sleep again when my phone rang, and the accompanying jolt of panic put an end to my plans of sleeping the day away.

Only one contact in my phone ever called instead of texting. Even my boss, clients, and parents texted. Even Ren's eighty-nine-year-old father. Snatching up my phone, I saw the name on the screen—Pamela Larson—and let out a despairing sigh. What now?

"Hey, Pam," I said briskly, as though we didn't both know how little I enjoyed our talks. "What's up?"

Her voice, quaky at the best of times, was nearly unintelligible now. "Claire. I haven't seen him since he came home from work on Friday. The house is dark… I hate to do this to you, but I'm so worried. I tried to call him this morning, and it went straight to voicemail. Should I call the police?"

"No, I'll take care of it. I'll head over now. Thanks for letting me know. Try not to worry, okay? I'm sure he's fine."

My grandiose plans for hair care would have to wait a bit longer. I got dressed in clothes I normally wore for organizing gigs in the messiest of houses—tight leggings, old t-shirt, older tennis shoes, and a denim jacket of 1990s vintage—and hastily re-tied my tangled ponytail before heading back down to the parking garage. I threw off my jacket as soon as I got in the Hellcat and cranked up the AC. It was going to be one of those days in Texas.

Pam hadn't seen Marty since Friday evening. It was Tuesday afternoon now. As hard as I fought to stay calm while I navigated to my ex-husband's house in White Settlement, I couldn't deny the reality of the situation. All Marty cared about was his job. To hear him tell it, the job was all he had left. If he missed work Monday and was still at home today, something bad must have happened. I should have been preparing myself for the worst, but a steady stream of unfounded optimism carried me all the way there.

I pulled into the driveway, doused Lucius' ungodly loud engine, and did a quick internet query on my phone. Was yesterday Memorial Day? Indeed it was. Maybe Marty had taken an extra day off. Steeling myself, I got out of the car and waved toward the neighboring house, from which I knew Pam would be watching me.

Though I knocked on the front door, it was more of a warning than a request to enter. I had a key, so I let myself inside and immediately recoiled at the smells that assaulted my nose. Spoiled food, unwashed laundry, stale beer, maybe a hint of vomit? Not death, though. I knew what death smelled like, and the absence of that unique aroma made me dizzy with relief. I left the front door open on my way into the living room.

"Marty?" I called, finding the living room empty. "Helloooooooo? Where are you?"

The house was cool, thank God. I couldn't bear the thought of how it would smell if his AC broke again. I opened every window I passed and switched on the ceiling fans, grabbing the first empty paper bag I came across and filling it with trash as I continued through the house.

The kitchen was as expected, not a single dish washed since the last time I'd been here. Trash overflowing, crusted food in pans on the stove, takeout containers on every surface, and of course those empty liquor bottles he didn't even bother to hide anymore. I breathed through my mouth, almost started cleaning, and changed my mind when I remembered I still hadn't found Marty.

Compared to the living room and kitchen, the rest of the house wasn't all that bad. The downstairs bedrooms, bathroom, and laundry room looked untouched and dusty. Upstairs, I followed my nose into the master bedroom and found him at last. Fully clothed, he was sound asleep on top of the covers, a neat little pile of puke lying next to him on what used to be a white quilt.

For ten seconds, I watched his chest rise and fall, and then I stepped into the hallway and sat down on the floor. From under my t-shirt I withdrew a tiny, golden cross on its chain, gripping it in one fist until my palm hurt. Finding him like this, right on the heels of that idiotic trip to Chicago, was too much. I let a few tears escape, but I managed to get a hold of myself before the real waterworks started. I had work to do, and little enough time to do it.

Easing to my feet, I waited for a spell of light headedness to pass before I returned to the bedroom. I'd slept through breakfast and hadn't had time for lunch, and now I'd be lucky if I had my appetite back by dinnertime. I opened the curtains and the windows, turned on the fan, and cleaned up the puke before shaking Marty awake. I left him to pull himself out of bed while I got the shower running.

He was on his feet when I came back, a good sign. At six feet, three inches and 180 pounds (last time I checked), my erstwhile husband was looking exceptionally haggard in the harsh daylight I'd let into his bedroom. He swayed, then sat, blinking at me as though trying to remember who I was.

"It's Tuesday," I said. "Do you have the day off?"

"The week." His voice was a painful rasp that made me clear my own throat out of sympathy.

"I wish you'd let me know. Pam was worried sick."

"I told her. She must have forgotten."

He stood again and peeled off his shirt, already heading for the shower. I left him to it and stripped the bed, returning downstairs to toss everything in the washing machine before tackling the kitchen.

Three hours later, I was on my way home again, dreaming of my own shower. Ceiling-mounted shower head, steamer, clean white tiles on the floor, spotless glass walls, overpriced shampoos and body scrubs and deep conditioners arranged by height, shape, and color. It was always my first stop after a particularly nasty clean-up. Today I took the extra step of working an entire bottle of conditioner into my dry hair, sitting on the shower bench while I carefully separated the dreaded tangles and steam saturated the air around me.

I enjoyed the steam and hot water until both ran out, threw on a robe, and made a beeline for the kitchen. Weak with hunger, I stood in front of the open fridge and hoovered up half an avocado, two slices of mozzarella, and a handful of cherry tomatoes before the hunger pangs faded away.

Then I had nothing to do but while away the hours until it was time to meet Ren for dinner. He'd chosen a pricy Brazilian restaurant downtown, which in my experience meant one of two things: He had exciting news to share with me, or he was going to give me a lecture.

*

Ren, or Preston Murphy Renner IV, was all of twenty years old when we met at my great aunt's funeral. My parents had chosen his father, Preston Murphy Renner III, as the conservator of the substantial inheritance Aunt Eva left me. Ren had taken over the reins when his father retired four years ago, and since then I'd enjoyed a much more agreeable and less risk-averse barrier between me and my fortune.

It had been Ren's father's idea to convert his conservatorship role into that of a financial manager when I turned eighteen, and at the time it seemed like a good idea. I knew nothing about money, and Mr. Renner had managed to grow my aunt's gift even as I spent it. He got my parents on board before approaching me with the idea. Though the arrangement was entirely voluntary, and I could take control of my own assets whenever I wanted, I had no intention of firing Ren. I'd seen enough of my own poor money management skills to know how lucky I was to have help.

As I followed the restaurant's hostess to the table where Ren was waiting, I couldn't help but smile to myself at the memory of eighteen-year-old me meeting Ren again when he had just celebrated his thirtieth birthday. I was immediately smitten. At six feet tall, with an athlete's build and an accountant's brain, he had an easy smile, perfectly styled dark brown hair, and big blue eyes. He'd shaken my hand like I was an adult, and he'd dropped some clever, off-color joke that made me laugh and his father scowl.

Now he was fifty, and time had been good to him. His brown hair was turning gray, his face was lined from decades of smiles and laughs, and he needed glasses to read; but to me he looked better every day. My schoolgirl crush was thankfully long gone—seeing him work his way through a pageant's worth of beautiful women one two-week fling at a time had done away with my mushy feelings—but I still nursed a soft spot in my heart for the man.

The moment I spotted him, sitting alone at a semi-private table, my smile faded and my heart sank. His smile of greeting was too tight, and he'd ordered a Manhattan for himself and nothing for me. It was going to be a lecture, I just knew it. I could turn around and leave, couldn't I? But that would be silly and cowardly, so I slid into a chair across from him and said something vapid in greeting.

"You look good," he said. "Chicago must have agreed with you."

"No, Chicago was a wind tunnel nightmare that tangled my hair so much I had to spend an hour and a half reviving it today. The food was good, though."

"You spent the afternoon at Marty's," he said. Not a question, not quite an accusation.

I didn't bother to ask how he knew. After ordering a glass of wine and accepting a menu from the waitress, I said, "Sure did. His neighbor called me. He'd been holed up for days. You can imagine the smell."

"Remind me why he's your responsibility?" Ren followed the delicate, sanctimonious question with a slow sip of his Manhattan. God, he could be insufferable.

I recited the answer I'd used so many times before. "Because I promised to stay with him for better or worse, in sickness and in health, so long as we both lived, and instead I left him alone to fend for himself while I went off to chase my own dreams. That's why."

"You left him because he broke your nose."

"The point is, I left him."

"Did he ask you for money?"

I appreciated Ren's attempt to steer the lecture into waters where he had any business whatsoever. Smiling, I shook my head. "He doesn't need money. He has a good job."

"For now."

My wine arrived, and while I tasted it, Ren ordered dinner for both of us. As the waitress sashayed away, her shapely figure drawing Ren's undivided attention, I watched him watch her. The was a time I would've given anything for Ren to look at me like that. When he was finished ogling, he turned to me with a guilty half-smile.

"Sorry. I know you don't like to talk about Marty, but I feel obligated to be the voice of reason. You don't owe him anything. I can't stand to watch him drag you down."

"No one owes anyone anything, when you really think about it," I shot back.

His mouth twisted in consternation. "I'm not sure I can agree with that."

"Change my mind."

"I'd rather not try. Tell me about Chicago. What happened?"

My tale of futility and woe in the Windy City got us all the way through dinner. I declined dessert, then summoned a rideshare to drive me home. Ren watched me tapping away at my phone with an air of polite indignation.

"Leaving so soon?" he asked once I'd scheduled the ride.

"I have to go to work. I have the night shift. Some contractor is updating the security equipment for a new exhibit, and Joe needed an extra pair of eyes. Apparently they're going to be at it all night."

"How can you stand having so much fun?" he asked.

"I need the money. My financial manager is a real miser." I stood, pulling on my jacket. "Thanks for dinner, Ren."

As I walked to the exit, deliberately *not* sashaying, I wondered if Ren were watching me go with the same quiet enthusiasm he'd shown for the waitress. I decided I didn't care, and I almost convinced myself that was true.

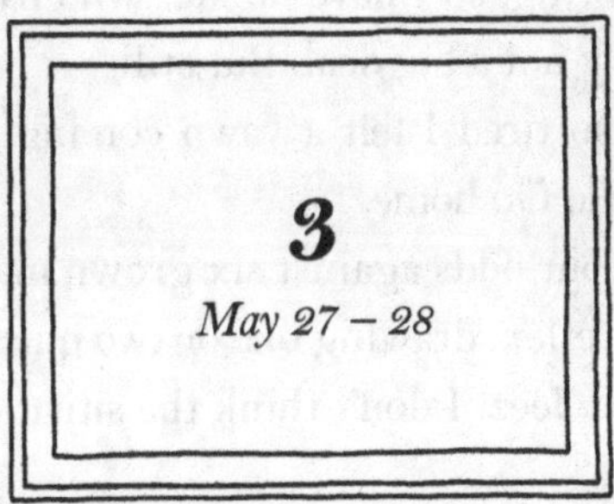


IN THE WOMEN'S LOCKER ROOM at the Kimbell Art Museum, I swapped out my designer jeans, cashmere sweater, and black leather pumps for the crisp white shirt, navy blue slacks, and black knitted vest that marked me as a security guard. Once I'd added the pièce de resistance, a pair of black orthopedic shoes, I stepped over to a full-length mirror to assess my appearance.

"Yuck," I concluded.

I braided my hair, donned my security badge on its generic lanyard, hid my necklace under my shirt, and clipped a small keychain to an empty belt loop. My transformation complete, I hurried to the gallery where a team of contractors was already at work.

They'd arrived early, which meant I was late. My boss, Joe, was watching over them in my stead. As I approached him from behind, I noted his tightly crossed arms and locked knees. His small, wiry frame was blocking the entrance to the gallery, so I cleared my throat to announce my presence. His narrow shoulders relaxed before he turned.

"There you are. Thanks for coming in."

"Happy to help. You look tense."

"Bit of a snafu. They didn't bring the staff they said they were going to bring, so I have no idea who half these people are. It's probably not a big deal. But still."

He sounded so tired I felt a yawn coming on. "I'll watch them like a hawk. Go home."

"I don't like your odds against six grown men, Claire."

I laughed on reflex, drawing one or two quick glances from the contractors. "Jeez. I don't think the situation is that dire, do you?"

"It never is until it is."

"So why'd you call me?" I asked, already knowing the answer.

"No one else available on such short notice. If you don't feel safe, you don't have to stay. I won't hold it against you."

"I'm not worried, but if you are, keep an eye on us from the back office. If you happen to fall asleep, so much the better for you. I'll be fine."

Joe nodded solemnly. "I called Rick, too. He'll be in in about an hour to back you up."

Rick, a seventy-seven-year-old retired CPA, was the only security guard on staff who was more useless in a physical confrontation than me. I couldn't help but be curious about Joe's heightened state of awareness. Watching the six-man crew at work, I saw a well-oiled team focused on their individual tasks. They were mounting cameras, splicing wires, aligning sensors, and calibrating pressure-sensitive switches, all in the name of upgrading the gallery's security for the incoming exhibit. The men looked pretty trustworthy to me—but then again, I'd once loaned my bike to a woman I met at the bus stop.

"Keep your head on a swivel," Joe said.

I watched him go, then turned back to observe the crew at work. One man, who I assumed was in charge, had set up a laptop on an empty pedestal and was staring intently at the glowing screen while the other five milled around him. I spared him a cursory glance before moving to a better position in the doorway between the under-renovation gallery and the adjacent one, which was full of early American furniture and textiles. Not my favorite pieces, but valuable all the same.

To a man they ignored me, hardly speaking as they went about their tasks. I watched each man work for a few minutes at a time, and after an hour I was furious at myself for not grabbing a coffee before I started my shift. I paced just to stay awake. The more my eyelids drooped, the more my gaze wanted to settle on the man with the laptop.

My backup, Rick, appeared in the doorway and greeted me with a polite nod. Though he was getting along in years, he was a big guy—tall, broad-shouldered, with a massive beer belly distending his vest, and hands that could palm a basketball. His physical presence brought relief I hadn't expected, and suddenly I was relaxed enough to roll my shoulders back and stretch a little. When my gaze settled once more on the man with the laptop, I saw him looking not at his screen but at Rick.

For a moment he studied the older man, his expression neutral in the LED glow. Then he turned to me, and I resisted the instinct to look somewhere else. I wasn't a fan of being studied, no matter the reason. Rather than losing the staring contest I'd started, he smiled and left his pedestal station to walk over to me.

When he was close enough, he held out his hand. "I'm Fred. Fred Laubenberg."

"Claire." I shook his hand, receiving a rather aggressive extra squeeze that set me on edge. There was something so off about the guy—not that I could articulate what—that I was absolutely certain he'd given me a fake name. But that couldn't be true. Joe had vetted these guys, right? Or was Fred one of the surprise new faces?

I lost my train of thought when he said, "I would've introduced myself sooner, but I didn't know you'd—Are they making you two stick around all night?"

"Yes, we'll be here until you're finished." With a smile, I added, "It's just museum policy."

"Well in that case, I hate to ask, but… Do you think we could get some water, maybe coffee? I was in charge of refreshments, and I dropped the ball."

So that was his reason for sizing Rick and me up. Which one looks more likely to fetch us a snack? I took a bit too much pleasure in replying, "I'm sorry, there's no food or drink allowed in the galleries."

His eyebrows shot up. "Even the empty ones?"

He had me there. The mention of coffee had weakened me, and his openly pleading expression finished me off. I sighed. "I guess you've got a point. I could use a coffee, too. Can you spare someone to help me carry everything?"

"I can spare myself. I'm not needed at the moment."

I explained our errand to Rick as we left the gallery, and he added a black coffee to my list. Finding myself walking side-by-side with Fred through the dark, deserted museum, I felt the same mental tug that had convinced me to text Ren when I was walking through downtown Fort Worth alone in the predawn hours. How easily this stranger had separated me from Rick, and now he was following me into the Staff Only area. Boy, was I dumb.

I shook the thought away. That was Joe talking, Mister Paranoid himself who didn't trust his own mother. That was why Joe was head of security and I was just a guard. I decided to let him be the suspicious one. He was probably following our progress on CCTV anyway.

We made it to the breakroom without exchanging a word, but as we gathered up bottles of water, filled paper cups with coffee, and sorted through the selection of chips and other empty calories, Fred asked, "So, what's your secret talent?"

Frowning, I asked, "My what?"

"Your talent. You're a security guard, right? What can you do?"

"I can stay on my feet for hours and stare at people if they get too close to something."

"Oh, come on. There has to be a reason you're the one babysitting us."

We divided up the loot and headed back to the gallery. I said, "If you want to believe I'm some kind of secret weapon, I won't stop you." Glancing warily at his profile, I asked, "Why do you ask?"

He laughed. "Oh, we're gonna rob the museum. Didn't you know? I wasn't expecting one of you to hang around all night, let alone two. What does the old man do? Ex-military? Is he hiding a Desert Eagle under that gut?"

"That's not funny."

Lowering his voice to a conspiratorial whisper, he replied, "I think it's pretty funny."

"Just walk in front of me," I ordered.

Laughing to himself, Fred complied without argument. When we got back to the gallery, I passed Rick his coffee with a whispered, "I've got a bad feeling about this guy."

"You've got a bad feeling about someone? Must be pretty serious."

"Can you go see if Joe is still here? And awake?"

Nodding, Rick took his coffee and departed with a sullen, "This is why we need radios. I've been saying it…"

"Yeah, yeah." I took up my post where Rick had been standing, blocking the gallery exit somewhat less effectively than he had. I watched Fred pass out the food and drink, for which none of his staff bothered thanking me. He took up his post in front of his laptop again, and while I sipped my coffee, I stared at him with my most deadpan, unfriendly, "Don't get even one centimeter closer to that Rembrandt" expression.

The caffeine-and-anxiety cocktail perked me right up, and soon I felt like I could do this all night and into the morning if needed. Eventually I would need sustenance, but the chips and cookies in the breakroom held no appeal for me. After I'd been standing at the entrance for a few minutes, I felt a tap on my shoulder and jumped halfway out of my shoes. Rick did have a secret skill: He could be as silent as a Prius if he felt like it.

"He's wide awake now," Rick said.

"Good. So am I."

"How much longer are they going to be?"

"No idea. I'll ask."

Personally I didn't care how long the contractors planned to work, but I wanted an excuse to peek at Fred's computer screen. I carefully wended my way through the equipment, cables, and men surrounding Fred like a minefield and brazenly studied his screen for a few seconds. He didn't snap the laptop closed, which I took as a good sign.

"My boss wants to know when you'll be done."

Without looking at me, Fred answered, "It'll go a lot faster if you and Sergeant Brewski get lost."

I said nothing, and after an uncomfortable silence, Fred finally moved his eyes from the screen to my face.

"Sorry. We're getting there." He pointed to his screen, where a black window displayed white text that I took for code of some sort. It was gibberish to me, but I gazed cooperatively at it as he explained, "The new cameras aren't communicating with your network. I've got to figure out what's going on there. Hopefully we won't have to wake up your IT guy. Then we need to test everything—all the alarms—and if those are fine, we'll be done. Could take twenty minutes, could take four hours."

"Anything I can do to help?"

He grinned at me. "Just keep hanging around looking good, and we'll all have a better night."

I made a face and walked away, resuming my position at the entrance to the Early American gallery. Fred favored me with one last smirk before returning to his stupid laptop.

Now I studied him with more purpose, sincerely believing I'd have to describe the man to a police sketch artist at some point. At least that's what I told myself.

He was younger than me, but not by much. I'd guess thirty-five, thirty-six. He did not look like a Fred. There was a Scandinavian look to him, and not just because of the straight, blonde hair and blue eyes. Something about the shape of his nose. Or maybe it was the too-long hair and stubbly beard that gave him a modern day Viking vibe. He wasn't tall though, for a man of Nordic descent. Roughly my height, though my hideous orthopedics added about two inches to my five-foot, nine-inch frame. Under his professional, blue polo and cargo pants—I *hated* cargo pants—he was clearly well muscled.

Why would he tell me I looked good? I knew for a fact that I looked ridiculous. The uniform made men look official and women look frumpy, no matter how they were shaped. Even female cops in their tactical vests and utility belts looked more feminine than I did. "Fred" was obviously trying to patronize me, to assert dominance. For the first time in a while, I felt a little glowing ember of unabashed antipathy settle in my stomach. I usually found something to like about people, even the unlikeable ones, but there were occasionally exceptions.

Fred Laubenberg. What a dumb, obviously made up name.

Mentally, I settled in for many more hours of keeping myself awake with coffee and dislike. Fred and his team wrapped it up less than an hour later, declaring the alarms and cameras to be working perfectly. In minutes they'd packed up their equipment, cleaned up the few minor messes they'd made, and started filing out of the gallery. Rick followed the five underlings while I held Fred back.

"Wait a minute," I ordered. "My boss needs to sign off on everything. He'll be out in a second." Unless he's sound asleep, I added to myself.

Fortunately, Joe was awake and watching and had seen the crew wrapping things up. He appeared in short order and made Fred walk him through everything they'd done, how it was all expected to function, and what to do in the event of a malfunction. I left them to it, dismissing myself to the locker room to change back into my normal clothes.

When I returned to the gallery, Fred and Joe were still

talking. Fred shook Joe's hand, had the audacity to wink at me, and left.

Joe pressed a piece of paper into my hand without comment.

"What's this?" I asked.

"His phone number." I could tell by my boss' tone that he was not impressed. "Unprofessional, if you ask me. Want me to file a complaint?"

I sighed. "No, it's okay. I'll settle for staying home next time he's doing work here. Is Rick gone already?"

"Took off like a racehorse."

"Is there anything else you need? Do you want to test the alarms again?"

"Yes, but you're going home." He checked his watch. "Reagan will be here in about an hour. I'll have her check everything out."

"Suits me. Good night, Joe."

"Night. Thanks for your help."

Such as it was, I thought.

Dawn was breaking as I stepped outside, and I gave serious thought to how I was going to get my sleep pattern back on a normal schedule. I'd have to stay awake all day, somehow, and set an alarm so I didn't sleep more than eight hours tonight. A couple days of that ought to sort me out. Lost in these pragmatic thoughts, I didn't notice the gaggle of admirers around Lucius until I was a few yards away.

Stopping, I pressed the remote start and felt a stab of vindictive pleasure as three of the crew, including Fred, leapt back in alarm. Laughing, they retreated to their van, which was parked a few spots away; but as I got closer, Fred came back.

Maybe I *would* file a complaint.

He asked, "Did you get my—"

I shoved the piece of paper into his chest, where he reflexively caught it as I pulled my hand away.

"—number. Okay, message received. Nice car." He grinned at me again. "Nice jeans."

I snapped, "You know you've got some nerve. This is where I *work*."

"Well, where do you meet people? At bars? Online?"

I was so surprised by his defense that I couldn't think of anything to say. He uncrumpled the paper I'd forced him to take, carefully folded it, and held it out to me.

"Call it temporary insanity. Redheads drive me crazy. At least wait 'til I'm out of sight to throw it away."

I took the paper, if only to end this interaction. He waited until I'd slipped it into my pocket to climb into the driver's seat of his work van. With a wave, he drove away. I stood by Lucius, savoring the predatory rumble of his idling engine, for ten full minutes before climbing in and heading home.

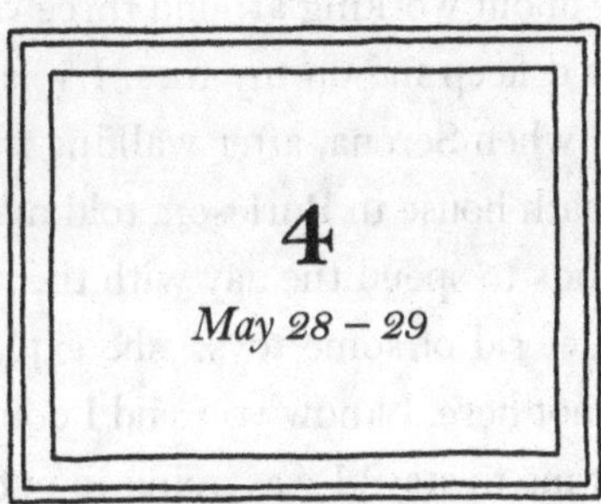



KNOWING I'D NEVER BE ABLE to stay awake until a reasonable bedtime without something constructive to do, I waited until 9:00 a.m. and texted a new client to ask if she wanted to move our appointment up a couple days. She texted back immediately in the affirmative.

In addition to my part time job at the museum, I ran a one-woman professional organizing business. Most of my clients were messy people on the cusp of turning into hoarders, and I had the luxury of being able to undercharge them. I felt bad about undercutting my competition, but other organizers were so expensive that most people—especially the low-income families who needed help the most—couldn't afford them. Ren called it my community service, as though I were making up for some petty crime. I'd never given him the satisfaction of asking why.

Serena Platt, a young mother of three children under six years old, had contacted me a few weeks ago. At the time, I didn't have any openings, having set aside today in case my trip to Chicago ran long. Now that I had the time, I couldn't wait to get started on her home. She'd sent a few photos, warning me that, "This isn't even the worst of it."

I wasn't crazy about working around three young children, but I knew they'd keep me on my toes. I was actually a little disappointed when Serena, after walking me through her three bed, two bath house in Burleson, told me that she'd arranged for the kids to spend the day with their father.

"We *have* to get rid of some toys," she explained. "It'll be easier if they're not here. I know you said I don't have to help, but do you want me to stay? I was going to put in a few extra hours at work."

"You don't have to stay. Do I have your permission to throw away anything that looks like trash to me?"

She hesitated, looking away into abstraction while I waited patiently. I never threw away any of my clients' things, not even a used tissue. The question was only meant to provoke exactly the sort of response Serena was giving me. She was definitely stuck in a hoarder mentality.

"I'd rather you didn't..." she finally muttered, clearly ashamed of herself.

"Say no more. I'll still pick out things I think are trash, but I won't actually throw them away. Does that sound okay?"

She nodded. After a few more formalities, she burdened herself with an enormous, tattered suitcase of a purse and departed.

It was a good day. Left entirely to my own devices, I made quick work of sorting out the presumptive trash, donate, sell, and keep items in their own piles in the living room. Once all the other rooms were empty, I gave them a thorough cleaning. There was always cash hiding in a house like this, and I was pleased to have found nearly $100 in small bills and loose change to present to Serena. I moved the probable trash to the back porch, the donate and sell items into the master bedroom, and the keepers onto the kitchen table so I could clean the living room.

I was writing out an organization plan for Serena when she returned. It was after four in the afternoon. I thought she'd looked tired when she left, but now she looked positively exhausted. Hoping to brighten her day a bit, I showed her the cash I'd found along with two checks that looked like they hadn't been deposited. Both were less than ninety days old, thankfully.

To my horror, the young mother looked at the cash, then at the checks, and burst into tears.

"Oh no," I breathed.

"I'm s-s-sorry," she gasped, forcing a laugh. "I just can't believe—This is over five hundred dollars. I can't believe I just—luh-lost it. I'm such an idiot."

"You are *not* an idiot."

"I b-bet you've never lost a check for…" She picked up one of the checks. "Three hundred and six dollars and fifty-two cents."

"I also don't have three little kids," I reminded her.

In fact, I had zero children, and all things considered, that was unlikely to change. She looked up at me through watery eyes and nodded, wanting to be comforted.

I walked her through the organization plan, which she seemed excited about. A good sign. When she asked about paying me, I told her I'd be back in a week to see how she was doing, talk about investing some money in better storage, and see how the kids felt about parting with their precious toys. I'd send an invoice after that.

I left her with a stern, "The trash on the back porch. It's very important that you throw it away yourself. Try to have that done by the time I come back, okay?"

"I will."

She wouldn't, but I accepted her answer and left. I felt as tired as she looked, but it didn't hit me until I was out of things to do. By my own self-imposed rules, I couldn't go to bed until nine o'clock at the earliest. I had over four hours to kill and no spark of inspiration about how to kill them.

Serena's house hadn't been all that dirty, only messy. Nevertheless, I made a beeline for the shower as soon as I got home. That ate up half an hour. I went shopping, found a new dress that went great with a pair of Jimmy Choos I'd found last week, and set my will toward thinking of a place to wear them. This was no easy task on a Wednesday, and I seriously considered giving Fred a call and letting him take me on the most expensive date he could be coerced into. Once I'd talked myself off that ledge, I admitted defeat and settled for the only other activity that could do the trick: going to the movies.

An unnecessarily long superhero flick kept me awake until after ten, which meant I could sleep past six. I was so strung out that I considered ducking into a bar after the movie instead of walking straight home, but Fred's snide comment about meeting people in bars changed my mind. It also made me realize that I wouldn't be getting him out of my head as easily as I'd hoped.

He was good looking, I had to give him that. Charming, in a very annoying way. He probably wasn't accustomed to being shot down, but something made me suspect he usually set his sights on younger women. Much younger. To a twenty-something on the prowl, he would be irresistible. Perhaps he'd grown bored with easy conquests; men tended to prefer a challenge, which was honestly the only thing I had going for me at this point.

My cynical inner monologue got me all the way home and into bed, where I promptly fell asleep without setting an alarm.

*

I slept for eleven hours straight and woke up Thursday morning as disoriented and hungry as I'd ever been. I rushed to the bathroom to take care of some urgent business, brushed my teeth, and downed several glasses of tap water.

Had I slept any longer, I'd have been late to my shift at the museum for the first time ever. Dressing in a fugue, I made it out the door and to the museum a scant four minutes before my shift was supposed to start.

Tired as I still was, I couldn't miss the scrum of activity inside. There were no visitors, but there were plenty of police officers and some profoundly upset older people I recognized as donors. The latter had been forced to congregate in the lobby, while the former created a barrier at the door through which it didn't seem I'd be allowed until Joe showed up to usher me inside.

"What happened?" I demanded as soon as we were out of earshot of the donors.

"Break-in. Last night." His teeth were clenched so hard I could barely understand him. "Listen, did you keep Fred Laubenberg's number? Did you call him?"

"Yes, and no. What did they take?"

"We're still going through everything. Nothing big. So far we've got some Roman-era coins, a few smaller statues from the First Nations gallery, and one Turner."

"The little one?"

"Yeah, the little one. It doesn't add up to much, even including the Turner, but the patrons are upset as you saw. Most of it was from Leonard Money's collection."

"So someone knew what they were doing."

"That's the consensus. Turns out he wasn't quite as insured as he claimed to be. Fortunately our policy will cover it." He shook his head like a dog, peered at me, and muttered, "Why am I telling you all this? God, I'm tired. You need to talk to the police."

"Me?" I squeaked. "Why me?"

"Calm down. They're questioning everyone."

Getting interrogated by two burly young Fort Worth PD detectives wasn't how I pictured spending my lunch hour, but it certainly wasn't boring. They could see right away that I wasn't suffering from a guilty conscience, so the interrogation was more of an interview. I went through everything I'd done for the past few days, assuring them I'd never met any of the men on Fred's crew, including Fred, prior to Tuesday night. I explained how I'd spent the intervening hours, and they seemed satisfied. We exchanged contact information, they asked me to give them a call if I thought of anything else, and that was that.

The rest of my shift was devoted to helping Joe with the inventory. At the final tally, the museum was missing seven Roman coins which had shared a display case, four Navajo wooden figures, a child's rocking chair from the Early American gallery, a Duccio triptych, a handful of small paintings by lesser known artists, and Joseph Mallord William Turner's *Study for Glaucus and Scylla*. This last was worth more than the rest combined, because the British landscape painter had only done a single study for the grandiose *Glaucus and Scylla* which also graced our permanent collection.

The study was on loan from Leonard Money. In fact, of everything that was taken, the only thing that didn't belong to him was the little rocking chair. Its theft felt personal, as though Fred wanted to me to know that he'd noticed how intent I was on guarding the Early American gallery.

I finished up with Joe, clocked out, and walked through the thinning crowd of police and museum big-wigs to the bench that sat before my favorite painting, Gustave Caillebotte's *On the Pont de l'Europe.* I plopped down in front of the outsized canvas and gazed up at it, taking a half-attentive inventory of my exhausted body while the soothing blues and grays of the Frenchman's masterpiece washed over me.

What a bizarre few days it had been. Museum heists didn't happen every day, and there I was in the hectic center of one. I'd told the detectives about "Fred's" joke that he was going to rob the museum and about him giving me his number, and I'd gladly handed it over when asked. Why I still had the little slip of paper in my pocket, they hadn't asked. I was glad they hadn't, because I didn't know. Unfortunately, I'd memorized the number.

I refocused on the Caillebotte. I counted the rivets in the bridge at the top center of the painting. Rising to my feet, I moved to within a foot of the canvas and counted them again. Renewed energy surged through me. My heart began to race. There were supposed to be twenty-six rivets, not counting the ones in another group in the top right corner. Exactly twenty-six. There would be twenty-seven if Caillebotte hadn't left a blank spot in the top row, but he *had* left a blank spot. I was sure he'd done it on purpose, to create tension and mystery. Why was a rivet missing? Was the bridge sound, or would it fall? Did the gentleman gazing disconsolately at the train in the distance hope the bridge would fall, the train would derail, and life would return to what it had been when he was a boy?

I counted the rivets four more times, but there was no need. The extra rivet where none belonged was proof enough.

This was not Gustave Caillebotte's *On the Pont de l'Europe.*

CLAIRE, *WHAT ARE YOU DOING?* *What the* heck *are you doing?*

My inner voice was sounding particularly stressed out as it repeated the question over and over. I refused to answer. She was *my* inner voice; I could ignore her if I wanted to. If I could. She was persistent, hammering me all the way home and through my Thursday evening whole-apartment cleaning ritual.

I hoped the question would drive out the phone number I'd unintentionally memorized, but I wasn't so lucky. Once my apartment was spotless and I had a box full of items to donate, I was forced to accept that the two things were related. What was I doing? Why couldn't I forget Fred's phone number?

I'd left the museum without saying a word to anyone. There was no doubt in my mind that whoever had stolen all those relatively obscure pieces from Leonard Money's collection—Fred and his crew, presumably—had also replaced Gustave Caillebotte's *On the Pont de l'Europe* with a very skilled forgery. I was less certain, but still mostly convinced, that the extra rivet had been included on purpose. The forger's signature. They could never resist signing their work.

Why hadn't I told Joe? The Caillebotte was one of the most valuable pieces in the entire museum. It was supposed to go back to the Musée d'Orsay in Paris in two months. If I didn't speak up soon, the French museum was going to get a lovely but worthless forgery in place of one of the best-known and most loved examples of French Impressionism in the world. Someone in France would see what I'd seen, and then the Kimbell would be in the hottest of hot water.

Maybe someone else would notice before it returned to France, so I wouldn't have to say anything. The extra rivet had stood out to me like a glowing beacon. Thousands, probably millions of people adored that painting at least as much as I did. Someone else would notice.

*Call Fred and demand the painting back!*

Yeah, right. What I needed to do, what a good and smart person would do, was call the police and then Joe and tell them they needed to add the Caillebotte to their list of stolen items. So why wasn't my pious inner voice suggesting that? Why let Fred know I knew what he'd done? Who would benefit from that?

This time the voice was silky with suppressed mischief as it so helpfully answered, *You would.*

Maybe wine and YouTube would shut her up. I poured myself a glass, turned on the TV, and scrolled through the newest videos posted by my favorite organizing gurus. They were always thinking of the most creative ways to declutter, the most novel approaches to convincing a proto-hoarder to turn aside from his or her dark path.

I did pick up some useful tips, but after eight videos, three glasses of wine, and a bubble bath, I was out of ways to distract myself. I was also drunk. Still in my bathrobe and toying with the idea of sleeping naked, I found my phone charging on the nightstand and composed a text.

"It's Claire. I'd like to have dinner with you tomorrow night."

A few minutes passed. I began to doubt my confidence that he'd reply at all. Then, in two separate texts, he answered.

"What a coincidence."

"I'd like that, too."

I was right about his age, if the capital letters and correct punctuation in his texts were any clue. Having cleared the hurdle of making contact, I managed to stay awake long enough to solidify our plans. Eight o'clock, il Corso, don't make me feel overdressed.

*

Most of Friday was a blur. I did follow-up visits at two homes I'd cleaned last week, had lunch with Ren (who was delighted to hear about my upcoming date), dropped my donations off at the Salvation Army, and went shopping to restock my fridge and wine rack.

I needed every moment of the day to figure out how to play my cards at dinner. I knew what I knew—that Fred was involved somehow in the theft of the Caillebotte—and I knew what I wanted—his assistance in finding and, if necessary, stealing Aunt Eva's Wyeth—but what did Fred-or-whatever-his-real-name-was need to know?

Eventually I'd have to tell him why I'd established contact. The real question was, could I pad the odds a little that he'd cooperate with my scheme? My scheme was blackmail, so he wouldn't like it no matter how I served it up. But if he liked *me* enough… maybe he'd make the whole thing easier. I was tempted to run it all by Ren, but ultimately I decided to leave him out of it.

My brand new dress and matching Jimmy Choos were in place, as was my hair. Fred had said he liked redheads, so I was letting my hair down for this one. I spent two hours curling it into a perfect cascade of copper waves, but the effort was worth it. I added a touch of makeup, trying not to make any vain attempt to hide my lack of youth under layers of gunk. A little mascara, a bright red lip, a couple dabs of blush, and I was ready to go.

My Choos weren't made for walking, but the restaurant, il Corso, was only a quarter mile from my front door. It was a slow walk, but I made it to the restaurant with a few minutes to spare. I remembered something about the swanky Italian joint right about the time I arrived there: il Corso was inside a hotel. Somehow I felt that sent the wrong message. Embarrassment quickly overshadowed all the other things I was feeling about tonight, and before I could rethink it, I pulled out my phone and called Fred.

"Hey, you," he answered right away. The man sounded pretty pleased with himself.

"Hey. Um, I'm going to have to take a rain check."

"You're kidding. What happened?"

"Nothing. I just… I forgot il Corso was inside a hotel. Um…"

"And you feel that sends the wrong message?" he finished, echoing my thoughts verbatim.

"Uh. Yeah. Sorry."

"Okay, I get that. Now that you've sent the right message, do you still want to come inside? The truffle mashed potatoes smell amazing."

"You're already there?" I asked.

"Yep. I just grabbed a seat at the bar. They said it'll be about an hour before they can seat us."

I pictured that hour, grimacing. But I was making him like me, right? I asked, "Order me a drink?"

"Oh." He sounded surprised by his quick victory. "What'll it be?"

"Surprise me."

"You got it." He hung up without saying goodbye. Another power move.

He'd won that volley, but I'd take the match before the night was over. The thought made me smile to myself. Feet screaming in protest, I mounted the steps into the hotel and found my way to the restaurant on the ground floor. I spotted Fred at the bar and started toward him, though the seats to either side of him were occupied.

I sidled up behind him and asked, "Is this seat taken?"

Revolving toward me on his barstool, Fred greeted me by putting a hand on my waist, looking me up and down, and saying, "Well look at you." I swatted his hand away, but before I could answer, he nodded at the man sitting next to him and said, "I told you, man."

The man, a total stranger to me, swore and then vacated his seat. Fred gestured for me to sit, so I sat and asked, "Who was that?"

He shrugged. "I don't know. He wanted the seat I was saving for you, so I told him I'd let him have it as long as a sexy redhead didn't come looking for me."

"How nice of him, to let me sit here in the meantime," I said. A drink appeared in front of me, and I wrapped my hand around it without a second thought. "What's this?"

"Try it."

I took an obedient sip, frowned, and eyed him suspiciously.

"Wrong drink?" he asked.

"This is a gin and Topo."

"Hey, it was a wild guess."

"Hm." I took another sip for time to think. "I'll drink it. It's good."

Though his eyebrows pushed together briefly, he took the defeat in stride. He was nursing what looked like a rum and Coke, and he took a swig before asking me, "So, what changed your mind?"

"I changed my mind?"

"Come on. I thought you were gonna take a swing at me when I gave you my number."

I should have anticipated this, but I'd been too busy scheming my little scheme. I made a face that probably wasn't very cute, but it earned me a laugh. "Sorry about that. I was in a mood."

"Oh, a *mood*," he repeated with a sage nod. "Sounds very exotic."

I couldn't think of a response, so I took another drink and waited for Fred to decide what he wanted to talk about next. He just smiled at me, eyes glittering mockingly.

"An hour, really?" I asked, when I could bear his scrutiny no longer.

"That's what they said."

"I'm not sure I can make it an hour. I'm pretty hungry."

"Let's go somewhere else."

Without waiting for my response, he pulled out his phone and looked up restaurants in our area. I spotted my favorite pizza parlor and pointed to it.

"That's right—down the street," I said, stopping myself just before telling him it was across the street from my apartment. "We could walk."

He agreed, and we each paid for our own drinks before setting off into the muggy night. My five-inch heels made me the taller, and I was sure he'd throw some snide comment my way about it; but he seemed content to walk next to me in silence, smiling benevolently at passersby. His smile faltered when we reached the pizza restaurant to find it dark and empty.

I stepped closer to read a hand-written sign on the front door. "'Closed due to bereavement. Back in June.' June? Oh no... I wonder what happened."

"Do you know the owners?" Fred asked.

"No... but it's sad, isn't it?" A wave of emotion hit me out of nowhere, and I took a deep breath. This was not going at all how I'd pictured it.

He squinted at me. "Are you... are you choking up?"

"Don't look at me."

"Wow." He laughed, but it wasn't a cruel or mocking sound. "You are full of surprises."

"Mhm. Okay." I ran a finger under each eye, checking for smeared mascara. I was in the clear. "Look, please don't take this the wrong way..."

"Calling it a night?" he asked.

"No, I was going to say, I live right there." I pointed across the street. "I could make you dinner."

"Oh?"

"Just dinner."

"Lead the way." As we crossed the street, he added, "I'm not sure how to feel about you assuming I want to have sex with you."

"Feel however you want," I said dismissively.

We made it inside, up to the top floor, and through my door in companionable silence. I knew he'd have something to say when he saw how I lived, and he didn't disappoint.

"Oops. Vacant apartment." He took my elbow and tried to steer me back out the door. "We probably shouldn't be here."

"Oh, stop it." I shook his hand away. "I don't like clutter. Take off your shoes."

He frowned.

"Please," I added.

I'd already forgotten the whole point of this date. Wasn't I supposed to be endearing myself to him? Why had I thought I could do that?

I slipped off my shoes and asked, "Do you want a glass of wine? I have other stuff, too."

He followed me into the kitchen. "Wine sounds great. But if you were planning to get me drunk before you start asking about the break-in, I should tell you now: I'm not that kind of drunk."

Turning, I was startled to find him a mere foot away, now looking down at me. How the tables had turned.

I forced a smile and backed up, but he followed. Soon I was out of room to retreat, squished into a corner between my fridge and stove. He put his hands on the counter to either side of me. I might have been afraid, but for that same playful gleam in his eyes I'd seen at il Corso's bar.

"I'd really like to check you for a wire," he said, trying and failing to sound intimidating.

"I bet you would."

"Go ahead. Ask. I don't have anything to hide."

I wasn't ready to ask, and I certainly wasn't going to play this game according to his rules. I gave a nervous laugh and admitted truthfully, "I've been so wrapped up in my own stuff these past few days, I didn't even realize… The police have been questioning you, haven't they? They think you were involved."

"You're gonna stand there and tell me that just occurred to you?"

"Yes."

He leaned away. Running a hand through his hair, he said through a sigh, "They've interviewed my whole crew, even the ones who weren't there. And they've sat me down twice. Now I guess they're trying to poke holes in my alibi, or whatever it is they do. I thought…" He shook his head, betraying the first hint of real anger I'd seen. It seemed to be directed inward. "Crap. I really thought… I wasn't kidding about the wire."

"It makes sense they'd think you were involved. They're just doing their jobs."

If he noticed my failure to assert any belief in his innocence, he chose not to comment on it. Instead he said, "Yeah, I know."

"They interviewed me, too. And everyone at the museum."

Some thought made him laugh, and he asked, "Well, you realize how this looks now, right? If it's true the detectives didn't put you up to this, you and I both better hope they don't find out."

"Oh?" I asked, not getting it. He raised his eyebrows at me. "Oh."

I turned around and retrieved two wine glasses from the cabinet over my head and a bottle of merlot from the wine rack. Fred had a pretty good point. I already knew he was involved, and I'd now done such a neat job of making myself look like the inside man. While I uncorked the bottle and poured us each a glass, I heard him pace on socked feet into the living area. It was a small apartment, though the sparseness I enjoyed made it seem bigger than it was. There wasn't much to look at. Soon enough he paced back to me, and I handed him his glass.

"I'm not going to lie about this if they ask me," I warned him. "I don't have anything to hide, either."

"Getting our story straight. Good idea."

"We don't have a story," I shot back. "What do you want for dinner? I have a couple steaks I could reverse seer, if you don't mind waiting. And it can get a little smoky. Otherwise I could do a charcuterie board and we could just graze…"

He opened my freezer, pushed a few things around like he owned the place, and pulled out a frozen pizza. "Let's not overcomplicate this," he said, passing the cold box into my free hand.

While the oven preheated, I led Fred on a tour of the apartment. Since I was pretending the bedroom didn't exist, it was a quick tour. We walked out onto the balcony and admired the view, I showed off some clever hidden cabinets and other storage in the living room, and then I led him into the spare bedroom. Half office, half art gallery, it was easily the most cluttered room in my home; but it was a functional sort of clutter, which was allowed.

Ignoring my desk under the window, Fred went straight for the first painting hanging on the left-hand wall. I felt a pang of pride in my work: He'd gone left, not right, which meant I'd designed my gallery correctly. The artwork I'd amassed over the years was arranged chronologically by the date I'd acquired each, so he was studying the first painting I'd ever bought. It wasn't worth anything, but it meant a lot to me.

"I got that in Santa Fe when I was seven," I explained while Fred gazed at the generic desert scene. "My aunt took me to an art fair and said this one was good. Technically, she bought it, but she passed me the money before I gave it to the artist."

"It's pretty," he concluded.

"Yeah, that's what I said." I heard the oven beep and said, "I'll go put the pizza in. Don't touch anything."

When I came back, Fred hadn't moved much. He was standing in front of an empty frame, twelve by eighteen. It was reserved for Aunt Eva's painting, one of my earliest acquisitions, according to the date I should have acquired it. I breathed a sigh of relief that I hadn't gotten around to hanging the plaque I'd had made for it. I wasn't ready to talk about the Wyeth yet.

"That's a long story," I said with a laugh. "You haven't even gotten to the good stuff yet."

"I like to take my time," he said to the empty frame, smiling some private smile.

"Then I'll leave you to it. I'm going to change. Don't—uh—don't steal anything if you can help it, okay?"

"Funny."

Fred was making himself at home on the sofa when I emerged from the bedroom a few minutes later. He'd brought the wine bottle with him, setting it on the side table next to his elbow. I didn't have a coffee table, so I supposed it made sense. He was flipping through a book that usually lived on the shelf next to my TV—the catalogue from a Caravaggio exhibition at the Kimbell.

"Do you get these for free?" he asked, not looking up from a full-page reproduction of *The Cardsharps*.

"Yep." I sat down at the opposite end of the sofa. "But I only take the ones I really want. So." I cleared my throat, waited for him to look up at me, and tucked my chin to say too loudly, "Fred, what do you think about this break-in at the Kimbell? Crazy, right?"

His answering laugh was genuine, and I congratulated myself for breaking the ice. He sat his empty wine glass down and scooted over to sit right next to me, leaning toward my chest to reply, "I don't know anything about that, ma'am."

Then he pressed his lips to my neck. Perhaps I'd broken the ice a bit too well. With his hand on my waist and his lips moving down my neck, I felt an answering rush of heat that demanded I slide both hands into his hair. I needed to know if it felt as soft as it looked, that's all. It did.

He tried to tug my collar down, but the t-shirt I'd thrown on stymied him. He kissed me on the lips instead, pushing me backward against the arm of the sofa.

As his hand crept under my shirt and found the clasp of my bra, the oven timer saved the day with five insistent beeps. I slithered out from underneath him, stood up, and fled into the kitchen.

I heard him following, but I ignored him while I slid the pizza onto a cutting board and set it on the stove top. I reached for the pizza wheel, but he pushed it out of my reach, turned me around by the hips, and kissed me again. He was a quick study, keeping his wandering hands on the right side of my clothes this time. One weaved its way into my hair, while the other slid down around my butt, pulling me closer.

I couldn't think of a way to stop this, and I figured I had about ten seconds before I didn't want to stop it anymore. Panicking, I pulled away and out tumbled the words, "You stole my favorite painting."

He closed his mouth, opened it, blinked at me, and asked, "Run that by me again?"

There was no going back now. Still painfully aware of his hands on me, I whispered, "The Caillebotte. You replaced it with a fake. The other stuff was just a distraction, right?"

His grip tightened, and he kissed me again, just once. "Why don't you tell me how you reached this conclusion."

"Did you paint the fake yourself? Or did you hire someone to do it? It was good."

I swallowed, an uncomfortable lump forming in my throat. Ren's words came back to me as Fred held my gaze. *You're not safe just because you're not scared.* Should I be scared?

"Whoever it was, they signed it with an extra rivet in the bridge. I know that painting, Fred. That's not my Caillebotte."

He kissed me again. His lips, his nearness, his hands were all beginning to feel like a threat—so why did they still feel so good?

"Your favorite painting," he said.

"Your bad luck, I guess."

He thought for a moment, then asked slowly, "Who else have you told?"

I recognized neither the admission of guilt nor the opportunity to make myself safer with a little white lie; all I heard was an easy question to answer.

"No one. I haven't told anyone."

"Who are you *going* to tell?"

"Can you let go of me? You're scaring me."

His hands stayed in place, his voice hardening. "Good. Who are you going to tell, Claire?"

Okay, now I was scared. I forced the unwelcome feeling back and said firmly, "No one. If you help me."

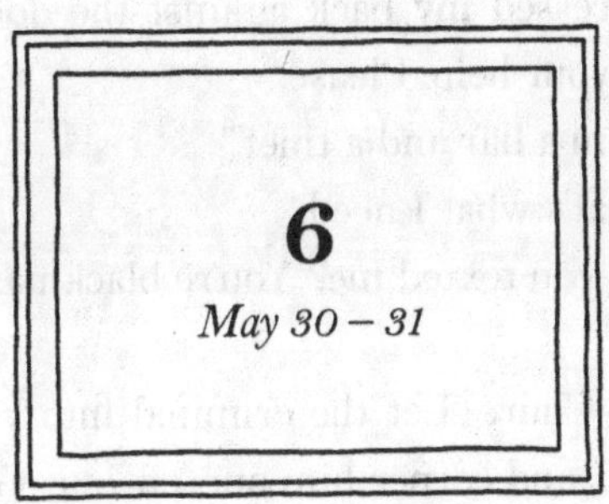


I HATED MYSELF FOR SHAKING so badly, knowing Fred could feel it. I could tell my brain he wasn't going to hurt me, but my body was not to be convinced. Waiting for his answer for what felt like an eternity, I kept my eyes on his lips. Meeting his gaze was too hard.

His lips pressed together into a hard line, and a quick burst of air through his nose was all the warning I got before he let go of me and backed away. For two seconds he studied me and seemed to struggle for words, then he returned to the living room and snatched up his empty glass, my mostly full one, and the wine bottle.

He passed my glass into my unresisting hands. After refilling his own and taking a measured sip, he asked, "With what?"

"First I want to know your real name. It's the least you could do."

That seemed to amuse him. To my alarm, he set his glass down again and strode toward the front door. I dashed after him. As he wrestled his shoes back on, I moved in front of the door to block his exit. Like I had the slightest chance of accomplishing that.

"Please." I pressed my back against the door as he came closer. "I need your help. Please."

"You think I'm a liar and a thief."

"You are. That's what I need."

"This is why you texted me? You're blackmailing me?"

"Yes."

"Real smart, Claire. Let the criminal into your home, get him all riled up, and corner him one-on-one. Great plan."

"I didn't rile up anything!" I took a deep breath. "You don't scare me."

"Oh, you're shaking because it's so cold in here, are you?"

"Well, are you going to hurt me?" I challenged, stupidly. "Or are you going to help me?"

"What makes you so sure Fred isn't my name?"

"I just know."

"You just… know."

"You don't look like a Fred."

"I don't want to hurt you. But if you don't get out of the way, I'll get you out of the way myself."

He moved even closer, and I squared my shoulders against the bracing, solid metal surface of my front door. More words came out of me, unassisted by my brain. "If you help me, I'll never tell anyone about the Caillebotte. You can keep it. Or sell it. Whatever you want. I won't interfere."

"Tell me what you want."

"There's another painting." For some reason, getting to this point felt like finishing a marathon. My shoulders relaxed, and I nodded toward the open door of my guest room. "The one the empty frame is for. I need your help to find it." Puzzlement clouded his angry expression, and I hurried to add, "It's a Wyeth. It's a portrait of my great aunt, Eva. Eva Riordan."

He stepped back, crossed his arms, and glowered at me in open disbelief. I tried to make his reaction make sense, but nothing occurred to me. He said nothing.

I went on, "No one believes me that it exists. My aunt left it to me when she died, but it disappeared. She only showed it to me once. I've been looking for it for thirty years and I'm sick and tired of getting jerked around by self-important art dealers and shady collectors. Whoever has it knows they have no right to it, and I want to find it and steal it back. I *have* to."

"Describe it," he ordered.

"The painting? It's a nude. In the desert… at sunset. I remember the colors. Aunt Eva's black hair. It must have been painted a long time ago, when she was young." He looked, if anything, even angrier. "I told you, I only saw it once. I was eight. She…" I trailed off, struck by another inconvenient tsunami of emotion. My voice thick, I forced, "She died two days later. Someone must have taken it. I want it back."

Fred came closer again, still furious, but I didn't sense any threat. He cupped my cheek in one hand, wiped a stray tear away with his thumb, and asked, "You're looking for an unknown portrait of Eva Riordan by Wyeth? *Andrew* Wyeth?"

"Yes."

His hand fell to my t-shirt, which he grabbed onto to haul me away from the door. The movement was so effortless, I abandoned any thought of physically preventing him from leaving.

"Wait. Please." My voice was so quiet, he might not have heard me.

"I'll call you tomorrow, okay?"

With that confusing statement, Fred let himself out and slammed the door behind him.

*

"He said he'd call me."

Ren frowned, taking in my sullen voice and slumped shoulders. I took a drink of my Bloody Mary, wishing he'd think of something else to talk about.

"Your tone and your words don't seem to match," he said lightly.

"I don't want to talk about it. What've you been up to?"

"Money stuff that I know for a fact holds no interest for you. When you invited me to brunch, I assumed you wanted to gush about your date. As your closest and only girlfriend, I obviously want to hear all about it."

I gave him an unwilling chuckle. A spark of inspiration made me say, "It's hard, you know… Most single women facing down forty… I guess I can't really blame him for expecting the night to turn out differently, you know?"

I was a terrible liar, which was only half the reason I did my best to avoid it. I watched on tenterhooks as Ren mulled over the ad-libbed falsehood. His fingers drummed against the table a few times.

"The truth must be pretty bad, for you to try that," he said.

I felt like banging my head against the table. "Okay. Look. I am not in the mood for a lecture. I'll tell you what happened, but not here. And you cannot tell *anyone* else."

"I wouldn't dream of betraying your confidence. You know that."

"Even if it makes you an accessory to a crime?"

A slow smile crept across his face. "You're messing with me."

I shook my head. In very short order, he'd paid the bill, summoned a taxi, and ferried us to his office. The building was a ghost town on a Saturday, empty but for a drowsy security guard who waved us toward the elevators without even glancing up from his novel. I refused to say a word until we were safely cloistered inside Ren's office.

"Okay, spill it," he snapped.

It wasn't like him to get snippy with me, and I felt myself physically and mentally shrinking away from his irritation.

In a softer tone, he said, "Claire, you're freaking me out. Please tell me what happened. Tell me he didn't hurt you."

"No. God, no, nothing like that. I mean…" I trailed away into silence. After plopping down into one of Ren's luxurious leather arm chairs and twisting my hands together, I felt safe enough to let it all out. "I think he wanted to. This guy… I don't even know where to start. I told you we met when he was doing some work at the museum, right?"

Ren nodded.

"And you know about the theft."

"Yes…"

I took a deep breath, then another. Technically, I'd promised Fred I wouldn't tell anyone what I was about to tell Ren; but Fred hadn't agreed yet to help me and probably never would.

"The police suspect Fred and his crew, and it's true. He… he pretty much admitted it last night. There's something the police don't know, though. Something else he took. I haven't told anyone and I thought if I—"

"Let me stop you right there," Ren said. "Did you try to *blackmail* an *art thief*?"

I looked up from a dismal study of my entwined fingers to see his face turning red. My non-answer was answer enough.

"Claire—just—what—why? Why would you do that? Why?"

"Please don't have a heart attack."

"I don't want to know what you're blackmailing him with. *Don't* tell me."

"Okay."

"You sprang this on him alone? In your apartment?"

"I wasn't afraid of him."

"You need to learn to be afraid. If you're going to pull stupid stunts like that—" He stopped himself, giving me an apologetic look. "Claire Bear. That was very, very risky."

He hadn't called me that in at least a decade. Feeling thoroughly chastised and as foolish as I'd ever felt, I crossed my arms and glared out his window at the Fort Worth skyline.

"Wait. He said he'd call you?" Ren asked.

"That's what he said."

As though Ren's question were a magic passphrase, a phone rang. We both checked our cell phones, but with a rush of disappointment, I realized Ren's was the one making all the racket. He glanced at the screen and pocketed the phone without answering it.

"I need to think. Will you do something for me?" he asked, almost pleading.

"Of course."

"Stay home today. Tell your doorman not to let him inside the building. Do that for me."

"I will. Ren… I'm sorry."

"It's okay. I'll bring dinner over tonight."

I agreed and left. Though Ren had also insisted I take a cab back to my apartment, a vindictive streak made me walk the mile and a half instead. It was a beautiful day, and I needed fresh air if I was going to be stuck inside for the rest of it. As soon as I got home, I made sure my organizing schedule was clear and called Joe to ask for the night off. I didn't care if doing so was suspicious; Ren told me to stay home, so I was going to stay home.

Around dinner time, my phone dinged with the arrival of a text message. Assuming it was Ren asking what I wanted for dinner, I was shocked to see Fred's name on the screen. I'd changed it to "Definitely NOT Fred," and the pettiness of me made me laugh.

He'd texted only, "Claire." The single word seemed to carry an imperious tone.

"What."

"I'm sorry for getting so upset last night. I need to talk to you."

"We're talking."

"In person."

"You can't come to my apartment."

"Burk Burnett Park? 6:30?"

Though I didn't appreciate the subtle reminder that he knew where I lived—Burk Burnett Park was feet from my building's front door—I felt an undeniable urge to comply with his request. I left him on Read while I called Ren.

"You okay?" was his greeting. "Getting hangry?"

"No. I mean, yes, but that's not why I called. He just texted me. He wants to meet at the park across the street."

"When?"

"In half an hour."

Ren fell silent, thinking. To my surprise, he asked, "Do you want to?"

"I—I don't know. I think so. I figured you'd tell me not to go."

"I don't like it, but I've been thinking… Maybe it's not such a bad idea to get some help. With the Wyeth."

I couldn't have been more surprised if he'd asked me to marry him. My voice jumped up an octave to ask, "Are you serious?"

"I've been watching you get nowhere with this for three decades. I'm sick of it."

"Wow."

"Tell him you'll meet him at six forty-five. That'll give me time to get to the park. Let's have a signal… Wear a jacket, and if you need my help, take it off."

"What if I get hot?"

"Deal with it."

*

Six forty-six found me sitting in the shade of a massive oak in the northeast corner of Burk Burnett Park. Though I'd come prepared in the lightest jacket I owned, the evening sun was brutally hot and I desperately wanted to take it off. I spotted Ren a few yards away, his nose in a book, sunglasses shading his eyes against the raking sunlight. Sunglasses would've been a good idea.

I took out my phone to text him, thinking the signal could easily be changed to putting my jacket *on*, but before I could compose the text, Fred appeared on the park bench next to me.

"Bring any friends?" he asked.

Refusing the invitation to turn and look at Ren, I said crossly, "I don't have any friends."

"Will you look at me?"

I reluctantly turned on the bench so that my body faced him, pulling one leg up to form a feeble barrier between us. With my back to Ren, I felt quite alone in the crowded, public park.

"I'm sorry," he said. The terse delivery was somewhat unconvincing. "I scared you. On purpose. That wasn't right."

"I think I'll survive."

"Your… uh… offer took me by surprise. And I didn't expect anyone to notice the Caillebotte, at least not so soon. Stupid rivet… I knew better. It was all ego."

"*You* painted it?" My heart thudded once against my chest.

"Yep. Took me six months. And it was all for nothing, apparently. I mean, who notices something like that?"

"I told you, it's my favorite painting."

"I really wanted that to be a God-honest date, you know."

I squirmed under his steady gaze and wrapped my arms around my propped-up knee. "Sorry."

"I like you."

"Oh. Still?"

With a wistful smile, he said, "Still."

"… Why?"

"Let's talk about this Wyeth. You told me it's a portrait of your great aunt and she left it to you when she died. That means you, your aunt, and Andrew Wyeth knew it exists. Who else knew? Anyone who's still among the living?"

I was tempted to answer right out again, but this time I thought better of it and asked instead, "Are you saying you'll help me?"

"Yeah, I will. It might be fate, after all. I bet there's a pretty good chance no one else is gonna notice the fake, if they haven't already. Just you."

I felt a surge of elation, followed by restraint. It wasn't time to start celebrating yet. "We'll probably have to steal it, if we can even find it." I rested my head on my arm, feeling oddly self-conscious about admitting, "I won't be much help there. I've never stolen anything."

He laughed. "Never? Nothing? Not even a candy bar?"

"Nope."

"You might find you like it." He caught a lock of my hair and twisted it around one finger. "If we're doing this, I'm in charge. Full-on dictatorship. Can you live with that?"

"Sure."

"If I decide I want to bring in outside help, that's totally up to me."

"Whatever you say, boss."

He almost smiled, adding sternly, "All you have to do is keep your mouth shut about the Caillebotte, verify the authenticity of your naughty Wyeth, and take it home when we're done. Clear?"

"It's a very tasteful nude," I argued. "But yes, clear. Are you going to make me sit at home and twiddle my thumbs while you do all the work? Because that's not what I had in mind."

"No, you're gonna help. However I want you to help, no arguments."

Though I grimaced, I answered, "Fine. Anything else?"

"Yeah. I still want you, and I plan to behave accordingly."

"That's not a good idea."

"I didn't say it was."

I stared at him, trying not to smile. He was already enjoying this, if that twinkle in his eyes was any clue. I asked, "You're going to boss me around just for the thrill of it, aren't you?"

"Absolutely."

"How confident are you that we can pull this off? Shouldn't we decide when to call it quits?"

"We can do it. Trust me."

"Trust who?"

He knew immediately what I meant, and for a moment a shadow crossed his face; but it was only a cloud drifting across the sun. He stretched one arm along the bench behind me, pulled me against him, and put his lips to my ear.

"Mikel Christenson. Pleased to meet you."

When he leaned away, I favored him with a smug grin. "That fits you better."

"Thanks. I better go. Tell that surly fascist guarding your door to let me in—we've got a lot of planning to do."

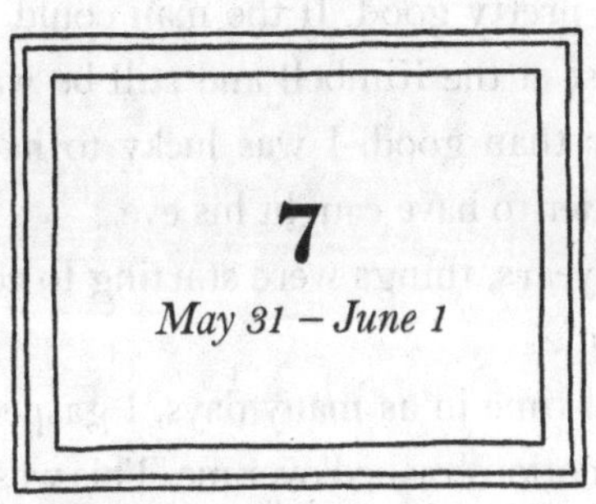


I SAT ON THE PARK BENCH long after Fred—Mikel—had gone. I answered a text from Ren, a single question mark, with a thumbs up, then watched listlessly as he left the park too. Still I sat, watching the sun sink behind the skyscrapers. The heavy air refused to cool down, so I stripped off my jacket at last and enjoyed the caress of a stray breeze on my arms and shoulders.

Ren could say it was risky and stupid, but my gambit had worked. Maybe Fred—Mikel, darn it—maybe *Mikel* and I would fail, but at least I'd be able to say I'd done everything in my power to find the Wyeth. And then, maybe, just maybe, I'd be able to admit defeat.

The very thought startled me, shaking me out of my reverie. I looked around the darkening park, assured myself no one was sneaking up on me, and returned to my thoughts.

*Could* I give up? I'd only given up on one thing my entire adult life—my marriage to Marty. That had nearly killed me. Did I really have to wait until things got that dire to look myself in the mirror and say, "Enough is enough, you did your best, and now it's time to move on"?

Then again, maybe Mikel and I would succeed. I thought our odds were pretty good. If the man could pull off a million-dollar heist at the Kimbell and still be walking free, he must be better than good. I was lucky to have crossed his path, even luckier to have caught his eye.

After thirty years, things were starting to come up Claire. It was about time.

For the third time in as many days, I gasped as a wave of non-specific emotion crashed over me. This was getting ridiculous. I was an emotional woman, sure, but why the drama? Almost as though in answer, my lower abdomen clenched in a painful spasm. I pressed one palm into my guts, groaning.

*Here we go again.*

For twenty-five years, I'd endured this nonsense, never knowing when or even if my next period would start. After each failed pregnancy—five in all—I'd enjoyed a few months of clockwork regularity. I got to see how "normal" women lived. Now I was shocked to feel this pain at all, even though my doctor assured me I wasn't menopausal yet. To hear her tell it, I'd clung so jealously to every egg in my body that I'd be fertile for another decade or more. Fat lot of good they were to me now.

I walked home, ran a bath, and took some painkillers. As they always did when the cramps appeared, my thoughts turned toward calling Marty. "I'm still in the game!" I wanted to scream at him. "Too bad you're too drunk to do anything about it!"

A cruel woman might be able to take satisfaction from that, but cruel I was not. What I wanted more was to call Marty, tell him to meet me for a date three to five days from now, and have sex with him every night until my next period came. He was the only man I'd ever been with, the father of five children we'd never gotten to meet. I would've stayed married to him no matter how drop-dead drunk he wanted to be, if only he could have stopped short of physical abuse. That was where I drew the line, and even then it was almost beyond my ability to do so. If it hadn't been for Ren, I probably wouldn't have been able to make that break. Ren had saved my life, hadn't he?

Could I call Ren in three to five days instead? How much convincing would he need? But I was being ridiculous—what about Fred-who-was-really-Mikel? He wouldn't take any convincing at all.

*Hormones. Stop.*

Dismissing thoughts of Ren and of Mikel before they could take any real form, I contented myself with a long, luxurious bubble bath, ate the rest of the pizza from last night, and finished off the bottle of wine before turning in for an early bedtime.

*

There was something I was supposed to do. I was certain of it. Something Mikel had asked me to do, or Ren? Both would be important. Unfortunately, I couldn't remember what it was. After sleeping in until after 10:00, I tuned back in to my favorite YouTube channels, cleared my schedule for the next two days, and poured myself a glass of breakfast wine. If influencers could drink mimosas before noon every Sunday, I could have a glass of wine for breakfast when my insides were being torn to pieces.

Wrapped in my biggest, fluffiest blanket, I sat on the sofa and nursed my wine while pain lanced through me at regular intervals. I'd given up on the painkillers, figuring I might as well savor the ache while it lasted. My stomach was reminding me of the existence of eggs, bacon, and cheese when my phone rang. Expecting Pam again, I was surprised to see the number for the front desk. I answered right away.

"Hey, Mr. Miller. What's up?"

"Miss Riordan, I'm sorry to bother you, but there's a gentleman here who…" Mr. Miller paused for a beat, for dramatic effect, "*insists* you invited him here for a meeting at eleven."

That's what it was! I was supposed to lift Mikel's ban on entering my apartment building.

"Oh, oh no, I'm so sorry. Yes, you can let him up. I meant to tell you about that yesterday. I'm sorry for the trouble."

"That's quite all right, Miss Riordan. Have a good day."

"You, too."

I jogged to the bathroom to splash water on my face, swish some mouthwash, and drag a comb through my hair. That last task was a lost cause, so I opted for a messy bun and called it cute. Thankfully I was already dressed—albeit in pajamas—so I was able to answer the knock at the door without any suspicious lingering.

I opened the door with a smile on my face for Mikel, only to find myself face-to-face with—I had no idea who this person was.

Before I could tell him he had the wrong apartment, the man forced his way inside and shut the door behind him. He locked it.

I retreated into the kitchen, casting about hopelessly for some kind of weapon. The man was a total stranger to me, but his expression left me in no doubt that he was in the apartment he meant to be in. He descended on me with slow, deliberate strides, filling my small kitchen with his bulk. I reached blindly behind myself, felt the handle of a knife in my knife block, and drew it. The menacing *snick* of metal on wood made him smile, and I nearly dropped the knife as fear numbed my fingers.

"Get out," I croaked.

My phone rang again. I'd left it on the sofa, so it was no more than something for us both to look at before our eyes met again.

"Where is Laubenberg?"

I surprised myself by replying without hesitation, "Who?"

"Fred Laubenberg. Tell me where he is."

"I don't know any Fred. I think you should go."

"I'll go when you tell me what I need to know." He took a long step forward, reached out, and plucked the knife from my nerveless hand. "Don't make this difficult."

Again, my phone rang. As Mondo turned reflexively toward it, I darted away and poured every atom of energy into reaching the phone before he caught up to me. What I'd do then, I had no idea, but the effort wasn't entirely wasted. I reached the phone and kept going, barely pausing to reach down and grab it. Some instinct told me the man was mere inches behind me, so I pivoted on one heel and headed for the bedroom. The maneuver gave me enough time to close my bedroom door, lock it, and answer the incoming call.

It was Mr. Miller again.

"Let him up, let him up!" I cried. That was all I could think to say before my door exploded inward in a shower of splinters. All on its own, my body turned away from the flying debris, and I dropped my phone. Mondo hit me like a wrecking ball, knocking me to the floor and landing on top of me.

"HEL—" I started to scream, hoping the call from Mr. Miller was still connected, but the man clapped a hand over my mouth and squeezed so hard I could only close my eyes and wait for my jaw to break.

"I'm going to cut off one of your fingers, and then I'm going to ask again."

A scream, muffled by his hand, was all I could do in my own defense as cold steel made contact with my right index finger. Instead of feeling its bite, I heard the man's voice again.

"One more chance: Where is Laubenberg?"

He moved his hand away. Gasping for air, I forced out the only thing that might help me more than a scream.

"He's—on his way up—right now—I swear—please!"

"Oh, really?"

Steel met finger again, and I tried to prepare myself for what came next. I barely felt the razor-sharp knife glide through the first few layers of skin, then the pressure disappeared as thundering footsteps tore through the bedroom doorway.

I opened my eyes just in time to see a boot fly through the air and make contact with my assailant's right temple. Mondo toppled over, eyes crossed, and lay still on the floor, my best knife still clutched in his hand.

Mikel hauled me to my feet and took my right hand in both of his. He swore, then dragged me out of the bedroom.

"Wait, my..." I tried to say "phone," but my voice didn't want to work.

Mikel forced me through the kitchen and out the front door, grabbing a hand towel on the way and wrapping it around my bleeding hand.

"Is your car in the garage?" he asked.

"Of course."

"Hey—stay with me. Come on." He pulled me toward the elevators. I hadn't even had a chance to put some shoes on.

I tried again to speak. I needed to tell Mikel that he couldn't get down to the residents' parking garage without my key fob, but my throat was suddenly so dry. He used a set of keys that I was certain belonged on Mr. Miller's belt to override the elevator's security and send us down to the correct level. When we saw Lucius, my voice finally started to work again.

"I don't have the key…"

"I do. Hey. Keep that towel wrapped tight, okay?"

For some reason I found myself looking at Mikel as though a long, dark tunnel separated us. I watched, swaying, as he dropped Mr. Miller's keys on the hood of another car before helping me into the Hellcat's passenger seat. Reality morphed into vague sensations of individual events.

The engine roared to life. My precious, totally unnecessary supercharger.

Sunlight flashed across my face, and I cringed away.

Mikel said, "Hey come on, it's not that bad. Keep your eyes open."

I asked, "What's not that bad? Where are we going?"

Firey pain shot through my right hand, and that was it for me.

*

The next thing I knew, I was lying on my back, staring up at the Hellcat's ceiling. By sound alone, I knew we were traveling at highway speeds—very fast highway speeds. My left hand sought my right, and I felt woolly towel rather than skin. I looked down, as much as I didn't want to, and saw a towel that was still mostly turquoise instead of the blood red hue I feared.

"There she is," Mikel breathed. "Crap, you scared me."

"He *cut* me."

"Yes, but it wasn't bad. I think you're in shock."

"He was looking for you."

"Yeah, I didn't see this coming. That backstabbing, greedy son of a…"

The engine noise took over for a few seconds. I tried to remember how I got here, but it was no use. I could only remember the knife.

"Where are we going?" I asked.

"I'm not a hundred percent sure. Are you hungry? Thirsty?"

"Yes."

"Okay, here's one of those giant gas stations. That's perfect. Any chance your wallet is in your pocket?"

"I don't have pockets."

"Okay. I've got cash."

I leaned my seat up and watched as we exited the highway and turned into a busy gas station. Mikel found a spot between two massive diesel trucks and killed the engine before turning to me.

"You with me?" he asked.

"I don't know. What happened? Where *are* we?"

"You were attacked in your apartment, I saved you, and now we're somewhere east of Tyler. You're in your pajamas, and I'm pretty sure you're both drunk *and* in shock, which is… fantastic."

It seemed important to ask, "How did you get inside my apartment? He locked the door."

"Your doorman gave me his keys. Smart guy."

"I need to call Ren."

"Who?"

Sighing as though answering his question represented the very depth of inconvenience, I recited, "Preston. Murphy. Renner. The Fourth."

After a protracted silence, he mumbled, "This just keeps getting better and better. Stay here, okay? I'm gonna grab something to eat and drink. You need anything else?"

"Tampons."

He swore again, pressed the Hellcat's key fob into my hand, and left.

I leaned the seat back again and closed my eyes. This was the perfect position in which to be flattened by a rush of nausea and then breathe through it, which I did with single-minded purpose. Maybe it was a hangover, maybe it was adrenaline withdrawal, or maybe it was something I didn't know about; but it was miserable. I had just reached the point where I was no longer worried about barfing when Mikel returned.

"You didn't even lock the door," he complained.

"I think I'm going to pass out."

He took my right hand and peeled away the towel, revealing a fair amount of blood that was starting to dry. The cut itself wasn't bleeding anymore, but the sight of the injury—just a half-inch long gash where the proximal phalange and metacarpal joined—made darkness creep around the edges of my vision.

Out of nowhere, rage reared its ugly head.

"Why am I being such a *wuss*," I cried, ripping my hand out of his grasp. I sat up, breathing hard. "I'm not even bleeding anymore. I—woah..."

My head hit the window.

Mikel's voice sounded far away. "Do me a favor and be a wuss. I know where to go, and we're only about an hour away. Once we're there, you can rest until this passes, okay?"

"Ugh gay."

The promised hour passed without event, and I managed to hold onto consciousness the entire time. We stopped again before a tiny log cabin surrounded by towering pines that blocked out almost all sunlight. About the length of a football field away, directly in line with Lucius' front bumper, was a glittering lake. The sun was behind us. I wanted to know what time it was, but didn't think to check Lucius' clock until it was too late and Mikel was pulling me to my feet outside the car. Dry pine needles stabbed into my bare soles, but only until he threw me over his shoulder in a fireman's lift and started for the cabin's front door.

Inside, the cabin was dark and smelled of mildew. Mikel deposited me on a ratty old couch, and I was too tired to protest. I stretched out, throwing my left arm over my eyes. My brain was starting to work a bit better, just in time for a painful, urgent pulse to start beating in my right hand.

I was vaguely aware of lights flicking on one by one. I heard a match flare to life, then smelled the sharp scent of burning sulfur that accompanied it.

"Yes. Burn it down. It's for the best," I mumbled.

"Huh?"

The couch sank as he sat down at my feet. A hand grasped my left ankle.

"I think that's enough histrionics, Miss Riordan," he said with measured tones. "I need a helper, not some fancy baggage."

"Wow," I said through a laugh. "That was *mean*."

"Do you have some kind of hang up about blood?"

I made him wait for my answer until after I'd sat up, pushed my wild hair out of my face, and yawned deeply.

"Yes, I do. I'm sorry. I think I'm better now."

"It's okay. I'm afraid of moths, so... basically the same thing."

I laughed again, enjoying the way it shook away the dregs of the last few hours. Throwing my arms around his neck, I gushed, "Thank you. If you hadn't gotten there when you did... Thank you."

"I never meant for you to get dragged into this. I just thought, 'Hey, she's cute. Maybe she'll go out with me.' It seemed simple at the time."

Nodding, I groaned, "I *really* need to call Ren."

"What is he, your guardian or something?"

"A friend. He'll be worried. Can I use your phone?"

"No."

He stood, easing away from me and toward a candle guttering on top of a rusted old wood stove. I watched the flame flicker and sputter. A faint hint of vanilla was now vying with the aroma of mildew, which I assumed was the point of the candle. There was plenty of light in the cabin without it.

"Why not?" I asked.

"Until I know what's going on, I don't want anyone to know where we are. Can you live with that? I'm not gonna keep you here against your will. But you'll be safer if you stick with me."

"I can live with that."

"You feel safe?"

I stared up at him, asking myself the question not in his

voice or in my own, but in Ren's. The honest answer was, "Yes."

"Good. Can anyone find your car? Are you using a GPS service or in-cab Wi-Fi, anything like that?"

"I'm a dedicated troglodyte."

"I'll take that as a no. Do you have a smart watch, tablet, anything that can connect to the internet or Five-G or—"

"Nothing, I promise. All I had was my phone, and we left it in my apartment with Mondo."

"Mondo? Never mind. Good. Okay." He sat down again. "So here's what happened: I met you in a public place, and the next morning you were attacked in your apartment. What did he want?"

"You. He kept asking me where you were."

Straightening up, he asked sharply, "When we met at the park, why did you change the time? To give someone else time to get there? Was Ren watching us?"

"Well, yeah." I sensed the accusation in his answering silence and cried, "Ren had nothing to do with this! He would never let me get hurt. Never."

"How can you be so sure?"

"He's been my friend almost as long as you've been alive. There's simply no way he has anything to do with this. It's not possible."

"Claire…"

My eyes darted to a plastic grocery bag on the table by the door, and I demanded, "Is there a bathroom in this place?"

"Sure."

He pointed behind me. I struggled to my feet, paused to let a bout of lightheadedness pass, and grabbed the bag on my way into the bathroom.

The cramping part was already over, which meant the rest would be wrapped up in a day and a half at most. Thanking God for small mercies, I muddled through the formalities one-handed and returned to the main room. Mikel had resumed his seat on the couch and was staring at the candle as though it held the answer to life, the universe, and everything.

Seeing a first aid kit at his feet, I sat down next to him and pulled the blue-and-white plastic box into my lap. Inside I found alcohol swabs, a topical antiseptic, an H-shaped bandage, and a couple butterfly sutures. I wasn't sure which kind of bandage to use, but I knew I needed to clean my cut ASAP. I unwound the kitchen towel from my hand again, and at my quiet hiss of pain, Mikel seemed to snap out of his stupor.

"Here, let me do that."

In case I passed out, he had me lean against his back and wrap my right arm around him so he could work on my hand. As he worked, he talked.

"I was worried you'd need stitches, but these butterflies will probably be fine. The trick will be keeping your finger relaxed and dry while it heals. Here comes the alcohol…"

I rested my head on his shoulder and breathed through the pain, but it wasn't too bad. I was starting to feel the first stirrings of real embarrassment. Was this mortal wound on my index finger no more than an XL papercut? Mikel kept talking, almost as though he couldn't help himself.

"Okay, I think I'll double up on the bandages. Butterflies, then the big one over top because it's waterproof. I think that'll work. I've been thinking, and what I can't figure out is how he found out about the Caillebotte. That must be why he sent someone after you. After you sprang your little blackmail scheme on me, I figured it might not be safe to go home, or to work, so I holed up at a crappy motel in Arlington. He didn't know where to find me, but he knew I'd been to your place. Was he watching you?"

"Who is 'he'?"

"Money. Leonard Money. The guy who's stuff I stole."

"OUR LEONARD MONEY? From the Kimbell?" I asked.

Without meaning to, I pulled my hand away as I sat back. Mikel grabbed my forearm and gently pulled me back.

"Almost done. Hold still. How many Leonard Moneys could we be talking about, Claire?"

I leaned my head against his shoulder again, sighing in defeat. "I can't believe it. That *snake*. Joe told me he was underinsured. To think I felt bad for him!"

"I don't know anything about insurance. I just know he wanted me to sell what I could and give him half the profit. He didn't know about the Caillebotte. That was my own deal."

"The guys on your crew must have known," I suggested.

There was a smile in his voice as he asked, "Oh, you think I needed a whole crew, huh?"

"You did it all yourself?"

"Those guys had nothing to do with the break-in. As far as I know, you and I are the only two people who know the Caillebotte at the Kimbell is a fake."

He was done bandaging my hand, but he didn't let go of it. I closed my eyes and felt his chest rise and fall as he lost himself in thought again. I was ready for the accusation when it finally came.

"Have you told anyone else? What about this Ren guy?"

"No one, I promise. I almost told Ren, but he wouldn't let me."

"When did you almost tell him?"

I thought back, struggling to remember what day it was now and how long ago I'd spilled the beans in Ren's office. It was right after brunch, which we'd normally do on a Sunday, but I wanted to talk about the date, so—

"Saturday morning. Yesterday."

"What exactly did you say to him?"

"If I tell you, will you drop it? Ren is like a big brother to me. He'd literally die before he let anything bad—"

"I understand. I'll drop it, just tell me."

I paused again to think. "I said... What did I say? I told him I tried to blackmail you. I started to say, there was something else stolen from the Kimbell that only I knew about, and that's where he stopped me."

The breath he forced in and out felt angry somehow, but he calmed himself enough to say levelly, "Okay. I see two possibilities, and neither seems all that plausible: Either someone overheard you and me in your apartment, or someone overheard you and Ren in... Where were you?"

"His office." I felt the question in his silence and explained, "He's my financial manager. He has a swanky office in downtown Fort Worth, not too far from my apartment. I seriously doubt someone was listening through the keyhole. What about someone you know? I mean, where are you keeping the Caillebotte? Is it safe? Could someone else have seen it?"

"It's safe."

"Fine, ignore my other questions," I huffed. "When you say 'someone overheard,' you mean someone who ran and told Leonard? And then he wanted to get in on this extra take?"

"Or kill me for using his job as a cover for my own."

"That seems a bit extreme," I whispered.

At this point Mikel was just holding my hand while I leaned against his back, and the arrangement felt so safe I decided to shut up and enjoy it. He started playing with my uninjured fingers, bending and flexing them with exaggerated gentleness. Soon he was talking again.

"We can probably get away with one night here, but then we'll have to move on. You need to rethink this thing, Claire. Circumstances have changed. As long as Leonard is after me, and trying to get to me through you, you're not safe. Can you stay with Ren? Do you have that kind of relationship? Or maybe with your parents, or another relative?"

"What about the Wyeth?"

"That's what I mean. Things are bad enough without trying to—"

"Oh no no no, we're not throwing in the towel already. So we have to make ourselves scarce while we look. Big deal. It's not like we were going to book spots on the local news channels to plead for its safe return. We'll work in the dark and live in the dark. Intrigue. Danger. I love it."

"You have a job," he reminded me.

"Two, actually. So Joe won't be able to reach me. My clients will think I ghosted them. So what? This may be hard for you to understand, but if I don't find that painting, I don't even—What will my life amount to? What will have been the point of all this?"

Having expressed as much to both Marty and Ren many times over the years, I knew Mikel would respond the same way they always had. You matter. Your life isn't meaningless. You have people who love you and need you. Blah, blah, blah.

"I get that," he said quietly. "I really do."

I pressed my face into his back and just breathed. I had no idea what to say to that.

"If you trust Ren so much, I guess I can too," he said. He pressed his phone into my palm. "Call him. We need to stay somewhere in the city, and I'm guessing he has a place or two to spare."

I had already dialed Ren's number and hit Send before Mikel finished talking. Ren answered on the first ring, his voice taut with suppressed anxiety.

"Hello? Who is this?"

"Ren, it's me."

"Claire! Where are you? What happened? Are you okay? What the—"

"I'm okay." I covered the microphone with one hand and asked Mikel, "Can I tell him I'm with you?"

"He'll figure it out eventually," Mikel said.

Ren was in full stride in the background. "… telling me someone attacked you in your apartment this morning and this art thief you've been running around with *abducted* you—"

"He didn't abduct me. Jeez. He saved me. I'm here with him now, and I told you, I'm okay."

"They said they found blood on the floor."

"And yet, I live. *Please* calm down. We need your help."

To his credit, Ren took the time to compose himself before saying, "All right. Tell me how I can help."

"We need a safe place to stay. Where we are now… it's not a long-term solution. Don't you have that apartment in Linwood, the short-term rental that you think I don't know is a love nest?"

Taking my jab in stride, he muttered, "Just a sec. Let me see if it's available."

I took the opportunity to put the phone on speaker and set it down on Mikel's knee. "He's checking," I explained.

"Love nest?"

"He's a mad man."

"I heard that," Ren said. "They just finished cleaning up after the last renter. It's all yours. I deactivated the listing."

"Thank you," I said. "We can be there in about two hours."

Ren reeled off the address and ended the call with an imperious, "I will meet you there."

*

As cozy as the spider-infested lakeside cabin was, I was happy to be back inside Lucius and roaring down Interstate 20 at exactly the posted speed limit. Mikel had wisely offered no resistance to me driving, which gave me two uninterrupted hours of taming 707 horses and thinking about absolutely nothing else. Mikel was silent for the entire ride, occasionally tapping away at his phone for reasons he didn't care to share with me.

He wasn't happy about our benefactor meeting us at the apartment, but he seemed to have concluded it was unavoidable. I was excited to see Ren until I parked in one of the apartment building's guest spots, turned off the engine with my right index finger per usual, and twitched in pain as my cut threatened to reopen.

"This might be a little dramatic," I said. "Maybe you should wait here? I'm not as sure as I'd like to be that Ren doesn't have the cops waiting for you up there."

"Fine time to tell me."

"Just take the key. I'll use his phone to call you once I know the lay of the land. If I tell you to lock the car, that's the signal to bug out. Got it?"

"Roger."

"Um… just in case." I grabbed his shirt with my uninjured hand and pulled him into a quick kiss. As I leaned away, he yanked me back and dragged me halfway into the passenger seat to kiss me properly. After a minute or so of that, I gave him a rather loopy goodbye and left him there in the Hellcat, hoping it wasn't the last time I'd see both of them.

I found my way to the correct apartment and, knowing Ren had beaten me there, I knocked on the door. Ren opened it and stepped aside, checking the hallway before locking the door behind me. Before I could explain Mikel's absence, Ren pulled me into a crushing embrace.

Voice muffled by my hair, he groaned, "You've really outdone yourself this time."

"Thanks."

He let me go and zeroed in on my heavily bandaged hand. "What happened? Where's Fred?"

"Ha! The last person who asked me that tried to slice off my second favorite finger."

"Good God, Claire…"

"It's not that bad. Did they arrest him?"

"The guy who attacked you? They didn't say. All I know is, he got out of the building about thirty seconds before the cops arrived. Your doorman wisely didn't try to stop him.

The size of him… They showed me the security camera footage to see if I recognized him."

"And?"

"Don't know him from Adam."

"Dang it." I pictured Mondo walking around Fort Worth, free as a vulture, and forced my thoughts toward less horrifying matters. I said, "Fred's name isn't Fred, it's Mikel, and he's waiting for me to give the all clear before he comes up. I thought you may have… you know…"

"Called the cops?"

"Yeah."

Ren pointed a maledicting finger under my nose and snapped, "The *only* reason I didn't was because I knew it would piss you off. Don't make me regret it."

"I told you he saved me from the knife guy, didn't I?"

"You're in this mess because of him. Why does he need to be here, anyway?"

I frowned at him, thrown off by his question. To me the answer was self-evident, but apparently Ren had credited me with more sense than I actually had. I saw the moment realization dawned; his face began to redden again.

"You're *still* going after the Wyeth?" he demanded.

"Don't fight me on this. Mikel is my best chance, and I'm not giving it up."

He gave me an unhappy nod of concession. "Fine. Do what you have to do." Smiling thinly, he asked, "You like this guy?"

"Yeah."

"Is that why you're being stupid?"

"Sure. Can I use your phone?"

He unlocked his phone and handed it to me, and I dialed the same number I'd memorized from the slip of paper Mikel had given me a million years ago. A pre-recorded message said the number was disconnected. I tried again, thinking I must have entered the wrong number, but I got the same result. Ren paused in the act of sorting groceries into the fridge, seeing me staring at his phone in consternation and trying not to panic.

"Can't reach him?" Ren asked.

"What number did I call you from earlier?"

"Just some unknown number. Check the call log."

I found the number and hit Send, and Mikel answered immediately with a generic, "Hello?"

"It's Claire. You got a new phone?"

"Yeah, this morning. Sorry, I thought I mentioned that."

"It's okay. You can come up."

"All right…" He gave me time to add something, perhaps a coded message about locking the Hellcat; but when I remained steadily silent, he said, "Be right there."

"I wonder why he got a new phone," I mused aloud.

"Guy like him probably gets a new one every week."

"Yeah… You're probably right."

Still mulling this over, I helped Ren unload the groceries. Red meat, eight different kinds of cheese, enough wine to open an Italian restaurant, a massive bag of avocados, three dozen eggs… the man knew me too well. He pulled out a giant box of mixed greens and shook it under my nose.

"Eat this too, Ron Swanson."

"Don't tell me what to do."

His response was lost in a series of booming knocks at the door. Mikel sure knew how to make an entrance. Giving Ren a quelling look, I left him to the groceries and hurried to let Mikel inside.

I opened the door to see Mikel standing with his back to the far wall in the hallway outside. He raised his eyebrows as though to ask, "Is it really safe to come in?"

"Come on," I said, waving my hand urgently. "Don't just stand out there."

Ren left off putting away groceries and paced into the entryway to stand behind me. Mikel nodded at him, stepped inside, and extended his hand in greeting.

"Mikel. Nice to finally meet you."

With the ghost of a smile, Ren took his hand and replied, "Preston. Likewise."

That seemed like the right time for me to duck into the kitchen and finish up. Trying to tune out their lowered voices, I made quite a meal of rearranging the items Ren had so haphazardly tossed into the fridge, then did the same for the dry goods and wine bottles. Ren had also purchased a bottle of my favorite gin and a six-pack of Topo Chico, which I eyed greedily while the entryway conversation moved toward the kitchen. Ren was really spoiling me. I stepped in front of the gin bottle as they turned the corner.

"Well, I'll get out of your hair so you can get to work on your conspiracies to commit things," Ren announced. "The keys are on the microwave. Is there anything else you need?"

I shook my head. "We're good. Thank you."

With forced optimism, we said our goodbyes, and then Ren was out the door and gone. The moment the door closed behind him, Mikel rounded on me and asked, "What are you hiding?"

"Nothing! What?" I crossed my arms. "Why?"

"You're so transparent. Take two steps to your right."

"No."

He reached blindly behind me and found the bottle of gin, which he withdrew with a magician-esque flourish. He frowned at the bottle, and then his gaze settled on the six-pack of Topo Chico. His eyes narrowed and moved to me.

"That *was* your drink."

"Technically, I didn't say it wasn't."

"Minx."

"We should get down to business, don't you think?" I asked.

"I'm ready when you are," he whispered, leaning in for a kiss.

I dodged away and retreated into the living room. "I mean the business of the Wyeth. Obviously."

He accepted my words with a stoic nod. "All right. I've been thinking about where to start, and if you've been after this thing for thirty years, I'd really love to know where the painting isn't. I'd say you're an expert in that."

"Oh, yeah. I've been all over the country, plus most of Europe and one exceedingly stupid trip to Argentina. No hablo Español." I smiled to myself, adding wistfully, "Ren always calls them my 'trips to Florence,' no matter where I'm going."

"Why Florence?"

"I never asked."

I made myself comfortable on the couch and waited for him to join me, but he picked up the gin bottle again and studied it. When I was about to wonder aloud whether he'd like to be alone with the liquor, he asked, "He got this for you? All this?"

"Yep. I'm sure you're allowed to partake."

He set the gin next to the Topo and opened the fridge. From between its open doors, I heard, "Good grief. Is this how you eat all the time?"

"What about it?"

He half-closed one door to level a judgmental glare at me. "When was the last time you got your cholesterol checked?"

"Six weeks ago, and it was the same it's always been."

"Four hundred?"

"Sixty-nine," I countered with a smug grin.

"Okay." He gave up on the food assessment and closed the fridge. "I can tell that's a conversation we don't need to have. Tell me about your 'trips to Florence.'"

"THE FIRST TRIP WAS WHEN I was eighteen. Ren's father was my financial manager then. He'd been the conservator of my money for ten years, and he'd just convinced me to continue the arrangement even though I was an adult and legally entitled to take control of my own assets. It made sense to let him do it. My parents weren't going to be any help at all, and Mr. Renner—"

"Why not?" Mikel interjected.

"My parents? They were the reason Aunt Eva's gift was being controlled by a conservator in the first place. They were and are—by their own admission, mind you—worse with money than an eight-year-old. My mom is a hoarder, and my dad is a compulsive shopper. They would've spent every last penny of it before my tenth birthday, and then their hoard would've crushed them to death. But in ten years, Mr. Renner more than doubled Aunt Eva's inheritance, and I had no idea how he'd done it. I still have no idea."

"How much money are we talking about?"

I studied the eager light in his eyes and said, "Don't worry about it. Anyway, when I turned eighteen, I convinced a few of my high school friends to take a graduation trip to Amsterdam with me. Since I was paying for their flights and hotels—once I convinced Mr. Renner to let me have the money—they didn't argue. What I didn't tell them was that I'd stumbled across a story online about a rich, crazy old man who lived in a mansion outside Amsterdam and had a massive art gallery that he only showed to his closest friends. The man claimed to have several pieces by an American artist—pieces no one had ever seen."

Mikel sighed. "This sounds super made up."

"Oh, of course it was. The day we got to Amsterdam, I dragged my poor friends to this mansion only to find a garden-variety art museum. I stayed mad for about half a day, and then we all had a great time in Amsterdam. I'd love to not count it as my first trip, but it was."

"I'm guessing the quality of your leads improved after that."

"Yes. I told Mr. Renner what I'd done, and he was mad, but he told me something I'll never forget. He said, 'This obsession is going to send you all over the map, and I know for a fact Eva would be tickled to death by that. All I ask is that you let me help you decide when and where to go.' And he did. Until he retired four years ago, I ran everything by him; and if he said not to go, I didn't go. Ren has been a little bit less… rigorous."

"How many times have you done this?"

"Eighty-two," I confessed. "I have been all over the map, and it's been fun, but… I really thought I would have found it by now. Sometimes I wonder if it didn't just get thrown away after my aunt died, and I've spent my life looking for a painting that doesn't exist anymore."

"Whoa." Mikel put a hand on my knee, his palm warm through the thin cotton of my pajama pants. "That took a depressing turn. You don't really believe that, do you?"

"I don't know."

"Someone else had to have known about it. Someone else had access to it."

"You're saying someone stole it?"

"It's the simplest answer."

As quickly as I could, I told Mikel the same story I'd told Maddie on the flight to Dallas. The safe in the basement. The briefest of looks before Aunt Eva shut it away again. Her death two days later, and my desperation as I realized the painting had vanished and there was nothing I could do about it. While I spoke, his expression moved from open curiosity to outright anger.

I finished my tale with, "What did I say that made you so mad?"

"Not mad," he said, distracted with his own thoughts. "Just... concerned. I'm sure you've already figured this out, but someone had to open your aunt's safe to dispose of the contents of her will. Who would that have been? Did you attend a reading of her will, or read it privately? How long after she died did her funeral take place? Was the will read before or after her funeral?"

"I see what you're getting at... If the painting was mentioned in her will, she would've had to give someone the combination to take it out for me. Right?" He nodded. "I have a copy of her will. It doesn't mention the painting. As to the rest... If I remember correctly, her funeral was a week after she died, but my parents and I attended a reading of her will a few days before. I have a vivid memory of my mom swearing for the first and only time in my life when Mr. Renner read out how much money Aunt Eva left me."

Sharply, he asked, "Mr. Renner? Ren's dad?"

"Well, yeah. He was the executor of her estate. That's how my parents met him."

"You're kidding."

"Why is that significant?"

"Are you serious?" He looked at me like I was crazy, or dense. "Who in the world was most likely to know the combination to Eva's safe, if not the executor of her estate?"

"I… guess I never thought of it like that."

"You said you asked people, adults, about the painting. Was he one of them?"

"I don't remember, I was *eight*," I snapped.

Anger fell over me, and I stood up just for something to do. I stalked into the kitchen, grabbed a bottle of wine, and began searching the unfamiliar, poorly organized space for a corkscrew. Mikel left me to it for a minute or so, then joined me in the kitchen. He slipped the wine bottle from my hand and set it carefully on the counter.

"It's a bit early for that," he said gently.

"Mr. Renner is like a grandfather to me. He loves me. He loved my aunt, too. There's no way—don't make me say this again—no *way* he—I mean, are you insinuating that *he* stole it, and all these years he's been letting me run around like an idiot searching for it? Is that what you're saying?"

"Yes, it is. You can be mad about it, but you should also consider the possibility that it's true."

"I *have* considered it. The painting wasn't in her will, and there wasn't anything else in that safe. So maybe she never told anyone the combination."

"Then how did she intend to leave it to you?"

"I don't *know*," I moaned. Painfully aware of how childish I sounded, I said, "I'm hungry, and I'm tired of wearing pajamas, and I *hate* this apartment. Why does everything have to be *white*?"

"Oooookay," he said, in a tone I'd use to soothe a cornered animal. He pulled me into a chaste hug and rubbed my back. "That's enough business for now, huh?"

I focused on the calming motion of his hand, up and down and up and down, and found my pulse slowing as the surge of anger faded away. "I forgot how emotional this makes me. I'm sorry."

"Give yourself a break. You've been through a lot today. Let's get you something to eat. What are you thinking, a big pile of cheese with bacon grease to dip it in?"

Laughing, I wormed out of his arms. "I'll make scrambled eggs." Seeing the keys on top of the microwave where Ren left them, I added, "He probably left us a key to the utility closet. I think he keeps a box of lost and found in there. Maybe we'll get lucky and find some clothes that fit."

"I'll look."

The familiar tedium of making scrambled eggs finished the job Mikel had started. By the time he returned to the kitchen, his arms full of clothes, I was perfectly calm. I divided the eggs between two bowls and passed one to Mikel after he piled the clothes on the kitchen island.

He took a bite, swallowed, took one more, and asked, "What did you put in these?"

"Goat cheese."

"This is some gourmet sh—stuff. It would go great on a

piece of toast…"

"Can't help you there. What did you find?"

Ren had been renting this apartment out since before Airbnb existed, so I expected a wide variety of forgotten items to choose from; still, I was surprised by how much Mikel found. I sorted through the items, checking sizes, and came up with enough clothes to get me through at least three days. No underwear, of course, but I'd never be desperate enough to wear second-hand panties. Along with the items Mikel had picked out for himself, I threw the lot in the washing machine.

At last, knowing I had clean clothes to change into, I took a shower and washed it all away—the attack, the pointless road trip to the Louisiana border and back, Mikel's aspersions against Ren's father, and the bandage on my finger which was supposed to be waterproof.

Though the butterfly sutures stayed in place, the cut began to bleed again as I climbed out of the shower. The sight of it seeping from under the sutures was bad enough, but when a big, fat drop landed on the bathroom floor, I almost went down under a wave of nausea. I rallied enough to wrap a huge, fluffy towel around myself and a smaller wash cloth around my hand before sitting down on the bed and calling, "Mikel?"

I wasn't sure he could hear me through the bedroom door and was about to call again when he let himself inside. He didn't have to ask what was wrong. He made me lay back, covered me in blankets, and ordered me not to move while he found a first aid kit.

While I listened to him search the small apartment, I lay there, breathing in and out and hating myself.

I couldn't handle the sight of blood. I couldn't see what was right in front of me, the possibility that Ren's dad—maybe even Ren himself—had known all along where the Wyeth was. I couldn't carry a child to term. I couldn't save my marriage. I couldn't find the Wyeth. I couldn't do *anything* I wanted to do.

Hearing Mikel returning, I swiped away a few hot tears with my left hand and forced myself to smile at him.

"Any chance you'll be fed up with me soon?" I asked lightly.

"Hm." He gave the question serious thought while he re-bandaged my hand. "If it weren't for you, I might not be in hiding right now. That's debatable. We don't really know how Money found out about the Caillebotte, or even if he did find out about it. Maybe he's pissed at me for some other reason. Maybe he just wants to tie up a loose end. *But* if not for you, I'd still be holed up in the stinking roach motel where I spent the last two nights, so that's a plus. I'd be alone, instead of being entertained by an interesting and attractive woman who can make scrambled eggs that taste like a gourmet meal."

"Oh, stop."

"I'd have to say, all things considered…" He smoothed out the new bandage, making me wait. "No, I don't see myself getting fed up with you in the near future, or at all."

Not to be mollified, I pressed, "And if we find the Wyeth? What happens after that?"

"Let's burn that bridge when we come to it."

With a full stomach, clean clothes, and the day threatening to end without any real accomplishment to my name, I was ready to dig back in to the nitty gritty; but Mikel insisted I needed the rest of the day off and all but forced me to agree that surviving a knife attack counted as an accomplishment. He poured me a glass of wine and put a decisive end to my business-minded thoughts by asking, "What's for dinner?"

The result of that debate was me, wearing a stranger's clothes and ill-fitting shoes to walk to a corner store two blocks from the apartment to acquire spaghetti. We'd tried calling Ren to use him as a grocery delivery service, but his phone had gone straight to voicemail. After an hour, when he still hadn't called back or answered my texts, we gave up on him. Mikel needed carbs, I needed underwear, and only one of us had to stay out of sight. Though Mikel protested, I convinced him the only thing that made sense was for me to run a quick errand, and I needed some fresh air anyway.

With the sun setting behind me, I set out for the corner store at a brisk walk. My scavenged flip-flops were a size and a half too big, but they were slightly better than going barefoot and didn't slow me down too much. I bought what I could at the store—they did not carry underwear, sadly—and emerged to find the sun gone and twilight setting in.

Directly across the street, taking up most of a bus stop bench, sat an enormous man who seemed to be staring straight at me. As he rose slowly to his feet, I accepted the evidence of my disbelieving eyes: Mondo was back in the fight.

WITHOUT A SECOND THOUGHT, I dived back inside the corner store. The employee who'd cashed me out asked, "Forget something?"

I stared at the teenage girl as though she were speaking Greek and hadn't thought of an answer by the time Mondo let himself into the store.

Piecing the scene together with incredible speed, the teenager asked, "Do you want me to call the police?" in a voice that I was sure had carried to every corner of the medium-sized store.

Mondo cast her a contemptuous glare before turning back around and exiting the store. I moved toward the employee, if only to set the heavy paper bags I carried down on the counter. I'd found a lot more than spaghetti.

"What was that about?" she asked.

If ever there were a time to not suck at lying, it was now. If she called the police, I'd have to lie to *them* about where I'd been since Saturday morning, who I was with, and other things I couldn't guess at the moment.

I scrabbled around in my muddled brain and came up with, "Can you believe I used to date that cave troll? I guess 'restraining order' isn't part of his limited vocabulary."

"Oh, yikes." She bit her lip, thinking. "All I can do is call the cops. If I try to keep him from coming inside, I'll probably get fired."

"I don't want that. Is there a back way out?"

"No, sorry."

"Can I use your phone?"

"Sure."

Rather than pointing me to the landline behind her, she pulled a bedazzled cell phone from her pocket, unlocked it, and handed it over. I dialed Ren's number. This time when the call went directly to voicemail, the irritation I'd felt before was gone. Now I was panicking. Knowing he wouldn't recognize the number, I left a quick voicemail.

"It's Claire. You-know-who found me somehow and followed me to the store. I'm inside now. Not sure what to do… Call Mi—Fred if you get this."

My next call would have been to Mikel, but I hadn't yet memorized his new number. I gave the phone back.

"Please don't call the police," I said through a sigh. "I don't want that kind of trouble. It'll just make him mad."

"You can't go out there," she argued. "He'll so be waiting for you."

"I know."

We both jumped as her phone rang from her back pocket. She checked the number and shot me an apologetic look. "It's just my mom."

While my impromptu ally took the call, I edged to my left

to see if Mondo was visible outside the glass front doors. He wasn't. Mind racing, I tried to look at the problem the way Mikel would. He was certainly more strategically-minded than I was.

Mondo had to have followed me to the store. From where? From the apartment? Had he known of my association with Ren, and somehow found a list of properties Ren owned? That didn't seem so far-fetched. It also seemed like the work of a cunning sort of person, not a pile of dumb ugly muscle. Someone had to be calling the shots and ordering Mondo around. Leonard Money? Had I known how to reach Money, I'd call him and tell him to leave me the heck alone; but that would probably do more harm than good.

I had to get back to Mikel somehow. What if another grunt was at the apartment right now?

"He probably doesn't know there's only one way out," I mused. "What time do you close?"

"Um… now, kinda. Sorry."

"Perfect. It's okay if you can't, but can you start closing up the store with me still in here? I want to make him think I'm gone."

"Oh smart! Yeah, I can do that. Just hide somewhere, I'll start turning off lights and stuff."

I took my paper grocery bags and sat down under the cash register, where I'd be invisible to anyone walking through the front door. As the store was plunged into darkness one light at a time, I heard two other customers leave. Then I heard one enter.

The teenager said, "Sorry, we're closed."

Oh, dear Lord. She was so tiny. Why did she sound so fierce? I had to fight past an urge to leap over the counter and throw myself between her and the enormous brute I knew she was talking to. Fortunately, Mondo didn't seem inclined to harm her.

He asked, "Where'd she go?"

"That lady you're harassing? Not that it's any of your business, but she's gone, okay? Now get out of here before I call the cops."

She seemed to be relishing her role in this drama of mine. Maybe she was a theater student. I almost believed her. Mondo stomped loudly through the doors, which thunked moments later as the girl locked them.

"Well now I'm sorta thinking I might get in trouble for letting you stay in here," she said quietly, voice echoing through the empty store. "Mom will be here in like five minutes to pick me up, and I have to set the alarm..."

I stood up. "I'm not staying. But if you have a hat and a jacket I can borrow, I promise I'll bring them back as soon as I safely can."

She dashed to the back and returned with a letterman jacket and a Cleveland Browns baseball cap, which she handed over without hesitation.

"I don't care if you bring the hat back, but that's my boyfriend's jacket, so, you know..."

"You'll get it back. Thank you so much."

As I started for the door, she asked, "What about all your stuff?"

"Oh yeah!" I leaned over the counter to grab the package of spaghetti out of one bag, slipped it into an inside pocket of the letterman, and said, "I can't take the rest, sorry."

She unlocked the door to let me out, and sooner than I would have liked, I was standing on the dark sidewalk with two blocks between me and safety. Two blocks in which Mondo was certain to be lurking, waiting for me to cross his path. I waved goodbye to the girl, pulled the cap down as low as I could, and started walking.

If he believed I'd really escaped out the non-existent back door, the only move that made sense was to book it back to the apartment and wait for me to appear. I wasn't within walking distance of anything or anyone else, unless I considered the three bars I'd passed on the way here possible refuges. I was tempted, but hiding wouldn't accomplish anything. I needed to get back to Mikel.

Mikel. Duh. Mondo was looking for him, not me. He must not know Mikel was in the apartment, otherwise he wouldn't have bothered with me at all. Cheered by the thought, though no closer to solving my immediate problem, I slowed my pace to give myself more time to think.

For the first time in my entire life, I wished I had a gun. I pictured shooting Mondo and changed my mind. Not for me, no thanks. I didn't need a gun; I needed to be invisible.

I tucked my hair up inside the cap, which was no easy task considering the sheer volume of it. Satisfied that my locks were hidden from sight, I slipped off my flip-flops and tucked them inside the jacket. As much as I hated the thought of walking barefoot down the sidewalk, it had to be done. I was out of ways to alter my appearance, so I spent the rest of the walk steeling myself. When I saw him, if I saw him, I wouldn't run. I wouldn't react to him or acknowledge him at all. I wasn't Claire, I was just some barefoot drunk wandering the streets alone.

It worked—mostly. I was within fifty yards of the apartment building's front door when I spotted him, leaning against the building in the shadow of a young oak. I forced myself to disobey the voice in my head telling me to run for my life, focusing instead on remembering the six-digit combination that opened the front door.

Once I reached the stairs, there was no reason to hope he wouldn't see through my paltry disguise. I heard him move and leapt up the last three steps, hammering the code into the keypad as fast as I could. He caught two handfuls of the letterman and I twisted out of it, leaving him holding the jacket while I threw myself through the door and closed it in his face.

Breathing hard, I stood in front of the door and stared at him. Good God, he was huge. The man was easily a foot taller than me, a cool 300 pounds of mostly muscle. He just stood there, a foot away on the other side of glass I was certain he could easily smash. For uncounted seconds, he glowered at me. Then he took a step forward, nose nearly touching the glass. Slowly, as though daring me to tell him not to, he reached down and tested the door handle. The handle swung loose, disabled by the electronic lock, while the door remained securely shut.

"You can't stay in there forever," he said. His gravelly voice was so clear, the glass might as well have vanished into thin air.

I wordlessly pointed to a sign attached to the inside of the door. It was blank on my side but said on the outside, if I recalled correctly, "NO LOITERING." He glanced at it, flashed me a wolfy grin, dropped the jacket on the ground, and left. Loyalty to the teenage girl and her boyfriend caused me to spend several minutes staring at the sad, crumpled heap of jacket, trying to work up the courage to dodge outside and grab it. Logic won out in the end, as it so rarely did with me, and I left it to chance that someone else would bring the jacket inside.

Legs shaking, I rode the elevator up and let myself into the apartment. The sight of Mikel sitting on the sofa, cocktail in one hand, remote control in the other, looking totally at ease and at peace with the world, made me want to scream.

He glanced at me, then did a double take. "Where'd you get the hat?"

"From the pint-sized teenage girl who just saved my life. Make me one of those?"

He brought his mostly-full glass to me and pressed it into my hands, asking, "What happened?"

I described the encounter and all I'd inferred from Mondo's sudden reappearance. Mikel nodded along, not disagreeing with any of my conclusions.

"I take it Ren didn't call?" I asked.

"No, he didn't."

I remembered I had a drink in my hands and gulped most of it down. "This is pretty light on the gin," I complained.

"I didn't know when you'd be back. Come sit down, you're white as a sheet."

"Yes, sir," I said.

He sat down next to me and slipped the cap off my head, letting my hair tumble free. Exhausted, I leaned forward and rested my head on his shoulder, letting him support me. I must have dozed off, because the next thing I knew, I was waking up alone on the couch with my feet tucked under a blanket and an older Roger Moore as James Bond movie on the TV. I watched listlessly as 007 out-skied several black-clad goons, looking improbably dapper in a bright yellow ski suit with red trim.

"It was a simpler time," I sighed.

As though in answer, Mikel asked, "You're sure?"

He was in the kitchen, his voice so low I knew he wasn't talking to me. I sat up and confirmed he was on the phone.

"Please be Ren," I whispered.

"All right. Yeah, I will. Bye." He hung up and met my eyes, reading in them the question I needed answered. "That was Ren. He's been getting grilled by the cops most of the evening."

"Why?"

"It's official, Ms. Riordan: You're the inside man on the Kimbell job. The cops think he's helping us hide."

"He is. Do we have to leave?"

"He doesn't think so. He told them he has renters here and put the fear of God in the detectives about bothering them. According to him."

"So we're stuck here," I concluded. "Between Mondo and the cops, neither of us can afford to show our faces."

"I agree. But we need help anyway, and it got me thinking…" He sat down by my feet. "Neither of us is any good with computers, and if we're gonna be stuck here, that's our only way to reach the outside world. I think it's time to bring in outside help."

"Weren't you monkeying around in the code for the security system at the museum?" I asked.

"No, I was watching Annika monkey around in the code through a remote connection."

"Annika?"

"My kid sister. If I can convince her to come here, she can come and go freely and help us track down the Wyeth. What do you think?"

"Per our deal, I think it's your decision," I said. "But, I agree."

"Good. Do we tell Ren?"

I hated the implication in his question, but it had to be asked. "I don't know," I said unhappily. "Do we have to decide tonight?"

"Nah." He found my feet through the blanket and gave them a playful squeeze, adding, "But we *do* have to decide how to spend our last night alone before my annoying little sister shows up."

"Well…" My gaze strayed to the TV, and I said, "This Bond flick isn't going to watch itself."

**11**

*June 2*

WHEN I WOKE UP AGAIN, I didn't know where or when I was. I was lying on my side and couldn't move, and light was flickering through the dark room. A TV was on. It must have been muted, because all I could hear was my own breathing.

After a few moments of quiet panic, I remembered the apartment and Mikel and falling asleep on the couch with him, serenaded by the cheeky antics of Sir Roger Moore. I was sandwiched between Mikel and the back of the couch, his broad back blocking the room from view.

I pressed a hand between his shoulder blades and felt his breathing change as he woke up. He rolled over to face me.

"What time is it?" I asked.

He pulled an arm out of the blanket that covered us both and checked his watch. "Just after four."

Tugging the blanket up over my shoulders, he draped his arm over me and pulled me even closer. I was suddenly hyperaware that two scant layers of clothing were all that stood between my body and his, and I wouldn't have minded at all if they both disappeared.

He seemed to be thinking along the same lines. Sliding one leg between mine, he grinned as I sucked in an involuntary gasp. His lips found mine, then moved down my neck while the pressure between my legs increased.

It took every last ounce of will I possessed to whisper, "Please don't do that."

The pressure disappeared at once, and I met his eyes as he leaned away.

"I'm sorry," was all I could think to say.

"Don't be." He kissed me once more. "I'm gonna take the bed, unless you want it."

"I'm fine here."

He left, and though I tried to fall back asleep, the effort was in vain. I endured a couple hours of feeling wretched and lonely, then rose with the sun and made myself a pot of very strong coffee.

Mikel emerged to the sound of steam erupting from the gurgling coffee pot. He was freshly-showered and clean-shaven, and his quiet "Good morning" did not come complete with a smile. All at once I felt so miserable, I considered calling off our arrangement. He came to stand in front of me, and I caught the scent of whatever soap or shampoo he'd used. He smelled so good I wanted to cry.

With a gusty sigh, he hooked a finger around the chain of my necklace and pulled it out from underneath my t-shirt.

Addressing the cross dangling between our noses, he asked, "This isn't just a pretty necklace or a family heirloom, is it?"

"No."

"That's… disappointing."

"I'm sorry you feel that way."

He finally smiled, though it was only a little one. "I'm just being honest. I'm not some twenty-year-old hound dog, you know. Still…" He shook his head wistfully. "Disappointing."

"When will Annika be here?"

"Nice segue. She'll be dead to the world until noon at the earliest. About telling Ren…"

I shook my head. "I trust him, but he doesn't need to know about your sister. If I'm wrong…" I shut my eyes, hating myself for saying it. "I don't want to put her in danger. It's bad enough asking her to be our errand girl with Mondo sharking around."

To my surprise, he laughed. "Trust me, she may not look like much, but she can take care of herself."

I found myself growing curious about this mysterious Annika. I asked, "How old is she?"

"Fifteen." Seeing my dubious expression, he added, "She was an accident."

"Mikel!"

"A *happy* accident," he said. An odd look crossed his face, and he volunteered, "Our mom was forty-six when she had Annika."

"That's incredible."

He shrugged. "These days? Not really."

The coffee pot dinged, and he moved away to pour us each a cup. I accepted mine with a stoic nod, still processing his words. Once I'd decided not to ask him why he told me that little bit of family trivia, I felt a sense of relief.

Renewed optimism flowed through me, and I asked, "Want to hear about the rest of my ill-fated trips? It'll help pass the time until reinforcements arrive."

Mikel agreed on the condition that I make another batch

of scrambled eggs with goat cheese. We spent the morning going over my decades of chasing the Wyeth. Judging by the questions Mikel asked, my search hadn't been entirely in vain.

He confirmed this by saying, after I'd finished my Chicago story, "I'd wondered about a few of those collectors myself. Good to know there's no reason to bother with them."

I nodded, feeling vindicated, until his words sank in to my tired brain. When had he wondered about the collectors I'd mentioned? It took me years to track them all down and confirm they didn't have the Wyeth. Hadn't Mikel only learned of Aunt Eva's portrait a few days ago?

I stared at him until he met my eyes, and I asked, "When?"

His lips pressed together into a hard line. He made me wait for what felt like an eternity for the answer, "Can we pretend I didn't say that?"

"No!" I stood up, though I couldn't have said why. "When? Tell me what you mean."

He shook his head, then checked his watch. "I'm gonna call her."

While Mikel talked to his sister, I remained on my feet, watching him. My mind was spinning, reeling. I tried to make it make sense.

Mikel couldn't have been talking about a time before he met me. I was the one who told him about the Wyeth. I distinctly remembered the way he'd reacted. I told him I was looking for it, he told me to describe it, and after I did, he stormed off. I'd assumed he didn't think my Aunt Eva's portrait was worth getting blackmailed over. An interesting find, but certainly not the Caillebotte's equal in terms of value and prestige.

But when would he have had time to identify the collectors I'd spent so many years tracking down? Saturday morning?

Maybe he was faster than I was—maybe Annika was his secret weapon.

I wanted to believe it, and I might have, were it not for the way he was acting now. He ended the call, and I moved toward the front door.

"Where are you going?"

I didn't know the answer until it popped out of my mouth. "The deal's off. I'm going home."

"No." He stepped between me and the door. "That's not a good idea. What are you gonna tell Mondo? You're not playing anymore? Think he's gonna buy that?"

"Get out of my way."

"You're safe here. Let's—" He put up his hands as I took a step forward. "Claire. Can we talk about this?"

"I don't want to. Are you going to stop me from leaving?"

Jaw set, he said, "Yeah. I am. You're making an emotional decision, and I'm gonna give you time to change your mind."

"Why?"

"Because you've seen it. I haven't. I need your help, too. That's how it is."

I took another step forward, near enough to reach for the door handle, and he put his hands on my shoulders. He didn't shove me, but we both knew one quick movement from him would send me flying. Like a lunatic, I wanted to fight him. I wanted to punch him in the face. He saw the wild light in my eyes and shook his head again.

"Don't make this worse than it already is," he pleaded.

I couldn't believe this was happening. Was it really just a few minutes ago that we were laughing about my stupid trip to Chicago? All the fight went out of me in an instant, and I could only gasp, "Please let me go. I just want to go home."

His hands slid around my upper arms, his grip making it clear that I wasn't going anywhere. With a pained look, he said, "We're the only two people in the world who can find that painting. It makes sense to work together, doesn't it?"

I said nothing.

His expression hardened, and he spat, "Fine."

He hauled me by the arm through the living room and into the larger of the apartment's two bedrooms, pushing me inside and closing the door in my face. I don't know how he did it, but in the two seconds it took me to get back to the door and turn the doorknob, he'd locked me in. The knob turned freely—the lock was on my side—but the door didn't budge. I set my shoulder against it and pushed, then backed up and gave it a half-hearted shove. All I achieved was an aching shoulder and a sinking feeling as I understood what just happened.

I wasn't Mikel's partner in crime anymore. I was his prisoner.

*

First I ruled out the window as a means of safe egress, making a note to myself to complain to the apartment's owner about the egregious safety issue this represented. What if there was a fire?

Then I ruled out starting a fire, because I couldn't be certain Mikel would let me out even to save my life. I verified there was no landline phone in the room, and the TV was the dumb kind without an internet connection—no email. All that took roughly five minutes, after which I was out of things to do. I sat down on the bed and fumed. Was I desperate enough yet to bash my way through the drywall into the next apartment? No, but I didn't rule it out. I picked out the exact piece of furniture I'd use to do it, and that was that.

After I'd whiled away about half an hour disassociating, my thoughts reignited and had nowhere to turn but Mikel and his betrayal.

Even though he hadn't come right out and said it, I knew what this morning's drama meant: Mikel had been looking for the Wyeth—*my* Wyeth—since before we met. How long he'd known about it, how he'd even learned of its existence, and whether he'd known when we met that *I* was looking for it too, I'd work up the courage to ask at some point. As to the last question, I thought I knew the answer. His angry reaction to me telling him about the Wyeth made a lot more sense if that was the first he knew of our parallel quests for the painting.

It made sense for him to be angry. There were coincidences, and then there were *coincidences*, and this was the latter. It was simply impossible that he and I could have crossed paths, let alone in the manner in which it happened, without some third party manipulating the situation. I was beginning to think Leonard Money, who I'd always thought of as nothing more than a charmingly neurotic and shy old man with excellent taste in art and cash tumbling out of his every orifice, was something else altogether.

When the bedside alarm clock read 1:33, I heard a faint knock on the apartment's front door. Standing up, I pressed my ear to the bedroom door and listened to Annika's long-awaited arrival.

Though muffled, her voice was clear enough to make out. It was unexpectedly low, sort of husky as though she were coming down with something.

"Do you have any food? I'm starving."

"A little, but that's part of the problem. We can't leave." Mikel was speaking more quietly, perhaps to exclude my prying ears, but I heard every word. "Did you happen to notice the guy I told you about when you were coming in?"

"There was a big guy sitting in a parked car I passed. Here, I got his picture."

After a pause, Mikel said, "Yeah, that's him."

"So if I want food, I have to go get it, is that the idea? You didn't mention that on the phone."

"Sorry. Did you bring the...?"

"Of course. Hey, where's your lady friend? Didn't you say she was here with you?"

"That's... complicated."

I heard Annika's disbelieving laugh, enjoying the thought of how uncomfortable Mikel had to be right now.

"Go ahead," I whispered, "tell your kid sister you're making her an accessory to kidnapping."

"I told her we were looking for the Wyeth, too. She didn't take it well."

A long, thick pause followed Mikel's words. I heard heavy footsteps clomping toward my door, then Mikel's wordless noise of protest as something bulky was shifted aside. The door flew open, and there stood about four feet, zero inches of skinny, livid teenager on five inches of platform boots. Mikel was right—she looked like she'd fit in my pocket with room to spare—but I was fervently hoping her rage wasn't directed at me.

"Did my brother lock you in here?" she asked.

I wasn't sure whether to laugh or cry, so I just said, "Yes."

She rounded on Mikel, crying, "What is *wrong* with you?

Did you seriously think I would be cool with this? I'm not helping you *kidnap* someone—"

"Keep your voice down," Mikel snapped. "I didn't kidnap her." His eyes moved from his sister to me, and he added with a touch of vindictiveness, "I'm giving her a chance to cool down, that's all."

Annika turned back to me. "Lady—I'm sorry, what's your name?"

"Claire."

"Claire, do you want to leave?"

"Yes."

"Then we're leaving. Come on."

Mikel watched us walk together through the living room, waiting until we were feet from the front door to say, "Ani, she's Eva Riordan's niece. She's seen the Wyeth."

Though Annika paused long enough to glance at me with frank curiosity, she said only, "Prolly shoulda been nicer to her, then."

Annika opened the door, and Mikel said only, "Claire."

I paused on the threshold, causing Annika to turn back and look up at me. She glanced from me to Mikel and back, her expression troubled.

"Okay, what is going on here?" she muttered.

"How long have you been looking for it?" I asked her.

"He's been looking my whole life," she said, nodding at her brother. "I started helping a few years ago. What's the big deal?"

"I didn't think anyone else knew about it."

"Isn't it kinda good that we do? We can help."

"There's three of us, and only one Wyeth," I argued.

Annika gave me a crooked smile. "That sounds like a problem for future us."

Mikel started to say something, but she shot him a look that clearly said, "I'm handling this." I couldn't help but like the girl, and not just because she was rescuing me. I'd spent most of my life obsessed with the Wyeth, and in a way, so had she. And though I'd never admit as much to him, Mikel had a point: We were a lot more likely to find it if we put our heads together.

But I was still furious. If Annika had showed up before Mikel locked me in the bedroom, things might have been different; but they were what they were.

"I'm going home," I said firmly. "I'll tell Ren to let you two stay here as long as you need to."

Again Mikel pleaded, "Claire."

"You can use the Hellcat, too. I'll take an Uber." Foreseeing Mikel's next argument, I said, "I'll stay inside until the Uber pulls up. Mondo won't try anything with witnesses around. He already proved that at the grocery store last night. I'll be fine. I'll talk to the cops and convince them I wasn't involved with the theft, and I'll draw Mondo away. I'll get him arrested."

"You're gonna lie to the cops about the last few days?" Mikel challenged.

"Yeah, I am. I'll tell them we went on one date, and I never saw you again."

He argued, "They have us on camera leaving your apartment together."

"Well—whatever, I'll figure something out."

Surprisingly, it was Annika and not Mikel who pointed out, "Lying to the police is actually really hard. You should prolly just not talk to them at all."

I didn't disagree, and Mikel seemed to be out of protests.

We stared at each other for a moment. He looked so unhappy my heart almost went out to him, but it wasn't difficult to dredge my anger back up and smother the sympathy.

"I just need some time," I said. "If you can't give me that…"

"How are you gonna call an Uber? You don't have a phone."

"I got it," Annika called. She had wandered into the living room and was sorting through the contents of a large suitcase she'd brought up.

"Thanks, Ani," Mikel said, voice dripping with sarcasm.

Annika got my address, secured a driver, and told me his name, the make and model of his car, and his license number. "He'll be here in five. Be careful. That big guy looked nasty."

MY STUPID, SOFT HEART was not happy about leaving Mikel and his sister. As I rode the elevator down, shod once more in ill-fitting shoes I'd stolen from Ren's lost and found, I asked myself why. Was I worried about them? Would I miss Mikel? Did I still care about him?

Was I afraid they'd find the Wyeth, cut me out, and disappear with it?

They'd had at least fifteen years, according to Annika. Somehow I didn't think I needed to worry about them suddenly finding it.

When I reached the lobby, which was deserted as usual, I took a second to search for the grocery store clerk's jacket. Though I found a small trove of forgotten items on a shelf next to the coffee bar, the jacket was obviously not among them. Moving to the front door to check for Rob in his black Honda Accord, I saw that someone had rescued the jacket from the ground after all. Rather than bringing it inside, they'd draped it over the railing. Again, I stayed the impulse to venture outside for it. A kind stranger might have picked it up, or Mondo might have set a trap. I'd grab the jacket on my way to the Uber.

I was searching the street for Mondo—sitting in a parked car, as Annika had seen him—when I felt someone standing right behind me. I started to step aside, assuming it was another resident trying to get out, and felt a massive hand wrap around my neck from behind. Something hard was pressed against my ribs.

The familiar, hated voice breathed, "We're going to walk outside, get in my car, and drive away. We're not going to make a scene. Right?"

"Why won't you just leave me alone?" I snarled.

The hand around my neck twitched. "And we're not asking questions. Let's go."

He pushed us both through the door and led me up the street. A black Accord passed us, the driver giving us an automatic, disinterested glance before scanning the street for a parking spot.

*Don't panic. Annika and Mikel will figure out what happened.*

Then what, though? They wouldn't know where Mondo was taking me.

*Okay, you can panic.*

"You're looking for Fred, right?" I asked. He'd let go of my neck, but whatever he'd pressed against my ribs was still very much there.

"Shut up."

"If you want me to help you find him, I'll help you. You don't have to—"

"I said shut up."

He pushed me toward a parked SUV and held me against

it with one hand while he pocketed something. It looked like a folding knife. From another pocket he pulled out a thick, black zip tie. After glancing up and down the street, checking for witnesses, he zipped my wrists together, opened the passenger side door, bundled me inside, and shut me in. As he moved around the SUV toward the driver's side, I tried to open my door, only to find the inside handle had been removed.

After he shoved his massive bulk into the driver's seat, slammed the door, and started the SUV, he turned to me. He reached into the back seat, grabbed something, and tossed it over my bound hands in my lap. It looked like an old hoodie.

"If you move, I'll skin you alive."

I stared straight ahead, praying involuntary tremors didn't count as moving. The SUV slid out of its parking spot, and we were off. As we passed the apartment building's front door, I turned my head just enough to see an encouraging scene: Annika was hanging out the door, talking to a man I assumed was Rob the Uber driver. She'd already figured out something was amiss, God bless her.

Within five minutes, we were on the highway, and I had to pee. I always had to go at the most inconvenient times. After another half hour of heading straight east, I began tapping my leg just to distract myself from the discomfort. Mondo endured it for another ten minutes before reaching over and slamming a hand down on my knee.

"Knock it off."

"Where are we going?"

"Shut up."

"What's your name? I've been calling you Mondo. I could stick with that..."

He swore under his breath and seemed to decide ignoring me was the only option. I perked up as we left Interstate 30 for the northbound Bush Turnpike, which was a toll road and happened to be the way to my parents' house in the Dallas suburbs. Even though I knew we weren't going there, the familiar path helped me relax enough to remember I ought to be paying attention to our route—just in case.

"I *really* have to pee," I whined. "How much longer?"

"Open your mouth again, and I'll tape it shut."

So I spent the remainder of the ride—all ninety minutes of it—with my lips pressed together and my bladder threatening to explode. I was near tears by the time we exited the turnpike. We wove through Plano toward Murphy, still sticking to the route I'd take to get to my parents' house until we turned off the main road onto a smaller, unnamed one that ended in a wrought iron gate. It was still familiar to me, but I'd never been there.

I was approaching the point of actual insanity and couldn't stop myself saying, "Hey, the house with all the statues."

He didn't answer. I'd driven past this house thousands of times, always glancing at the statuary littering the deep front lawn, trying to catch a glimpse of the house, and wondering who lived here. I was about to find out at long last. Mondo parked in the circle drive of a massive, rather ugly attempt at Romanesque architecture that I took for a house. I craned my neck to look back at the road, which was completely hidden by a forest of well-groomed, deciduous trees.

Mondo opened my door and dragged me out, and I just about did something I hadn't done since I was six. By the grace of God, I held it in until he ushered me through the unlocked front door and shoved me toward a powder room just off the marble foyer.

I shut myself in, locked the door, and started to panic when my zip tied hands wouldn't cooperate. An unhinged laugh popped out of me as I wrestled my pants down one side at a time, completing the humbling task not a millisecond too soon.

I emerged from the powder room feeling almost happy, somewhere between relaxed and sleepy. That had been quite the ordeal, and I had to forcefully remind myself the misadventure was beginning, not ending. Mondo's gigantic paw around my forearm and being frog-marched deeper into the house helped put an end to my contentment.

He led me toward a pair of closed, carved wooden doors deep in the interior of the first floor. After a perfunctory knock, he opened one door and pushed me inside without a word, closing it behind me. I wasn't surprised as much as I was resigned to see Leonard Money sitting on a leather sofa, clearly waiting for Mondo to deliver me. He stood up to greet me like a proper Texas gentleman, but there was no mistaking the malice in his gaze as he looked me over.

"Miss Riordan. You're a hard woman to track down."

With my wrists zip tied together and my burly abductor most likely stationed right outside the doors, I should have been scared—terrified. But Leonard Money was just so... unintimidating. He was stooped with age and shorter than me, as bald as a turtle, and slim in the extreme. Though he dressed nicely, he looked like he'd crumble at my touch. Only his eyes, magnified behind small, round glasses, looked truly alive. They remained fixed on me and filled with extreme dislike.

I burst out, "*What* is that guy's name?"

"Ken?"

"No, the big guy who brought me here."

"Ken."

Was he messing with me? I shook my head. "No. That can't be his name. I'll keep calling him Mondo. What the heck do you want?"

"I want that Caillebotte," he said, almost quivering with rage. "Tell me what you've done with it."

I blinked at him, failing to answer for so long that his face began to turn red.

"If you don't tell me, I will call the police and turn you in. I'll tell them you broke in and tried to steal more of my collection. They already know you were working with Laubenberg."

This was so ludicrous I laughed and said, "Okay. Do that."

"I'm glad you think this is funny. The value of the items you stole makes your crime a felony. You'll go to prison."

"Is conspiracy to commit a felony also a felony?" I shot back. "I'm not familiar with crime and punishment, but I just bet you are."

Leonard raised his quaking voice to call, "Ken!"

Mondo stepped promptly inside. My nervous bravado vanished at the sight of him.

"Beat some sense into this woman. Don't draw any blood. I don't want a mess."

I hardly had time to wonder if he was serious before a powerful backhand connected with my cheek, knocking me to the floor. Based on the metallic taste in my mouth, Leonard's simple instruction had not been followed. I was still trying to regain my senses when Mondo yanked me back to my feet and buried one fist in my stomach. I went down again, gasping for air. I couldn't draw a breath. My chest began to ache with the effort of trying to inhale. I was going to suffocate. I shrimped up into the fetal position and waited for the next blow, but it never came.

"That's enough. You idiot, you busted her lip open. Go get a towel or something."

I heard him stomp away. I'd had the wind knocked out of me a time or two, but it had been a while, and Marty didn't pack nearly the punch Mondo did. I couldn't remember what I was supposed to do. Put my arms over my head? Put my head between my knees? Raise my legs? I felt certain I'd die in less than a minute if I didn't figure it out.

Mondo announced his return by pulling me back to my feet and pressing a towel to my busted lip. By then I hadn't died thanks to the small, unsatisfactory breaths I'd been able to draw; but I was so angry I wanted to bite him. I settled for whipping my face away from the towel and spitting a mouthful of blood onto Money's Persian rug.

"Take her to the cellar," Moncy ordered.

He didn't specify whether I was to be beaten some more, so when Mondo deposited me inside a roomy wine cellar, I braced myself for another impact. He just shook his head, growled a sigh, and locked me into a room with hundreds and hundreds of bottles of wine.

"This could be worse," I whispered.

Energy was draining from my body, and I was losing the will to not think about what was still seeping out of my lower lip. I managed to find a bottle with a screw top, sit down in the corner, squeeze the bottle between my thighs to twist it open with my bound hands, and take a healthy swallow or four before exhaustion pulled me under.

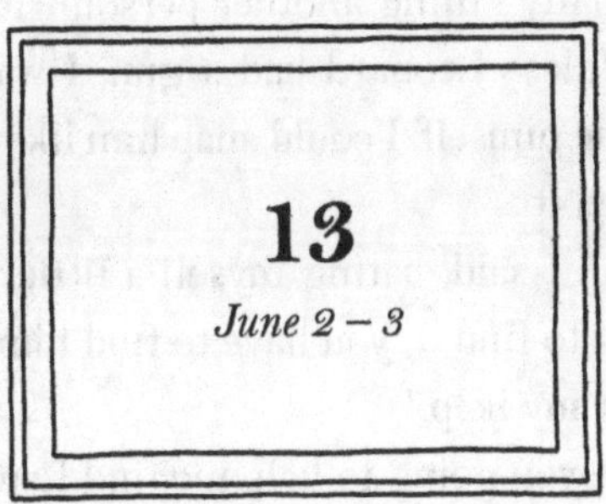


GENTLENESS, THY NAME IS NEITHER Ken nor Mondo. I woke up to the sound of a door slamming and could only cry out in confusion and alarm as I was yanked to my feet yet again. My back crashed against a pane of glass but didn't break it.

"Careful," Money hissed.

I tried to sink to the floor again, but Mondo didn't let me.

"Are you ready to tell us where the Caillebotte is?" Money asked.

I needed more sleep, more wine, and less Leonard to be coherent or clever. I just wanted him to go away. I moaned, "Yeah, I am." I then made my art history professors proud by reeling off, in passable French, *"Paysage aux meules de paille* is in a private collection. *Jeune homme a sa fenêtre* is at the Getty Center, I think. *The Parquet Planers*—sorry, I can't remember the French name—that's also in a private collection…"

"Enough. We both know I'm talking about the painting at the Kimbell. I'm out of patience. If you don't tell me where it is, you're not leaving this room alive."

I looked at Mondo, who would undoubtedly be doing the deed, and was surprised to see him frowning in what looked almost like consternation. Could it be that he drew the line just before actually killing another person? That would be a lucky break. Unless Leonard had a gun, I was sure he'd be unable to kill me himself. I could snap him like a stale cracker. I kind of wanted to.

"Fred knows," I said, hating myself a little. "He won't tell me. If you want to find it, you have to find him, and you can't do that without my help."

"And how are you going to help me find Laubenberg?"

"Give me something to eat, and I'll think of a way."

The two of them left without another word, and I sat back down. I found my bottle of wine and tried to take another drink, but pain exploded in my lower lip and I had to admit defeat. I put the bottle down and pressed my sleeve to my lip, trying not to pass out.

*It's not that much blood. It's not that much. Don't be a baby.*

I consciously rejected that advice and started to cry. How long had I been here? Were Annika and Mikel trying to find me? What if Leonard accepted my demand? I couldn't lead him to Mikel. I wouldn't. I wasn't smart enough to think of any other way out of this.

Mondo returned in a few minutes, bearing a bottle of water and what looked like a heel end of a loaf of French bread. He set the water down at my feet and tossed the bread at me.

Though I caught it, I snarled, "I don't eat bread."

He looked as though he'd like to take the bread and shove it down my throat, along with his fist, but he didn't get that far. A series of melodic chimes issued from a speaker by the door, followed by Leonard's voice snapping, "The police are here.

Go see what they want. Don't let them inside."

He left to do as commanded. I considered the hunk of bread in my hand, wondering how hungry I'd have to get before I ate it. A heck of a lot hungrier than I was now. I did chug the bottle of water, busted lip be darned, which revived me enough to realize the import of Money's words.

See what they want? Had he not called them himself?

Several minutes of uncomfortable ignorance later, I had my answer. The door opened to reveal neither Mondo nor Leonard, but a gaggle of uniformed police officers who all looked very stressed out. I couldn't believe my eyes. I managed not to start crying again, but only just.

One of them stepped inside and knelt down in front of me.

"Are you injured?" he asked.

I studied his stern, dark blue eyes and concluded he was there to rescue me, not arrest me. I shook my head.

"Okay. Come on."

He looped an arm under mine and helped me to my feet, then guided me all the way back up the stairs, through the house, and out to the circle drive. It was dark outside. From between two patrol cars, lights flashing obnoxiously, a familiar silhouette appeared and rushed toward me a bit too enthusiastically for my police escort.

"Take it easy," the officer warned, turning to get between me and Ren. "She's a little shaken up."

He passed me into Ren's arms, where I finally felt safe enough to fall apart. Ren half-hugged, half-carried me through the armada of police vehicles to the one in which I assumed he'd traveled here. How he'd managed to secure a place in a squad car, I could only imagine. He helped me into the back of the car, sliding in next to me. I threw my arms around his neck and clung to him like a drowning cat. I was already done sobbing, but I was shaking so hard I thought I might actually come apart.

"How?" I forced.

"We'll talk about it later. They're going to ask you to give a statement. You don't have to. They can't stop you from going home. You can talk to them later, after you've rested. That's what you should do."

"Okay."

True to his prediction, a different officer appeared and opened the patrol car door. They'd sent a woman to take my statement, a gentle touch that I appreciated—but not enough to disregard Ren's advice. I told her I wanted to go home, and she didn't argue. She radioed her comrades that she was taking Ren and me home, then led us to an unmarked car nearer the end of the long driveway.

Before we got moving, the officer rustled around in her center console for a moment before passing something into Ren's hands. It was a small, white plastic box. He accepted it without question, opened it, and pulled out a paper-wrapped alcohol swab. The car lurched forward, forcing us to buckle our seatbelts before he turned back to me.

"This is going to hurt," he warned.

"I don't care."

I endured Ren's somewhat clumsy attempt at first aid, which really only amounted to cleaning the dried blood off my face. Once that was done, I leaned against his shoulder and immediately fell asleep.

*

I woke up to the sight of Ren's house, bathed in darkness but for the flood lights directed at its façade from behind the manicured bushes in his front garden. The clock on the dash read 2:20. I didn't believe it.

"Wake up. We're here."

Still half-asleep, I climbed out of the car and stayed on my feet with the assistance of Ren's arm while he exchanged quiet words with the police officer. She drove away, he led me into the house, and I found myself in the tiny guest room where I'd spent more nights than I care to admit after drinking too much to drive myself home. Ren helped me into bed, and in seconds I was asleep again.

*

Something jostled the bed, flinging me out of a cozy, nonsense dream and into the too-bright reality of Ren's guest room. I moaned, eliciting a dramatic, verbal wince from someone sitting on the bed next to me.

A quiet, husky voice said, "Sorry, Miss Riordan. They were gonna let you sleep all day, but I really want to get down to business. Are you hungry?"

I recognized Annika's voice, but I didn't accept it. I was at Ren's house, not his rental apartment. I opened my eyes the tiniest possible amount and tried to focus on the shape hovering over me. Pixie-short, box-dyed black hair, too much make-up, black clothes—definitely Annika. Did she get smaller?

"I'm starving," I whispered.

"You literally slept for twelve hours. I couldn't stand it anymore."

"If you're here, does that mean Mikel is here?"

"Uh-huh. But if you want him gone, just say the word."

"Ugh. No. Look, I need to take a shower. Can you wait a few

minutes longer?"

"Sure, yeah. Take your time." She departed quickly, before I could even sit up. I'd worked my tired arms underneath myself and was halfway vertical when she reappeared, poking her head into the room to say, "He really wants to apologize, but he *sucks* at it. He won't say he's sorry unless he knows you'll forgive him."

I smiled weakly. Holding up my necklace, I answered, "I don't really have a choice."

"Oooooh. Gotchya. Okay, bye."

I made it into the shower without further interruption. Annika had said to take my time, so I did, soaking up the hot water until it was all gone. I'd raided Ren's collection of forgotten toiletries for a razor that looked unused and a tub of sugar scrub, the combined result of which was me feeling raw, shiny, and unusually clean—if a bit winded by the prolonged effort. I wrapped a towel around myself and left the ensuite bathroom to find Mikel sitting on my bed.

He stood up, and I took an automatic step back. Undismayed by this, he crossed the room in two strides and would have hugged me, if I hadn't swatted his arms away. Apparently, I was still mad.

I wanted to tell him to leave, mostly because of the towel situation, but I couldn't make myself say it. I knew if I told him to get out, he would. He slowly raised one hand to press his thumb gently against my lower lip.

"Please tell me this is the worst of it," he said.

I'd noticed a healthy bruise on my stomach where Mondo's fist left its mark, but technically it wasn't a lie if I thought the busted lip was worse. Sure it still kind of hurt to breathe, but my lip had bled, which I hated. I said, "Yeah. I'm okay."

"You left because of me. This is my fault."

"The way I remember it, you weren't going to let me leave at all. Maybe you should blame Annika."

He breathed a humorless laugh. "Yeah, right."

He kissed me on the cheek, and it felt right to wrap my arms around his waist and rest my head on his chest. He returned my embrace, and we stood like that for at least a minute before I was forced to conclude that the word "sorry" really wasn't going to make an appearance. He *had* said it was all his fault, which was true, so I counted it.

My reward for these mental gymnastics was his muttered, "Claire, I'm so sorry. I don't know what I was thinking."

"Are you sure?" I argued. "You told me what you were thinking. You want the Wyeth, and you don't think you can find it without my help."

"I could have done that without—I panicked. I'm sorry."

I sighed. "I've never been kidnapped even once in my whole life, not even that time I flew to Paris alone and went to a nightclub and accidentally dropped acid, and then it happens twice in one day. You were a lot nicer than Money and his goon, I'll give you that."

"Hm." He rested his chin on my head. "I bet they weren't thinking about how cool it was to have a beautiful woman held captive, totally at their mercy."

I pulled away enough to look up at him, stammering, "Were—were you?"

"Only for like, two and a half seconds," he assured me. His brow furrowed. "You told me about Paris, but you left out the acid."

"It wasn't relevant."

Carefully, he kissed me on the lips. "Does it hurt?"

"A little."

He kissed me on the jaw. "What about that?"

"Mikel, come on," I moaned. "I'm practically naked."

"Yeah, the towel's gotta go—"

"No." I pushed him away. "You do."

"Yeah, yeah." He looked at the bed. I was preparing to physically remove him from the bedroom when he said, "Ren found these for you. He told me he crosses his heart and hopes to die that the underwear is brand new."

I saw the stack of folded clothes and giggled. "Gross. Tell him I say thanks. I'll be right out. I can't wait to hear how you all pulled this off."

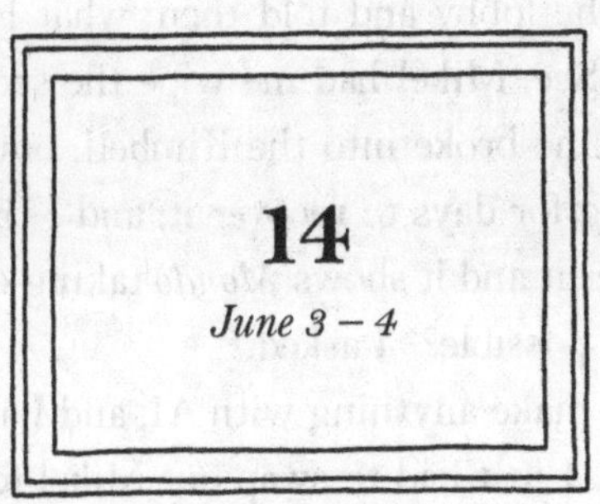



THE VICTORY BELONGED ALMOST entirely to Annika, who'd not only been the first to realize I was in Mondo's clutches but had originated the idea that she, Ren, and Mikel had turned into a reality. Since she was the star of the show, Ren and Mikel let her do most of the talking while wearing almost identical expressions of paternal indulgence.

She opened with, "So first of all, that big dude's name is *Ken*. Like, Ken and Barbie. Can you believe that?"

"Leonard told me," I said. "I didn't believe him."

"Right? Anyway, that Uber driver called me to say he was waiting at the curb for me, and I was like, you're supposed to be down there waiting for him, and he said there was no one, and I ran downstairs and saw for myself that you were gone. Then I saw that same jacket sitting right where I left it, and I don't know why I thought it was important, but I brought it upstairs and Mikel remembered it from your story and knew you wouldn't have just left it there, so we knew we had a problem.

"Mikel called Mr. Renner, and while we were waiting for him I got into the security camera feed from the apartment and saw what happened. I called the police right away from the phone in the lobby and told them what I saw, but then I had an idea. See, Mikel had me wipe the security cameras from the night he broke into the Kimbell, but their IT lady has been trying for days to recover it, and I thought, what if she *does* recover it and it shows *Mondo* taking everything?"

"How is that possible?" I asked.

"AI. You can make anything with AI, and I already had the video of Mikel. I just had to swap out Mikel for Mondo, and between the footage from your apartment and from the other apartment, I had more than enough to train the AI to make it look really convincing. The parts where I couldn't fudge it because Mondo's so much bigger than Mikel, I just cut in some static. That made it look even better, since it was supposed to be recovered footage.

"I dropped it into the IT chick's computer and made sure it was the first thing she saw when she got back from her lunch break. Then we just had to get Mikel's phone records from talking to Money to set everything up, make them look like Mondo's which was stupid easy, mock up a paper trail and pictures and stuff to make it look like Money hired Mondo to raid his collection for the insurance money. We got a copy of the insurance policies and included that with the whole packet, and we hired a courier to drop it off at Ren's office for Ren to take to the police. They had to find the security camera footage from the rental apartment themselves, though. I guess they did, since they showed up with guns a-blazin'."

"Annika tracked down Mondo's address, and I moved everything to his apartment," Mikel finished. "The police didn't find it until after they rescued you. Those two are out of our hair for good, thanks to this little chaos demon."

"It was fun," Annika said.

"You did all this *after* he took me?" I asked, aghast. All three nodded.

"We were highly motivated," Ren said.

"You guys are… This is… Wait." I peered at Mikel, asking, "So 'Fred Laubenberg' is totally off the hook for the break-in?"

"I am," Mikel said with a grin. "So are you. It was all Money and his hired thief."

"And no one knows about the Caillebotte?" I pressed.

"If either of them has mentioned it, the cops haven't seen fit to share that with us," Ren answered. "I doubt Money will let that cat out of the bag. That greedy old fart probably still thinks he can get his hands on it somehow."

"He will have other goons besides Mondo," Annika said by way of agreement. "Maybe they're not completely finished being a problem, but at least they're tied up for now."

"I still want to know how Money found out about the Caillebotte," Mikel said.

Annika piped up, "*I* didn't tell him."

"I only told Mikel," I put in. "Unless you count what I told you Saturday morning," I added, directing this at Ren. He shifted uncomfortably in his seat.

"I know you never mentioned Caillebotte by name," Ren said.

"Leonard's an art lover," I said. "Maybe he figured it out the same way I did." I didn't really believe that, but I didn't like the way Mikel was looking at Ren.

We all fell silent, thinking our individual thoughts. My stomach ended the moment by gurgling loudly.

"Claire's stomach is right," Annika announced. "I don't care if it's dinner time or not, I'm hungry."

It turned out everyone was running on empty, and after a quick discussion, it was clear we wouldn't be agreeing on what to eat. Annika wanted pizza, I wanted steak, Ren wanted a cheeseburger, and Mikel wanted tacos; so Ren ordered one of each from a delivery service, then found some cheese and crackers to tide us over while we waited. We were placing wagers on which delivery driver would arrive first when Ren redirected us.

"How about we get our story straight?" he suggested. "Claire will have to give a statement, today or tomorrow, and obviously it can't be one hundred percent true."

"Have the cops talked to all of you?" I asked.

"Not us," Annika answered. "They don't know we're here."

"I'm sure they want to talk to me," Mikel said with a grimace. "Making Mondo take the fall was clever, but they'll still want to know why I disappeared in the middle of their investigation and dragged Claire into it. It looks suspicious."

Ren said, "I don't know. Now that they've got their guy, why bother you?"

"Because Money and Mondo will be telling the cops I was involved. If I were them, I'd keep looking into that. It's still too big of a coincidence that I was working in the museum the night before it happened, then went to ground with a security guard from the same museum."

"Money thinks I was involved, too," I said. "But I don't want to lie. I'm not good at it."

Ren shot me a commiserative look but said, "You'll have to try. You can't tell them about the Caillebotte, right?"

I groaned.

"Right?" Mikel echoed.

"How about you all tell me what to say, and I'll memorize it?" I offered.

"Oh, I love these things," Annika said, bouncing up from her chair to stand next to Ren's enormous TV. "It's like a riddle: What do the cops know, what might they find out, and what can we get away with lying about? We need like a big whiteboard, or—Do you have an HDMI cable? Wait, never mind, I think I brought a couple."

With that, she galloped away, leaving the three of us somewhat winded. The doorbell rang while Annika was still gathering whatever it was she needed, so Mikel moved into the kitchen, out of sight of the door, and Ren answered it.

He came into the living room with two plastic bags. "Two down, two to go. Let's see who the lucky winners are."

Ren's cheeseburger and Mikel's tacos had arrived together, and I tried my best not to look sullen and mutinous as they politely set their dinners aside to wait for the rest of the food. Annika came back to the living room, armed with a laptop and an HDMI cable. She connected her laptop to the TV, set the screens to duplicate, and opened a new document in some program I didn't recognize.

I watched, almost forgetting how hungry I was, as she used her finger on her laptop's touch screen to draw two vertical lines on the document's white background, dividing the space into three equal columns. As soon as she lifted her finger each time, the program turned the wobbly segments into perfectly straight lines. Then she labeled the columns Know, Might Know, and Don't Know. The program turned her scribbles into typed letters, using a font that closely matched her handwriting. I was as mesmerized as a chimpanzee watching a magic trick.

Her pizza arrived, followed too many minutes later by my steak. While we all chowed down, we filled in the columns. Annika was right—it was fun.

"Ugh, I got pizza grease on my screen. Just a sec."

She managed to turn cleaning her screen into quite the ordeal; the girl clearly loved her gadgets. While she worked on that, I reviewed what we'd come up with so far.

We all agreed that the police knew Mikel—Fred, to them—and I met at the museum the night before the break-in and went on a date the night after. We thought there was a fifty-fifty chance they had reviewed the security footage from my apartment building's lobby, not just from the incident on Sunday but going back to before the break-in, which meant they'd know Mikel was at my apartment Friday night. They'd seen the footage of Mondo arriving on Sunday, followed by Mikel, and Mikel and me leaving together before Mondo made his escape alone. They'd certainly interviewed Mr. Miller about the incident, and we could assume he'd told them about my request that he not allow Mikel into the building. They knew Mikel and I had been in hiding, together or separately, from Sunday until I turned up alone at Mr. Money's house in the wee hours of this morning. As to Ren's involvement, all they knew was that a courier had dropped off a package from an anonymous source at his office yesterday, and per the written instructions with the package, he'd taken it to the Fort Worth detectives working the Kimbell case.

In the Might Know column, Annika had listed all our names under the heading Phone Records. Presumably the police had taken my phone from my apartment, placing it into evidence, and might have requested my phone records once they began to suspect I was involved in the break-in. None of the adults was much use helping Annika figure out how likely they were to have these records, so it remained a question mark. Since my car was parked at the rental apartment, we agreed there was a chance they'd figure out Ren was lying to them about me being there.

They didn't know where Mikel and I went when we left my apartment, or where we'd been since then. They couldn't know about the incident in the grocery store, nor in the rental apartment building's lobby. Annika had stolen, then permanently deleted all the footage from the cameras just to be safe. She'd left the footage from my building alone, knowing the cops had already reviewed it.

I felt like we were missing something, Annika was certain we were, and Mikel and Ren were ambivalent. Something about the exercise had put Annika in a grumpy mood, and she took her half-finished pizza to whatever room Ren had allotted her with a terse, "I'm going to work in my room. Don't break my laptop."

When she was gone, I asked, "How's she going to work without her laptop?"

"I don't even know how many computers that kid has," Mikel said.

Ren checked his watch. "I expected to hear from the Plano PD by now. I wonder what they're waiting for."

Whatever it was, the day drew to a close without a peep from the police. While Annika continued to sulk in her room, the three of us watched a movie, then its sequel. We all fell asleep on the couch, and I woke up sometime later with my head in Mikel's lap and my legs thrown over Ren's. They were both asleep sitting up, heads lolling back on the overstuffed sofa cushions. Feeling rather queenly between my two willing man-pillows, I savored my coziness and tried to fall back asleep. It was no use; I'd slept too much earlier.

I got up and decided to check on Annika. Ren's house was huge, three stories of oversized rooms and an inexcusable number of bathrooms, but I knew where all the guest rooms were and in which one he was likely to have billeted the teenage girl. I found my way to the third floor and the jack-and-jill bedrooms at the back of the house. Ren had converted one of the bedrooms into a panic room, which meant Annika was sleeping in the safest place in the entire house.

Except she wasn't asleep, not if the light and sound pouring from under her door was any clue. I knocked, and she whipped the door open so fast I leapt backward in surprise.

"Oh—it's you. Sorry. What's up?"

"Uuuuuuh… Are you okay?"

Annika's expression suddenly held so much world-weary ennui that I almost laughed out loud. I was glad I held it in, because something told me being laughed at was the very last thing she needed right now. She gave me a fake smile.

"No. I'm really mad, and I can't tell you why I'm mad, which makes me *really* mad."

"We can talk about it if you want. Or we can talk about something else. Or I can go away? Sorry, I forgot how to talk to teenagers the moment I turned twenty, and that was a long time ago."

This time her smile was genuine. "You're doing fine. Actually, I did see a hot tub in Mr. Renner's back yard. Any chance we could fire that up? I brought a swimsuit just in case, so it would be a shame not to use it."

I suppressed a grimace at the thought of what sorts of things had gone on in that hot tub. The water was chlorinated, so my disgust was probably groundless.

"I could use a soak. Let me see if I can find a swimsuit for me. You know how to turn the tub on?"

"I can figure it out. Meet you down there."

I let myself into Ren's bedroom on the second floor and easily located the drawer in his closet where he kept swimsuits and other garments for female guests' use. Sorting through them made me feel icky, but at least I was able to find a surprisingly modest one-piece swimsuit that still had tags on it. Ren and his borderline hoarding tendencies always came through. I changed into it, leaving my clothes in a pile on his closet floor, and grabbed two towels from his bathroom. I made a pit stop in the kitchen to grab a glass of wine for me and a Coke for Annika.

She had already removed the hot tub's cover and turned it on when I arrived. I flipped on the light, sending a pulsing, green glow across the ceiling of the ivy-covered pergola. Annika gazed up at it, looking deep in thought again.

"Your Mr. Renner sure knows how to live it up," she said.

Passing her the Coke, I said, "He is a bit of a libertine, but he's got a good heart."

As we climbed into the bubbling water, she argued, "Don't you think it's a little unfair that some people can't even afford groceries, and he lives like this?"

"No, I don't think it's unfair at all."

That was all it took to spark a prolonged political debate. I generally hated talking politics, but she made it fun and kept it friendly. Despite some unfortunately collectivist leanings, she was wiser and more mature than I'd given her credit for—certainly more than I was at her age. I was patting myself on the back for drawing her out of her bad mood when her gaze settled on a point behind me, her eyes flashed, and she abandoned the point she'd been trying to make about universal basic income.

"What are you two up to?" Mikel asked from behind me. I hadn't even heard the back door open.

"We're solving all the world's problems, obviously," I said.

"Room for one more in there?"

Annika climbed out, grabbed a towel, and snapped, "It's all yours." In a kinder tone, she told me, "Thanks for the food for thought, Claire. You might not be entirely evil."

"Gee, thanks."

Mikel waited until she was inside to ask, "Evil?"

"Who raised that girl? She thinks libertarians are, by definition, irredeemably evil."

"Ah. Well… actually, I raised her." He took my empty glass and headed inside, calling, "I'll bring you a refill."

His casual admission made me realize we had a lot to talk about, but I was still annoyed that he'd sent Annika scurrying back under her rock. When he returned in swim trunks with two glasses of wine, I couldn't make myself return his smile.

He climbed in, sitting directly across from me, and asked, "What's on your mind, Red?"

I smirked at the nickname. I didn't hate it. "A lot. But mostly… How did you find out about the Wyeth? And when?"

"Ah. I… really don't want to tell you that."

I took a drink of wine to hide my expression and concluded, "Wow, that was honest."

"I'm sorry. I will, but not yet. Later."

"Fine. Why is Annika so mad at you?"

"Is it not obvious?"

"Obviously not."

He sighed. "She thinks I'm leading you on. Thinks I'm a heartbreaker. Sorry, there's no way to say that without sounding self-serving."

I wasn't sure I believed that explanation, but I didn't feel like calling him out. Instead I said, "I thought I was the one leading you on."

"You definitely are," he said, not sounding at all put off by it. "But she's seen me fall for women before. She thinks I fall too fast and too hard, and… She's not wrong."

"And what's become of these unfortunate women?"

"If you ask me, they're all way better off. I don't think I've ever broken any heart but my own. Try convincing your kid sister of that, though. She really, really liked some of them."

"Please don't tell me your body count. I don't want to know."

Laughing, he said, "I wasn't planning to. Worried I'll break your heart?"

"No." I took another drink. The wine was making me mawkish and overly honest. I didn't have the will to fight it. "I've had five children, and they're all in heaven waiting for me. That's where my heart is. It's as safe as it can be."

I looked at him, worried about how he'd react. He was frowning down at the surface of the water, deep in thought.

"Should I have kept that to myself?" I whispered.

"No. I'm glad you told me. I just wish you hadn't had to go through that. I'm sorry."

"Me, too. But you can't fight city hall, right?"

"City hall?" he echoed. "What does that mean?"

"Oh, it's something my mom is always saying. It just means some things are out of our hands, and getting mad about it isn't going to solve anything. At least, that's what she means when she says it."

"That's… that's BS. You have every right to be mad about it. *I'm* mad about it."

"You can be mad for both of us. I just want to keep plodding ahead."

He waded over to sit next to me, wrapping one arm around me. Though the kiss he planted on my cheek was gentle, his tone was playful when he asked, "One?"

"One what?"

"That's your body count, isn't it? One."

Reddening, I mumbled, "I don't see how that's any of your business."

"You brought it up. Besides, considering how persistently I'm endeavoring to double it, I'd say it's my business."

Turning to him, I asked seriously, "Maybe you could do me a favor and not try so hard? This is difficult for me, too."

"It is?"

Studying his openly gratified expression, I mouthed, "Very."

He kissed me on the cheek again, and I could feel his smile against my skin. He said, "Cool."

"Will you tell me about the Wyeth now? It's later."

"Hm." He drummed his fingers on my shoulder. "Nope. All I'll say is, I've never laid eyes on it. Until you told me you were looking for it too, I wasn't even sure it really existed. I *am* sure that I didn't have an ice cube's chance in hell of finding it without your help."

THE LAST HALF HOUR I SPENT with Mikel in Ren's hot tub was playing over and over in my mind, creating a pleasant distraction from reality. He'd been a perfect gentleman, but we'd managed to have our share of fun anyway.

Summoned by the detectives who were working the case against Leonard Money and Mondo, I rode to the Plano Police Department headquarters with Ren and obediently rehearsed my story with him. We'd only had a couple hours to put it together before the detectives called Ren and asked me to come in at 9:30. I couldn't remember ever being so nervous to talk to a cop.

Ren and I had decided not to bring a lawyer. I wanted to appear as open and cooperative as possible, and I hadn't been charged with a crime or even openly accused of one. Annika had vehemently poo-pooed this decision, but she was outnumbered three to one. Make that two and a half to one and a half. She was probably right. This was not going to go well.

Once we arrived, I was ushered into an interview room

while Ren was politely but firmly told to wait in the lobby. I found myself facing four detectives, not the two I'd expected. The pair from the Fort Worth Police Department had joined us, a fact which I felt I should've been made aware of sooner. I expressed as much to them, and my complaint was met with badly feigned expressions of regret for the oversight.

If their intent had been to make me feel defensive and ganged up on, it worked. They sat me down in a corner of the interview room and arrayed themselves in a semi-circle between me and the closed, windowless door. There was simply no way this hadn't been choreographed to make me uncomfortable. Just before they dived into their questions, I finally understood that I was not there to give a victim statement; this was another interview. Maybe even an interrogation.

Annika's words came to me, reminding me I could leave at any time. Just get up and leave. I didn't need their permission, and I didn't need to explain myself.

Except that I was me, and I'd never *not* feel the need to explain myself.

"How are you feeling, Miss Riordan?" one of the Plano detectives asked.

I knew what he meant, but I said, "I feel like you're trying to make me uncomfortable. I kind of feel like leaving."

Plano Two (I'd forgotten their names the moment I heard them) said sympathetically, "I know, these rooms are terrible. We did have a love seat in here at one point. But… trust me, you wouldn't want to sit on it after what happened."

"Well." I cleared my throat. "How does this work? I've never given a statement before. Do I just… talk?"

Plano One said, "No, we'll walk you through it. Do you want anything to eat? Some water or coffee?"

*What I want is for these two yahoos from Fort Worth to wait their turn.* I hesitated, thinking a request for coffee would sound normal and non-guilty. *Say what you want to say!*

"Coffee would be great," I sighed. Then I forced out, "And I'd like the detectives from Fort Worth to leave. I'm sorry, I don't remember your names. It's hard enough talking about this in front of two strangers."

One of the Fort Worth detectives, the younger of the two by far, frowned and said, "We do have some questions for you, Miss Riordan."

Plano One piped up in my defense. "You can ask them when we're done. This won't take long."

In short order the number of officers arrayed against me had been reduced by half, and I had a steaming Styrofoam cup of coffee in my hand. I felt so much better, even a little smug, that I wondered whether that hadn't been their intention all along.

The Plano detectives pulled the narrative out of me one question at a time, capturing the whole thing on a voice recorder on the table next to me. My story and the truth had a lot in common, with one outstanding detail: I'd asked Fred Laubenberg to drop me off at a big box store a short distance from my apartment, then taken a cab from there to Ren's house. I hadn't seen Fred since. I'd been walking from Ren's house to a nearby strip mall to buy some real shoes when Mondo (I did remember to say "Ken") grabbed me.

They seemed dubious about certain details but didn't outright accuse me of lying. How had I called a cab, when my phone had been left behind at my apartment? I'd used a phone inside the store. Had I asked Laubenberg to come to my apartment Sunday morning? No, it was just dumb luck.

Did he still have my Challenger? I had no idea. Why hadn't I reported it stolen? I was getting around to it.

Plano Two was more interested in clarifying every last detail of my quality time with Leonard Money. Knowing they'd be soliciting the same details from him, I stuck to the gospel truth and only omitted any mention of the Caillebotte. The way I told it, they were looking for Fred. I had to believe that if Leonard or Mondo said anything at all, their stories would roughly align with mine whether they liked it or not.

If I'd suspected the Fort Worth pair was listening in, this was confirmed when Plano One said, "Thank you, Miss Riordan. We'll get this typed up and get your John Hancock on there. Refill on that coffee?" and the other two detectives let themselves back into the interview room as though that was their cue.

"I'll have a water," I said sourly. "I have to go to the bathroom."

Plano Two escorted me to the ladies room, where I sat in relative peace and quiet and forced my brain to think and my lungs to breathe. This wasn't so easy or pleasant in the pee-and-Pine Sol-scented bathroom, but I gutted it out.

The Plano detectives and the Fort Worth detectives had different priorities. Leonard Money's crimes—if I counted the insurance fraud and Kimbell break-in—straddled their jurisdictions, but the assault, terroristic threats, and my favorite, "imprisoning or restraining another without consent," all happened in Plano. If Ren's prediction were right, they'd end up turning their case over to the Fort Worth Police Department, but for now it seemed they were focused on gathering statements and evidence of crimes in which I was 100% the victim.

The Fort Worth guys, on the other hand, definitely still thought I might be involved in some crimes. Victim or not, the way they looked at me—not to mention their insistence on shoehorning themselves into today's interview—made it clear they thought I was hiding something.

Which I was, which was why I was hyperventilating on a weirdly tiny toilet in the ladies room at the Plano Police Department headquarters.

*Just stick to your guns, and if you can't answer a question, don't. Couldn't be simpler.*

To my dismay, the Plano detectives only stayed in the interview room long enough to see if I needed anything else, then they abandoned me. Clutching my bottle of water, I watched the Fort Worth detectives put on a little production. One of them pulled a plain manilla folder from his shoulder bag, opened it, and arranged several small stacks of paper on the table. From my vantage point, they looked like bank records or something along those lines. The other guy sat in his chair, leaning forward, elbows on his knees and hands clasped together, and stared at me.

I found the courage to say, "Y'all still think I had something to do with the Kimbell, don't you?"

The guy at the table said, "What you are, Miss Riordan, is an accessory after the fact. That's a choice. That's a crime. Do you understand that?"

"I can understand it without agreeing with it," I snapped. "And it's just Claire."

"Fair enough. I'm Art, by the way," the older one at the table said. "That's Wayne. Like we said, we've got some questions for you, and I'm sorry to say I don't think you're going to take too kindly to them."

"Art. That's funny."

"That's why I got this case," he said with a genuine smile. He rearranged his face into a neutral mask and said, "Let's start with a simple one: What happened to that little blue hotrod of yours? The…" He checked some handwritten notes. "Hellcat?"

"I don't know. Fred took it."

"By force?"

"Not really. He dropped me off at Target, and I didn't ask for my car back, and he didn't offer. I just wanted to get to Ren."

"Ren is Preston Renner?" Wayne asked. I nodded, and the younger detective fell silent again.

"Did Laubenberg say where he was going?" Art asked.

"No."

"What about why he went to your apartment Saturday afternoon and again Sunday morning. Did he tell you that?"

I hadn't realized Mikel made a visit on Saturday, but I wasn't surprised. "We didn't talk about it. We didn't say much at all. I was kind of in shock, and I was just glad he was there."

"So you've been at Mr. Renner's house since then?"

"That's right. I didn't think it was safe to go home."

"We talked to Mr. Renner Sunday evening. He said he didn't know where you were."

I sighed, "Can you give him a break? He was just trying to protect me."

"I understand that," Art said. He didn't fire off another question right away, giving his partner time to interject.

Wayne asked, "When did you first meet Fred Laubenberg?"

"At the Kimbell. It would have been… last Tuesday night? He and his crew were installing a new security system for a special exhibit."

"And that's when he gave you his phone number?"

"Yeah. Well, it was Wednesday morning by then..." I fell silent, suddenly unable to speak.

Mikel's phone number. He'd given it to Joe, who'd given it to me. Then I'd given it to Wayne, one week ago, before forgetting Wayne's name, the piece of paper, and even the fact of that first interview. Judging by the way both Wayne and Art sat up straighter, they hadn't forgotten.

Art said, "Miss Riordan—Claire, sorry—I've got some phone records here. These ones are yours." He passed me a stapled stack of about three sheets. "I've highlighted a couple different numbers, if you want to take a look. The first one there, from last Tuesday, in yellow, whose phone number is that?"

My mouth was almost too dry to allow me to say, "That's Ren's number. His cell. I texted him when I got home from a trip early Tuesday morning."

"Okay. And then down there in green, a few texts Thursday night and a call Friday night. Who's that?"

"That's Fred. We—we went out on a date."

While he let me stew in that, my eyes roved down the page and saw a lot of green and yellow, all ending abruptly on Saturday. I recognized the three calls from Mr. Miller Sunday morning, but Art hadn't seen fit to highlight those. Maybe he ran out of colors.

I felt a spark of hope. I was overreacting, wasn't I? Mikel got a new phone on Sunday. They didn't have that number. Unless they'd—

"Now these are Mr. Renner's records," Art said, swapping out the papers in my numb hands. "You're in pink. Mr. Laubenberg is still in green. Can you hazard a guess why

Laubenberg called Mr. Renner Saturday morning, and Mr. Renner returned that call later that afternoon?"

I studied the dates and the phone numbers. I had introduced Mikel to Ren Sunday afternoon, at the rental apartment. I was absolutely certain of that. They couldn't have exchanged phone calls the day before. These records were simply wrong. Since I couldn't say that, I said nothing.

A memory flashed in my mind: Ren and me in his office after brunch on Saturday. His phone ringing. Him ignoring the call. I looked at the time and date stamp of Mikel's call to Ren's cell. They were a perfect match.

I couldn't hold it in anymore. I blurted, "You're lying. You made all this up."

"What makes you say that?" Art asked.

Unbridled stupidity was the honest answer. I pressed my mouth shut and shook my head.

"All right. Now this block here I circled, this was all while Mr. Renner was hosting us in his office for an interview on Sunday. That's when he lied to us about knowing where you were, if you recall. This call and these texts—whose phone number is that?"

I didn't recognize the number, but it wasn't difficult to guess based on the date and time. It was Mikel's new phone number. He and I had tried to reach Ren before I'd stupidly decided to go fetch groceries myself. Under that, when I was at the grocery store, was the call from the clerk's phone to Ren. Had they tracked her down and figured out she worked a couple blocks from the rental unit? Did it even matter? I was so lost and confused, all I knew for sure was that my goose was cooked.

Art finished waiting for my answer and said, "You may be

glad to know we found your car, Claire. It's parked at the same address one Robert Fuller was summoned to by this number..."

He passed me another stack, this one much thicker. Among the hundreds of texts was one phone call highlighted in yellow. Next to the number, someone had written 'Fuller'. I searched the top of the page and nearly fainted when I saw the name: Annika Christenson.

Art and Wayne gave me a few seconds to process this before Wayne asked gently, "Are you ready to tell us the truth, Claire?"

What I was ready to do was sink through the floor and disappear forever. Perhaps find a nice, cozy subterranean tunnel to call home. Maybe my eyes would adjust to the low light, like Gollum. I could live on rats and pet snakes people flushed down the toilet. Annika was right all along, wasn't she? It's hard to lie to the police, even if you're a good liar; and you *always* bring a lawyer.

Underneath the sense of defeat and the feeling that I'd just stepped into a bear trap was a growing anger. They'd lied to me. Somehow, for some reason, Ren and Mikel knew each other. Maybe not before I met Mikel, but certainly before I'd introduced him to Ren. And they'd pretended they'd never met. *They lied to me.*

All I could do was meet Wayne's muddy brown eyes and nod once.

# 16

*June 4*

REN STOOD UP WHEN HE saw me coming back down the hall, flanked by Planos One and Two. I'd been in the interview room for about three hours, so it made sense for him to look worried and irritated. He drew me into a hug as soon as I was close enough, saying nothing until the detectives were gone.

"You look shaken up. Did it go okay? Why did it take so long?"

"I… it was fine. I'm just tired. They wanted to go over every little detail ad nauseam. I guess it's good they're taking this so seriously, huh?"

"Did they say what happens next?"

Oh, did they. I took a deep breath. "Yeah. They said they'll call if they have any more questions. I may have to testify, but that won't be for a long time. They got my phone back from the Fort Worth cops." I pulled away from Ren and showed him my phone. "It's stone dead."

"We can charge it in the car. Let's get out of here."

Ren rushed me out of there like he thought they were about to lock us in. Now that I knew he'd been lying to me for days—maybe even longer—I couldn't blame him for wanting to put some distance between himself and the law. The more I thought about it, the worse it got.

I'd concluded that Ren had convinced Mikel to contact me after our disastrous date. I'd told Mikel about the Wyeth, he'd gotten angry, and he'd called Ren the next morning. I didn't know why yet, but I knew Mikel'd had a change of heart. He was all charm when we met again at the park.

"Nice to finally meet you," he'd said. Like he didn't know exactly who Ren was.

My thoughts must have been doing something to my face, because Ren asked, "Are you sure you're okay?"

We were almost to the highway, and it was going to be a long drive from Plano, northeast of Dallas, back to Ren's house in Benbrook, southwest of Fort Worth. I'd slept through the trip last night and wished I could do it again. My thoughts were chaos, an all-out war between loyalty to Ren and affection for Mikel on one side, and my wounded, seething ego on the other. Already I regretted the deal I'd made with Art and Wayne, but there was no going back. Unless I wanted to give prison a try.

Just to give my hands something to do besides smack Ren around, I picked up my charging phone and turned it on. As it came to life, voicemails and text messages began pouring in. I ignored the unknown numbers, attempts by potential clients to secure my organizing assistance. They'd have moved on to other organizers by now. I took a few seconds to text Serena, the young mother whose home I'd cleaned and organized last Wednesday, before reviewing my voicemails.

My heart stopped. I had a voicemail from Marty's neighbor, Pam.

Ren heard me gasp and asked, "What? What happened?"

"Pam called. It was—oh, it was just a couple hours ago. I have to call her back."

Under his breath, he asked, "Do you?"

I ignored him and hit the Send button. Pam answered so fast, I knew she'd been sitting by the phone. "Claire?"

"Is he okay? What happened?"

Her tremulous voice sounded odd, as though she were fighting back some unwieldy emotion. "I am not sure. I called him last night to make sure he had gone back to work, and he said he did not want to talk to me and he would call me this morning. He has not called and I have tried to reach him, I even went over there and knocked on the door—"

I lost the thread of her words, distracted by astonishment. Pam, Marty's agoraphobic and mostly handicapped neighbor, had actually walked over to his house and knocked on the door? That was a first. I tuned back in to her babbling voice.

"—did not answer, so I called you, and the call went straight to voicemail. I am glad you called back. I do think you need to go check on him. Will you?"

"Of course. I'll be there as soon as I can."

I ended the call, and before I could say anything else, Ren barked, "No. I'm not taking you to Marty's house. Forget it."

"Then let me out here, and I'll get there myself."

"No."

"This is imprisoning or restraining another without consent," I recited. "That's the same thing Mondo and Leonard did to me. If you don't let me out, you're committing a Class A misdemeanor."

"As thrilled as I am that you know that, I think I'll risk it."

"You are *so mean!*" I cried. "It's not up to you whether I try to help Marty—"

"Well it shouldn't be up to you!" he fired back. He wasn't going to go easy on me this time. "The man stole years of your life, treated you like a dog, and broke your nose! All he deserves from you is disdain. You're too soft-hearted."

"I'll be as soft-hearted as I want to be," I muttered. "I'm gonna be soft-hearted even harder."

"That doesn't even make sense."

I unplugged my phone, which wasn't even up to a 10% charge yet, and took my chance when we stopped at the underpass to get on the turnpike. Throwing myself out the door, I skipped between two cars in the next lane and hit the sidewalk running. I knew Ren wouldn't actually chase me, but I wanted to leave him in no doubt that his only choice was to head home and let me do what I wanted.

When I'd reached the parking lot of an auto body shop at the corner, I turned back and saw Ren's Denali continuing south under the turnpike. He was actually going to turn around and come after me!

Powerwalking across the lot and through the shop's front door, I found myself inside a small lobby smelling of grease and popcorn. A man about my age sat behind the desk, regarding me with open suspicion.

"You here to pick up?" he asked.

"No. I'm just trying to get out of sight for a minute."

"Git outta sight?" he repeated, as though I'd just told him to give me everything in his pockets. "This look like a hideout to you? G'won, git."

"All right, sorry. Jeez."

I left, feeling deflated. The worst part about what I'd done was that I was still wearing the sandals I'd scavenged from

Ren's lost and found after Mondo robbed me of those stupid, too-big, pink flip-flops. This pair was slightly too small, and I hadn't had a chance to buy real shoes yet. My dogs were barking. The second worst part was realizing I hadn't done it because I was so desperate to get to Marty; I just wanted to get away from Ren.

*That lying, manipulating, no good son of a gun.*

Unfortunately, my phone didn't have enough battery power to arrange a ride to Marty's house. Defeat was simple, but not easy. Still seething, I crossed the street to a carwash that looked a bit friendlier and texted Ren to tell him where I was. He pulled to a stop outside the front door a couple minutes later, and I climbed inside.

"Are you ready to act even half your age now?" he asked.

"Don't talk to me."

He complied, and we spent the remainder of the ride in tense silence. My legs and arms were so tightly crossed that they didn't seem to want to uncross when we reached Ren's house. I got them to cooperate and followed Ren inside, ignoring Mikel and Annika's greetings and shutting myself into my room. I found an old charger in the nightstand and plugged my phone in.

Predictably, Pam called again when I'd had time to get there and still hadn't shown up. I sat down on the bed to answer it so I wouldn't have to unplug my phone.

"Are you still coming?" she asked. She sounded a little testy.

"I'm working on it. I don't have my car right now."

"Oh… all right. Do please hurry, Claire."

Now I was mad at her, too. If she was so worried, why didn't she do something about it? Why did it have to be me? It wasn't like she needed my permission to call the police and ask them to do a wellness check. Marty worked in a SCIF, and he didn't have access to his cell phone at work. Of course he wouldn't answer it, because he was at work because it was a work day! It was all too much.

I heard a light knock at the door and ignored it, to no effect. The door opened, and Annika stepped inside.

"Was it that bad?" she asked.

"Yeah. It took a lot longer than I thought it would."

"But did they believe you?"

I tossed my phone on the bed and sighed. "Honestly? I don't know. If they thought I wasn't telling the truth, they didn't come right out and say so."

This lying thing was getting easier and easier. Pretty soon I'd be as skilled as Ren and Mikel.

Annika sat down next to me and said, "You look super stressed out and like… kinda mad."

I told her about my need to get to my ex-husband's house, and Ren's refusal to help me. Then I had to explain why Ren hated Marty so much, and why I didn't. By the time I was finished spilling my guts, Annika knew more about my marriage than my own parents did. I felt bad about trauma dumping on a teenage girl, but somehow I knew she could handle it.

She surprised me by asking, "Don't you know how to defend yourself?"

"Defend myself? How?"

She held up her hands, wiggling her fingers. "These bad boys. You know, punch, scratch, kick, and bite? Every girl should know."

"That's not really my style."

"Maybe it should be." She stood up. "I'll teach you a few things when you get back, but for now, just be the cat."

"Now there's a cat involved?" I asked.

"Yes, a cat. Just imagine you're holding a big, fat, happy, purring cat. Right now, go on."

Cooperatively, I mimed holding a large cat in my arms. Whether she meant to or not, she was cheering me up already.

Annika said, "Now imagine me dumping a bucket of ice water on you. What do you think the cat's gonna do?"

"Jump down. Maybe scratch me."

"What if you try to hold onto it?"

I laughed. "It would shred me to ribbons."

"Exactly. Just be the cat."

She then convinced Ren to give me the keys to his Denali, through means unknown. Mikel insisted on accompanying me to Marty's house, and refusing to allow him to do so gave me a stab of vindictive pleasure. It was nearly 3:00 p.m. when I set out once more, this time for a much shorter drive to White Settlement. Marty wouldn't be home from work yet, so all I had to do was let myself into the house, confirm the absence of his dead, decaying body, and report as much to Pam.

When I pulled to a stop in his driveway, it occurred to me that letting myself inside wasn't going to be so easy this time. The key to his house was hanging on a hook in my kitchen. And the key to my apartment was with the key to the Hellcat. I wasn't sure where those had ended up.

Thankfully, I'd been down this road before. Letting myself into the back yard, I found a ladder behind the shed, leaned it against the house, and climbed up to the back patio. The sliding door in Marty's bedroom was always unlocked despite Marty's insistence that he took home security very seriously. I stepped inside, closed the door behind me, and felt the first happy feeling I'd felt all day.

The bedroom was clean and fresh, the bed was made, and the laundry hamper was empty. The master bathroom was in a similar state, even the mirrors free of toothpaste specks. Most of this was the work of my own hands, but it was encouraging to see that Marty hadn't undone it in the week he'd been left to his own devices.

I checked every room of the house to be sure, but I already knew he wasn't there. He was at work, and I was breaking and entering for no reason at all. At least the trip had given me a break from those two miserable liars whose names I refused to think.

I called Pam and told her all was well, then found a notepad in the kitchen to leave Marty a note. I told him I'd been there because Pam asked me to, how I'd gotten inside, that he needed to remember to lock the sliding door, and that I was proud of him for keeping the house so clean. There were still empty liquor bottles in the kitchen, but at least they were in the recycling bin where they belonged.

Back up to the bedroom I went, because I had to leave the same way I came in. Expecting to bask in the sight of Marty's clean bedroom one more time, I was instead greeted by a total stranger standing in the middle of the room, waiting for me.

I TURNED ON MY HEEL and sprinted for the stairs, but he was faster. Where Mondo was big and heavy, this guy was gracile as a deer and seemed to be composed primarily of stringy, iron-hard muscle. He tackled me to the floor, rolled me over, and pinned my elbows to the floor with his bony knees.

The question-and-answer session I expected didn't come. The man didn't say a word. He just pulled a gun from his waistband—Marty's revolver—and pressed it to my temple.

That was the moment to make my peace with God. I didn't even consider it.

In a heartbeat I was so angry, so mind-boilingly consumed by rage, that I wanted nothing more than to grievously injure this man before he killed me. I heard him pull back the hammer and did the only thing I could think to do: I squirmed and wriggled and bucked like a mad woman—like a cat drenched in ice water.

The gun went off, nearly deafening me, but wherever the bullet went, I was reasonably sure it wasn't in me. I didn't feel any pain, only more rage. The more I fought, the angrier I felt. This worthless piece of garbage didn't know me from Eve, and he was trying to take my life.

I found his right hand, the one with the gun, and wrapped both my hands around his wrist. Though he'd grabbed a fistful of my hair, it wasn't enough to stop me from sinking my teeth into his hand and biting until I felt the skin break between my teeth. The gun fell to the floor, and I rolled on top of it, the taste of blood filling my mouth.

No amount of vim could keep the thought of blood from making me woozy, but I fought through it. What choice did I have? With the revolver digging painfully into my back, I locked my legs around the man and started clawing, punching, hammering, and even slapping with both hands until he managed to free himself. He stumbled backward to his feet, found the edge of the stairs, and tumbled head over heels all the way down to the first floor.

The silence following his descent was deafening. I sat up, hands fumbling for the revolver. I had no idea how to use it. Marty had tried to teach me a few times, but his words always went in one ear and out the other. I knew the hammer had to be pulled back, so I did that, then pointed the little gun at the top of the stairs and waited, breathing hard.

I heard the front door open, then light footsteps fleeing down the front sidewalk.

I actually laughed. Had I—had I *scared him away?*

Rising to my feet, I peered over the banister to make sure he was really gone. The lout hadn't even bothered to close the door behind him. I trudged downstairs, closed and locked the door, and stumbled to the living room sofa. I collapsed onto it, still struggling to catch my breath.

It had been a quick victory after all, but I'd used up every drop of energy doing it. With the gun in my lap, I stayed on the sofa until I could breathe again, and then stayed a little longer. I couldn't really think straight. What was I supposed to do now? I could wait for Marty to get home and tell him what happened. I could call the police. I could just leave. I could walk over to Pam's house and make her tell me whether she'd had anything to do with this.

She had sounded so strange, almost like she was reading a script. I'd ask her about it later. I found my note in the kitchen and amended it with, "Give me a call when you get home."

I added my phone number just in case he'd lost it again. Leaving the gun next to the note for dramatic effect, I again climbed the stairs. Noting the bullet hole in the drywall, I concluded I really hadn't been shot. I didn't care to think how narrowly I'd avoided that. I let myself out the sliding door, climbed down, replaced the ladder, and left the back yard. Stopping in sight of Pam's kitchen window, I stared for about a minute, wondering if she'd have the nerve to come outside. She didn't.

I didn't remember the drive back to Ren's house. The next thing I was aware of, I was parked in his driveway, sobbing my guts out. My entire body hurt, and I was afraid to look in a mirror. I could see my hands, though, and the marks left by my unhinged attack. My knuckles were raw and red, bleeding in two places, and I'd broken all my fingernails off. Bruises were blossoming on my forearms and likely in a lot of other places as well. But I won.

Ren was going to have kittens when he saw me. Seeing no way to avoid this, I went inside.

I found them clustered in the kitchen, snacking on cheese

and crackers again. Ren and Mikel had beers in their hands, and my appearance interrupted Annika in the middle of an impassioned argument in favor of allowing her to drink a beer, too.

"How'd it go?" Ren asked automatically, before the state of me could sink in. He paused, stared at me for a second, and breathed, "Good God, Claire. What happened?"

Mikel and Annika turned to see what the big deal was, and the former dropped his beer and ran over to me. I wasn't really sure why until my legs gave out, and I found myself held upright entirely by the support of his arms. I smiled weakly at Annika.

"I did like you said, Ani. Like a cat." Darkness crept around the edges of my vision, and I told Mikel, "I'd like to go to sleep now."

*

I woke up in bed, and I wished I hadn't. I hurt. Darkness had fallen outside, and my room wasn't much brighter. By the feeble light seeping under my closed door, I could see the shape of someone lying in bed next to me. Without moving, I took stock of my body.

My head hurt, but that was manageable. Little aches and pains lived here and there in my arms, legs, and back, but the worst of it was my hands. They seemed to be on fire from wrist to fingertip, my pulse beating hard beneath at least two layers of bandages or gauze. There was also a large bandage on the inside of my left forearm. I had no memory of getting injured there, but that didn't mean much.

My lower lip felt swollen, too, which was annoying. That had been healing nicely, but I supposed my attacker could have landed a blow there and reopened the cut. I had no clear memory of the fight.

I moved just enough to peek under the blanket that covered me to my chin. I was only wearing a bra and underwear. The movement roused the person next to me. I could tell it was Mikel just by the sound of his sigh.

"Are you awake?" he whispered.

"No."

He rolled over to turn on a light, then turned back to me. Without a word he picked up my hands one at a time and looked them over. I assumed the lack of blood seeping through the bandages was taken as a good sign.

"Did you undress me?" I asked.

"Annika took care of that. There was a lot of you-know-what on your clothes, and she had to check you for other injuries."

"Was I asleep or unconscious?"

"I don't know. How do you feel now? Do you want some painkillers, or...?"

I pressed one hand to his cheek, taking in the exhaustion written in every line of his face. "I'm sorry. I shouldn't have gone. Or I should've let you come with me. Either way, I'm sorry."

"Don't tell me," he said. "Ren's ready to first-degree murder your ex. If you feel like stopping him, I don't think he's left yet."

I frowned. "Marty? Why?"

"Why? He beat the crap out you, Claire! How can you—"

"He didn't do this to me. He wasn't even there."

That woke him up. He sat up on one elbow, halfway pulling the blanket away from me. I pulled it back automatically, tucking it back under my chin.

He asked, "Who?"

"I don't know who it was." My head started to pound, and I shut my eyes and waited for it to pass. "I have to be dehydrated or something. If I'm going to explain this, I only want to do it once."

Mikel left at once to bring Ren, who appeared in my doorway looking so positively hawkish that I blurted, "Take it easy. It wasn't Marty."

"Then that makes it okay," he said.

"I didn't say it was okay, I just said you don't have to blame Marty."

"If you're gonna give her crap, you can leave," Mikel said. Ren turned to him, nonplussed.

"You're telling me what to do in my own house?" he asked.

"Sounds like it," Mikel shot back.

"Oh, stop it," I moaned. "Ren, I'm sorry. I should've listened to you."

Not to be won over that easily, he asked, "Is there any reason to hope that means you'll listen to me in the future?"

"I mean… you can always hope."

His dumbfounded laugh, his shaking head, his crossed arms, I'd seen it all before. He wanted to stay mad at me, but he couldn't. Mikel wasn't as familiar with Ren's moods.

"Seriously, man. Don't give her any grief."

"I'll give her whatever I want to give her," Ren snapped. He asked me, "What'll it be? Wine? Tylenol? Cheese platter?"

"Yes," I said. He started to walk away, and I arrested him with, "Wait. First, let me tell you what happened. I can't make sense of it on my own."

He remained in the doorway, Mikel sat on the bed, and I

made short work of the tale. The two of them were immediately in agreement that my attacker was another one of Money's goons, the existence of which Annika had already foretold. With no way to know how many more violent sociopaths he could throw at us, we all agreed it was best to stick together from now on and only leave the house if we absolutely had to.

"Do we tell the detectives?" Ren asked.

I shrugged, and Mikel said, "I vote yes. If Money's still calling the shots from jail, they need to shut him down."

"We don't even know he is in jail," Ren pointed out. "He could've been released on his own recognizance. It happens, especially with elder defendants. And he's got money, which means pull."

"Then I don't see any point in telling the cops," I said. "It'll just give them an excuse to interview me again. I don't like it."

As the tie breaker, Ren concluded, "I don't see what's to be gained by telling them. Seems like we're on our own here."

"Where's Annika?" I asked.

"Asleep. It's nearly dawn. She was pretty upset," Mikel said. "I had to give her drugs to get her to sleep."

"Drugs?" I repeated, appalled.

"He means NyQuil," Ren said.

"Oh. I am *starving.*" I started to get up, remembered what I was wearing, and thought better of it. "Can you two get lost? I need to get dressed."

"You need any help?" Mikel asked.

I ignored him, and Ren dragged him out of my room and shut the door. I actually could have used some help, but I muddled through just fine and found my way to the kitchen. Weak with hunger and aching with thirst, I found a half-empty bottle of water on the kitchen island and helped myself to it. There was plenty more to be had in Ren's pantry, but I thought about walking all twenty feet to get there and decided to sit down instead. Ren read my mind and brought me two bottles of water.

He said, "Don't take this as encouragement in any way, but I'm impressed. Sounds like you came at that guy so hard you scared him off."

"Maybe." I took down half of one bottle in two huge gulps, burped, and said, "Or maybe I put up too much of a fight to make it look like suicide. I think that's what he was trying to do."

"Either way. Well done."

"I don't know what came over me. I was just… so mad. Blind with rage. It was scary."

"So Money wants you dead now?" Mikel asked. "Why?"

"If he was one of Leonard's guys, it makes sense," I argued. "I'm not going to help him find the Caillebotte, and the fewer people who know about it, the better. Right?"

"How did he know you'd go to Marty's house alone?" Ren asked.

"Beats the heck out of me." I picked at the label on the plastic bottle, thinking.

Now that my brain wasn't desiccated, I remembered that I was on a mission. The Fort Worth PD wanted information about the heist, including Ren's involvement if he was involved, and they wanted me to get it. If I didn't, couldn't, or wouldn't, it was no skin off their noses. They'd prosecute me for lesser crimes and call it a day. Art and Wayne hadn't set a time limit on this demand, only telling me that the sooner I came through, the less time they'd have to wonder if I would.

They knew Annika was involved, which meant they knew Mikel's real name and what I assumed was a long and colorful criminal history. As far as they were concerned, he was an even bigger fish than Leonard Money. Ren was a normal-sized fish, and I was a minnow. A bait fish. Just a dummy who didn't come clean to the cops soon enough.

Bringing up the heist now would be awkward at best, suspicious at worst. I wasn't anywhere near ready for them to know I knew they'd lied to me about knowing each other. There was exactly one way, in my limited imagination, that I could get some solid evidence.

I asked, "Will you tell me where the Caillebotte is?"

Taken aback, Mikel asked, "Why?"

"Why do you think? The next time someone threatens to murder me if I don't tell *them*, I'd like to be able to comply."

I had achieved awkward but avoided suspicious, so far as I could tell. Mikel didn't answer, and Ren felt it necessary to save the moment by asking, "What do you want to eat?"

"Everything you've got," I answered.

While Ren whipped up a feast of scrambled eggs and bacon, Mikel changed the bandages on my hands. My knuckles didn't look that bad, but I needed to do something about the ragged, snapped-off edges of my fingernails. The earlier cut Mondo had inflicted was healing well. After Mikel was done with my hands, he moved on to the bandage on my forearm. I was curious to see what was under it.

"I do not remember that happening," I breathed when he pulled the bandage away.

It looked like someone had branded me with a long, narrow object that tapered at either end. The whole thing was about two inches long. At one end, a splash of burned skin appeared like a tiny firework exploding toward the longer burn. I had no idea what I was looking at.

"You said the gun went off," Mikel explained. "Looks like it barely grazed you. It must have been nearly touching you when he pulled the trigger. See the powder burn there? You didn't feel it?"

"No."

He smiled, tugging my hair. "Luck of the Irish, huh?"

"Oh yeah, that's me. So lucky."

"Eureka!"

Annika's boisterous shout carried easily from the third floor to the first. Standing in the kitchen with Mikel and having just won the argument about who was going to load the dishwasher, I waited in silence with him for her to gallop down two flights of stairs and into the kitchen to explain herself.

She dashed in, carrying her laptop, and set it down on the kitchen island between Mikel and me. Ren was at work, and I had a feeling he was going to be sorry he missed this.

"You are *not* going to believe this," she crowed. Her happiness was infectious.

"Give us a chance to, kiddo," Mikel said.

"Okay, okay. Look. Eureka, Montana."

Mikel and I looked at each other, then at her screen. It was just a map with a town in northwest Montana, near the Canadian border, marked with a red pin.

"What about it?" he prompted.

"Paul Pearson. Heard of him?"

"Yes," Mikel and I said in unison. I added, "Have you?"

"Well, I hadn't. But now I have."

Paul Pearson was one of the best-known actors of the 1970s and 80s. A heartthrob if ever there was one. The last I'd heard of him, he'd emerged from relative obscurity to play the bad guy in a flop Sci-Fi thriller with B- and C-list actors two years ago. He was still handsome, despite pushing eighty years old. For the life of me, I couldn't guess what he had to do with the Wyeth.

Annika explained, "He was really close with your aunt. Like… really. If you get me."

"They were lovers?" I asked.

"Yeppo. I take it by your expression, you didn't know that."

"She didn't discuss her love life with me. I was eight."

"Well, thank goodness for trashy tabloids. Claire, Pearson has the painting."

Her pronouncement was met with crickets. I stared at the red pin, trying to find some clue to Annika's complete confidence. I came up empty handed.

Knowing his sister and her ways much better than I, Mikel didn't seem confused at all. He just asked, "He lives in Eureka?"

"Yes. He bought a big, fancy, rhinestone cowboy kinda house there—on a hundred-acre ranch—ten years ago. He's retired and lives there with his current wife and occasionally some of his kids."

"How do you know he has it?" I asked.

"Well, it was something you said last night," she answered. I racked my brain, hardly remembering said conversation.

It had been just over a week since the attack at Marty's house, and Mikel and Annika had been stuck inside the whole time. I'd ventured beyond the safety of Ren's door just once, with Ren, to dash to my apartment and grab a couple suitcases worth of clothes, shoes, and other bare necessities.

Annika had refused to allow this excursion without first teaching me the basics of self-defense, to which I submitted with as much attentiveness as I could. I couldn't imagine breaking someone's nose with the heel of my hand or sending my knee smashing into another person's groin, but I learned how to do it anyway.

Once my apartment supply run was complete, only Ren was allowed to leave his house at all. He was back to work and business as usual, no longer lying to Detectives Art and Wayne about the fact that I was living at his house.

I'd screened daily calls from the detectives, and I wasn't sure I could hold them off much longer. I didn't have anything useful to tell them, and I'd long since come to regret—and privately repudiate—my deal with them. They were bugging Ren now, but he was standing his ground. They weren't allowed inside his house, but he couldn't stop them from hanging around outside. Mikel and Annika were much better at staying out of sight than I was.

I'd set an auto-reply for new client inquiries, which was annoying but necessary. Joe had called to regretfully inform me that, although he knew I had nothing to do with the break-in at the Kimbell, he'd had no choice but to let me go so he could hire a replacement. The museum directors were hounding him to beef up security, anyway. That left me jobless, not to mention halfway homeless. My rent and utilities were still being paid, but I wouldn't be returning to my apartment for good until I was sure it was safe. As much as I disliked "stuff" in the abstract, I did miss my own specific possessions more and more every day.

Last night, in a red wine sort of mood, I'd tuned out of Ren, Mikel, and Annika's conversation to journey mentally to my bedroom, pull a medium-sized, blue box from the top shelf of my closet, and sort through its contents. Inside were the only things I'd allowed myself to hold onto out of pure sentimentality—not including the paintings in my art gallery—unused toys, sonogram pictures, sympathy cards, a baby blanket, a teddy bear that weighed exactly 184 grams and still smelled of peppermint and lavender.

Mikel had yanked me back into the present—last night's present—by poking me in the thigh and asking, "Right?"

"What's right?" I'd asked.

"Your aunt threw a party the night before she showed you the painting?" Annika had pressed.

"Oh yeah." Why that thought had led me on a walk down World's Most Painful Memories Lane, I'd had no idea. "I was in my room for most of it. I think my parents had told her to keep me away from her friends. She was always throwing house parties."

Her house—that was why I was feeling nostalgic. For three days, fires had been springing up and raging out of control through Southern California. Many people suspected arson, but that hadn't been confirmed. Homes, businesses, car collections, beloved family pets, and even human lives had been lost. Aunt Eva's 100-plus-year-old mansion in Pasadena was among the thousands threatened with total, fiery annihilation, and I'd been worried sick.

Drawing me back out of my thoughts yet again, Annika had asked, "Do you happen to remember who was there?"

"No. She was going to show me the guest book the next morning, but I think she was drunk and forgot. She showed me the painting instead."

The memory ended, I continued to stare at the map of Montana, and I asked, "The thing about the guest book?"

Nodding happily, Annika said, "Yeah. I found it. I stayed up all night tracking it down. It was in a collection of personal writings and sketches auctioned off by Sotheby's just last year. The bidder—anonymous, sadly—donated a lot of it to the Getty Center. The guest book isn't on public display, but it's been digitized. I got a list of everyone who was there the night before your aunt showed you the Wyeth."

I gaped at her, mouth hanging open, until Mikel tapped me under the chin.

His voice was a study in fraternal pride. "Well done, kiddo."

"Holy moly," I agreed.

Mikel asked, "How'd you narrow it down to Pearson?"

"Thanks to his anal retentiveness, that's how. When he moved from Hollywood to Eureka, he re-upped his insurance and gave them a list of everything he was taking with him." She opened a different window and pointed to a line of text on a poorly scanned document. "One oil painting, twenty by twenty-six including frame, nude in the desert, unsigned and unattributed, value estimated at twenty-two thousand dollars."

I was no great shakes at mental math, but thankfully Mikel showed his work out loud. "That's a big fat frame—four inches thick all around if the painting is twelve-by-eighteen—but it's possible."

"Twenty-two thousand dollars!" I cried. "It's worth ten times that! More!"

"But he'd have to get it appraised and attributed to Wyeth to get that price tag," Annika reminded me. "I know it's kinda circular reasoning, but if he doesn't want anyone to know what he's got, he has to undervalue it."

"Keep convincing me," Mikel said.

Smirking, Annika opened a third window. "I knew you'd say that. Eva Riordan's death was unattended. That means the police had to investigate her cause of death. Claire, thanks to you, we know the painting was still in Eva's safe the morning after the party. Pearson and everyone else was gone by then—it actually says so in the guest book. But look who the police interviewed when they found him at Eva's house the day *before* the funeral."

There, in plain handwriting on a dated Pasadena Police Department form, were the words "Interviewed visitor at victim's home, Mr. P. Pearson of Hollywood, CA."

I didn't bother reading the narrative that followed. A soaring feeling in my heart told me this was it. Finally, after thirty years and thanks to Annika, I'd found it.

How in the world was I going to get my hands on it?

*

That discussion was tabled until Ren got home from work Friday evening. While we waited for him, we each celebrated in our own ways. I cleaned Ren's entire house (his housekeeper had been gently encouraged to stay away); Annika spent the whole, sunny day switching between the pool and hot tub; and Mikel availed himself of Ren's in-home gym, in-home theater, cavernous master bathroom, and full pantry. We all had a good day, except the homeowner himself.

Ren came home at 7:00, bearing with him a storm cloud of indignation. I hurriedly threw together the best Manhattan I could make, which wasn't very good but better than nothing, and brought it to him in the living room. Mikel and Annika lingered in the kitchen, letting me deal with the grump.

"Thanks, Mrs. Brady," Ren sighed, accepting the drink and knocking back half of it in one gulp. "You look like something wants to explode out of you."

"It's true, but tell me about your day first. It was bad, wasn't it?"

An evasive look in his tired eyes was gone before I could be sure I'd seen it. He took another, smaller drink. "Art and Fart came to my office," he said, using his unaffectionate nickname for Wayne. "They thought they could embarrass me into giving my consent for them to enter the house. Clearly they've figured out Mikel and Ani are here. I've already told them you are."

"Did it work?"

"They certainly embarrassed me, but they're not getting in here without a warrant. Unfortunately, I think that's in the works."

"I have an idea."

The words came from the living room doorway, from Annika. We both looked up.

"How long have you been eavesdropping, young lady?" Ren asked.

"Long enough. Sorry to steal your thunder, Claire, but we found the Wyeth. It's in Montana."

Ren perked up, meeting my eyes. I nodded.

Annika went on, "As Mikel has so gleefully informed me, I can't go to Montana to get it. He and Claire can go, but I have to go to summer semester."

I stared at the teenager, blurting, "There's absolutely no way *you're* in summer school."

"There is if my meddling brother signs me up for twelve credit hours, forging my signature!" This last she shouted toward the kitchen, from which issued a self-satisfied laugh.

"Oh, college," I said. "That makes more sense."

"Yes. Classes start next Thursday. So here's my idea: I'll stay here and be Claire, and that ought to get the fuzz off your back. With no one in the house, they'll have to find some other place to look for Mikel and me, and they won't be looking for Claire in Montana or anywhere else."

"I am literally two of you," I argued.

"But our voices sound really similar. Say I'm indisposed when the detectives come inside. Taking a shower, or a deuce. It won't work over and over, but if all they need to do is confirm you're here and we're not, that's the problem solved."

Ren looked at her like he was seeing her for the first time. He swirled his glass and muttered, "Claire, I'm frightened of this child. She's smarter than me."

"It's probably best to do what she says," I agreed.

Annika said, "Great. I'll go tell my brother that he's getting his way, yet again."

After she'd gone, I perched on the arm of Ren's chair and swiped the glass from his hand to steal a drink. He accepted it back with a sarcastic, "Thanks."

"I'm not crazy about this," I admitted. "Annika will be safe with you, but… Ren… I can't go to Montana with Mikel, just him and me." I turned to keep the doorway in view, just in case Mikel felt like eavesdropping as well. I lowered my voice to say, "He'll eat me alive."

"Is that not good? I would've thought that would be good."

I stared at him, trying not to smile.

"Hey, I'm straight, not blind," he defended. "He's a good

looking guy, right? He's got that Encino Man look going on. You're a fan."

"Yeah. So what? I'm not sure our relationship is really… like that," I said.

Ren asked, "Not like what?"

"It's not a long-term thing. We find the Wyeth, I take it, he gets to keep the Caillebotte, and that's that. Right?"

"Why?" he asked.

"Oh, come on. How else could it be? It's not like I can live happily ever after with someone who's always one step ahead of the law."

"Why not? You're going to write the guy off just because he's a petty criminal? You're better than that." I didn't know what to say to that. He gave me a delicate tap on the chin and said, "He should be so lucky. Just stick to your guns, Claire Bear."

"What do you mean?"

"I mean certain things are important to you. These exhausting principles and morals you've imposed on yourself. If he can't respect that, he doesn't deserve you. Right?"

"Meaning if he *can* respect that, he does?"

"Well, *I* like him. He's not afraid of you, which makes him a cut above the rest. Besides." He finished his drink, pressed the empty glass into my hands, and said, "You're getting ahead of yourself. Quit overthinking everything. I bet you he isn't."

*

Annika flatly forbade all three of us from so much as Googling "Montana" on our phones or computers. Scaring us dinosaurs stupid with talk of onion routers, VPNs, and the like, she secured our unanimous agreement that all travel arrangements would be made by her and her alone.

When Ren asked her how she planned to pay for all of it, she said only, "Emergency funds."

We decided not to ask for more detail. Having gained our cooperation, she had one more piece of business to take care of before we went to bed: Detectives Art and Fart.

She devised a plan that required me to meet with them tomorrow, in Ren's house, and I had no choice but to agree. Ren called Art to arrange it, then declared he would not stay awake a moment longer. We all went our separate ways, though two of those ways weren't quite as separate as I would have liked. Mikel trailed me to my bedroom, stopped me at the door, and gave me a good night kiss.

As he had the last five nights in a row, he asked, "Want some company?"

"Not tonight," I said, as per the routine. Had I known the first night that I'd be repeating the line, I'd have chosen something a bit less open-ended, like "No."

He shrugged off my answer and walked away, and I looked up at the ceiling to whisper, "Anytime you want to make this easier, I sure would appreciate it."

Annika and I were shut in the hall bathroom between the foyer and the kitchen at 9:00 the next morning, per her diabolical plan. It wasn't a big bathroom, so she was forced to perch on the sink while I sat on the closed toilet. To amp up the awkwardness, we couldn't talk to each other. We just sat there, waiting. Finally, a rap on the door.

"Hey Claire? They're here."

Annika answered, too loudly, "Okay, give me a sec!"

I flushed the toilet, she waited a beat and turned on the tap, and the sound of running water helped mask any telltale sounds of her folding herself into the cabinet under the sink. She barely fit, the P-trap digging into her abdomen, but she didn't seem to mind. She flashed me a thumbs up before I shut her in, turned off the tap, and opened the door.

"Sorry," I said to the two detectives waiting outside with Ren.

Wayne made no attempt to hide a searching glance into the bathroom. There was clearly nowhere for anyone else to hide—no one larger than Annika, anyway. She had insisted on being the one to call out, so she had only herself to blame for her current predicament. She had to stay there until after the detectives were gone, while Mikel had the luxury of cooling his heels in the attic with all of his stuff and all of hers.

If the younger detective thought my voice had sounded strange, he didn't mention it. He followed Ren and me to Ren's study, with Art bringing up the rear. Ren was kind enough to give us the room, so I made myself comfortable in his desk chair while the two detectives seated themselves in the matching armchairs across the desk from me.

"You're a hard woman to get a hold of, Claire," Art said.

"I haven't wanted to talk to you," I said flatly. "I haven't learned anything."

They shared a frown. Wayne asked, "Do you need some extra motivation?"

"Look, I don't know where Fred is—"

"Mikel," Art corrected.

"Whatever. He's always been Fred to me. If I could track him down, I'd try to get some information from him, but he obviously doesn't want to be found."

Wayne rose to his feet.

I asked, "Finished already?"

"I'm going to have a look around," he said, ignoring me to direct his answer at his partner. "You can handle this."

I wasn't even a "her" to the guy. I was a "this." Scowling, I watched him go and kept my eyes on the closed door until Art cleared his throat to regain my attention.

"Try not to let your dislike for my partner distract you. You still want to help us, right?"

"You mean, do I still not want to go to prison? What the heck do you think?"

"Why aren't you going home?"

My gaze fell to the surface of the desk, and I whispered, "I can't. It's… I just…"

"What happened to you was traumatic. No one is denying that."

"I feel safe here."

"Mr. Capelli told us he had to let you go, because you won't come to work. You're just going to stay shut up in here forever?"

"Is that a crime?" I snapped.

"No, but it's unfortunate. Wayne may be a sourpuss, but I feel for you, Claire. I would think you'd want to get this all resolved as quickly as possible."

"Helping you make a case against Fred won't stop Leonard from wanting to harm me. Are *you* going to convince him I didn't help Fred and Ken take his stuff?"

"I would if I could. I can't figure out why he wants to hurt you at all."

"Well, it's not *my* job." He didn't answer, giving me time to regret my bad attitude. It worked. Through a sigh, I said, "I'm sorry. If I had anything, I'd tell you. I swear."

"Nothing on Mr. Renner?"

"Ren? I've been through this house a dozen times. There's nothing to find."

"What about his office?"

"You want me to search his office?"

"I'd like you to try."

Twisting my mouth, letting my distaste for the idea simmer for a moment, I eventually said, "I'll try. That's that best I can do."

"Fine. Then if you don't have anything to tell me, I'll be on my way. Don't leave the area."

"No plans to."

That final statement, along with the misleading comment about going through Ren's house, were the only lies I ended up telling. I credited that fact for the speed with which I wrapped up the interview, which meant Wayne the Fart had that much less time to search Ren's house. Not that I was worried he'd find Mikel or Annika, but I wanted the two detectives gone.

By 9:30, they were. Annika freed herself from under the sink, Mikel emerged from the attic, and we spent the rest of the weekend making plans for Montana. Mikel and I would have to drive there, and we couldn't take my car or Ren's. We couldn't rent a car, and we couldn't buy one. All agreed that left but a single option: borrow one. Annika was fresh out of cars, but I happened to know two people who hadn't gotten rid of a single automobile since 1982.

*

On the pretense of acquiring a car for my use around town, Ren drove me to my parents' house after he got home from work the following Monday. Their three-acre property in Lucas was another multi-hour drive across the entire DFW metroplex from Ren's house, but we got lucky. Rush hour traffic had died down, leaving no accidents in its wake along our route. We got there in record time, so the mid-June sun was still shining cheerfully down on a scene of wholesale bedlam.

I stepped out of Ren's pristine Denali and had to take a pause to let the view wash over me. I counted two additional cars, a new collection of what looked like feeding troughs for cows, a claw-foot bathtub with dead lantana in it, and a gargantuan, spindly antenna affixed to the roof. I could only imagine what they'd done with the inside.

Condition-wise, the house was still holding up. When he wasn't trolling thrift stores or the internet for crap to buy, my dad took great pride in keeping the gutters clean, mowing and edging the yard, power-washing the siding, and other such conscientious chores. He had himself convinced this made his collection of unnecessary things look "quaint."

"Okay," I said to Ren, who was watching me apprehensively. "I think I'm ready."

He took my hand and walked me up to the front door.

As frustrated as I was with them, I loved my parents more than life itself. When my mom opened the door, my dad standing behind her left shoulder, I only took a heartbeat to notice their patent attempt to hide the inside from view before their smiles melted my heart. My mom yanked me into a hug, my dad shook Ren's hand, and then we traded.

They stepped out onto the front porch and shut the front door behind them, not even bothering to make excuses about letting us inside. My dad already had two sets of car keys in his hands.

"So the two that run best are the van," he pointed at an off-white, unmarked utility van parked just in front of the Denali, then at a ruby red Jeep Grand Cherokee next to it. "And the red Jeep there. Jeep needs some work on the suspension, but it should get you from A to B. Which one you want?"

"Um…" I pretended to think about it, studying the two cars with an uneducated eye.

Ren figured out I wasn't going to say it, so he piped up, "Actually, we need both. Is that okay?"

"Well shore, but… how y'all gonna get home?" Dad asked. "I wouldn't mind driving that luxury tank around town, mind you."

"Sorry, Lee," Ren said. "We actually brought another driver with us. *Claire*," he said pointedly, "is going to explain that to you."

"Could we go inside?" I asked.

"Oh, I don't think so," my mom said. "It's kind of a mess. I know how that stresses you out."

I considered pushing back, but since I was about to ask her and Dad to do something they wouldn't like, I let it go. "Fair enough. The thing is, I've got a friend who needs a car, too. Only for a few weeks, a month at most. He can't afford to buy one right now, but he'll pay you monthly to sort of lease it, if that works."

"Oh, he don't need to pay us nothin'," said the retired man who was probably bidding on sixteen different eBay items at once as we spoke. "But we'd need to meet him. What is he, hidin' in the car?"

I nodded.

Mom asked, "Uh… why?"

I took in a slow breath of air. Since I couldn't lie to my parents, the best I could do was be as blunt as an antique ax. I said on the exhale, "He is wanted by the police."

While I basked in their round-eyed stares, Ren added, "Not for anything violent."

"Claire Evelyn Riordan," my mom whispered. "I think you better tell us what's goin' on."

"He's helping me find Aunt Eva's painting," I said. "The police think he's the one who broke into the Kimbell, and if they arrest him, he won't be able to help me."

I could feel Ren's eyes searing my flesh and refused to look at him. That gem of a half-truth was entirely my on-the-spot invention, and I wasn't about to let his disbelief ruin it.

Shaking her head, my mom mumbled, "You are somethin' else, Claire."

"I have to ask. You don't have to say yes."

"Well, let's meet this fella," my dad said.

Ren used his key fob to open the Denali's back hatch, out of which Mikel climbed. Now that I saw him through my parents' eyes, I wished I'd asked him to shave and cut his hair. There was nothing I could do about it now, so I waited in silence for him to reach the front porch.

"Mr. Riordan, Mrs. Riordan," he said, shaking their hands in turn. "I'm Mikel. It's a pleasure to meet you."

My mother had been struck dumb, so my dad handled the platitudes. "Likewise. How'd you come to meet our daughter?"

"At mass. On Mother's Day, actually."

I almost fainted. I'd *told* him not to say that! To my astonished relief, my mom smiled and my dad nodded. He got lucky.

"What do you do for a living, Mikel?"

"I work for a security contractor. We did some work at the Kimbell recently. I, uh… I guess Claire already told you all about that."

I cut in, "I didn't. That's why they think he had something to do with the break-in. Just because he was there."

"Bad luck. But, if Claire trusts you, I s'pose we can. S'long as we won't get arrested for loaning you a car," he added with a chuckle.

We all joined in, the nervous edge to our laughter going unnoticed by both of my parents. While my dad carried on with the friendly interrogation, I told my mom, "I actually really have to pee."

"Oh, fuff, you just want to look at the mess we've made."

"Two things can be true at the same time. Make it three—I want to see Dolly."

"Well, I can't hide it from you forever, can I? Come on in. Watch where you step."

*

Half an hour later, Ren, Mikel, and I were driving three vehicles in convoy away from my parents' house. Our paths soon diverged, Ren and me taking the direct route back to Benbrook while Mikel set off alone on the scenic route with the luggage we'd transferred from the Denali to the van. I was in the Jeep, which did indeed need significant suspension work.

Alone in the noisy, rather smelly car, I fought for my composure. The inside of my parents' house had been so much worse than I'd expected. I hadn't said anything about it to them, knowing my words would fall on deaf ears, but the hoard was officially out of control.

Dolly, my parents' eleven-year-old golden retriever, was in good shape and had a relatively clean spot to herself in the climate-controlled garage. Everything else was beyond salvation. The entire house needed to be burned to the ground.

To keep my breakdown at bay, I replayed my reunion with Dolly. I hadn't seen her in over two months, and she was all wiggles and licks and tail wags, like she'd been as a puppy. Dolly had been Marty's gift to me after we lost our first, and within a month she had been re-gifted to my parents. A drunk and a potty-training puppy don't mix. My parents had been overjoyed to take her, even after the stern talk I'd had with them about keeping her clean and safe.

Now Dolly's snout was white, and she didn't get around

quite as easily as she used to. These thoughts only accelerated and worsened my breakdown, so I gave up and let it come, hoping I'd be all done by the time I got back to Ren's house.

I was, but my red face and puffy eyes told Ren all he needed to know. Annika was shut up in her bedroom, presumably still in the testing phase of her apparatus for quickly moving her gadgets out of sight in the event of a surprise visit from the detectives. Mikel was off on his own errand of last-minute preparation. I sat on the couch with Ren, still crying but not nearly as hard as before.

"God, Ren… I can't even describe it. It's so, so much worse than it was just a couple months ago. I thought when we got them evicted from the last place, they'd take the chance for a fresh start. I mean… *where* do they get the money to buy all that junk? *You're* not giving them money, are you?"

"Absolutely not."

"I just can't believe it. How can they *live* like that?"

He put an arm around my shoulders and gave me a bracing squeeze. "I know I've said it a million times before, but I'll say it again: They're happy. They want to live like that. I know that doesn't make it okay, but it makes it better, right?"

"Mmm," I moaned, mostly agreeing.

"Focus on one thing at a time. Bring home the Wyeth, and then we'll figure out how to help your parents."

"Once and for all?"

Another squeeze. "Once and for all. Now go to bed. You've got a long day tomorrow."

# 20

*June 17 – 18*

As I walked down the cereal aisle, searching for the specific box of diabetes Annika had requested, I felt a pang of regret. This would be the last time in a while that I'd participate in one of her devious, complicated little schemes. I was going to miss it. I was going to miss *her*, and Ren, and Ren's house, and Texas, and so many things.

I found the cereal, which was the last item on my list, and got through the checkout quickly. The receipt was what I needed, so I made sure to stick it safely in one of the grocery bags, which I set in the passenger seat of my parents' borrowed Jeep as I climbed into the driver's seat. Though I'd argued for a more realistic list of bacon, eggs, cheese, avocadoes, and the like, Annika had insisted the cops couldn't possibly know what kinds of food I liked. And she wanted chocolate-frosted sugar bombs.

Turning to look in the back, I saw Annika stretched out on the seat, her nose buried in her phone. She felt my gaze and asked, "Find everything okay?"

"Yeah. You want to say goodbye, or you want to play games?"

Though her large, dark eyes darted to me, she shook her head. "I'm not so great with goodbyes. Just take good care of my brother, okay?"

"I will."

"Camera is panning away. You're good to go."

I assumed that meant she was watching the feed from the store's external security camera, not playing a game. I hurried to shrug out of my jacket.

"Okay, bye," I breathed.

I jumped out and power-walked over to the van, where Mikel was waiting. We both watched the Jeep in silence, waiting until a be-wigged and jacketed Annika climbed from the back into the driver's seat. I shook my head.

"She couldn't pass for me if her life depended on it. She can barely see over the steering wheel..."

"The disguise is just a backup," he reminded me. "Ren's got Art and Fart tied up at his office. Hey." He tugged on my hair, pulling my attention away from the Jeep. "Try not to look so excited."

"She doesn't even have a driver's license."

"Claire. She has *your* driver's license."

"That's not what I mean."

Mikel's scenic route from my parent's house had kept him away all last night and included a stop at a location he refused to disclose, from which he'd acquired cash, fake IDs, assorted gift cards, cheap burner phones, and other odds and ends for our cross-country road trip. According to the Nebraska driver's license he'd given me, I was Annette Carter, two years younger and thirty pounds heavier than Claire Riordan. His license, declaring him to be Craig Carter, was a closer match for his identifiers. I pulled mine from my pocket and studied the photo, angling it this way and that in the sunlight. It looked so real, I knew no one would question it.

"How'd you do this?" I asked.

"Carefully. Actually, I'm exhausted. Want to take the first leg?"

"Sure thing."

We switched places without getting out of the van, and then there was nothing left to do but hit the road. Facing a twenty-seven-hour drive, I longed for my phone and my trusty road trip playlist; but Annika had that, too. To make the boredom complete, Mikel fell asleep as soon as we hit the highway, leaving me alone with my thoughts.

Ordinarily, my thoughts were productive, hopeful, and organized, and I enjoyed being alone with them. At the moment, they were in disarray. Everything I could think about was repellant to me, and I wouldn't let my mind linger on anything long enough to really think it through.

I'd either go to prison at the end of this, or live the rest of my life in hiding. Next.

I'd made my parents accessories to my crimes. Nope. Next.

I hadn't heard from Marty, or Pam, since the latest incident with Money's goon. Next.

Mikel and I had to make our funds hold out as long as possible, which meant Annika had reserved one room, not two, in Eureka. Oh, God, next.

I still hadn't confronted Ren and Mikel about their perfidy. Ugh. *Next.*

Mikel had been looking for the Wyeth for at least half as long as I had. I still didn't know how that had come to be.

Was he really going to let me walk away with it when this was all over?

The playlist ended there, because it had to. I turned on the radio, adjusting the volume down to keep from waking Mikel.

*

Twelve hours on the road got us to Denver well after dark Tuesday night. I would've stopped sooner, as both Mikel and I were fading fast, but Annika had arranged for us to stay with some "friends" in Lakewood, a firmly middle-class, northern suburb. Since Annika claimed never to have left the state of Texas, I wasn't quite sure how she came to call these people friends; but Mikel didn't question it, so neither did I.

Once Mikel's lengthy nap had ended somewhere north of Wichita Falls, we'd enjoyed hours and hours of conversation that never threatened to touch upon the stickier points of our relationship—friendship—alliance—whatever. We talked about our parents, school, jobs, even our love lives. His was a little bit more interesting than mine, to say the least.

Mikel's comment about raising Annika turned out not to be an exaggeration. She'd been four years old when a car crash killed their parents and left her miraculously unharmed, but she remembered it. Mikel, twenty-five at the time, had been forced to assume the roles of mother and father. He claimed he couldn't take credit for the way she'd turned out, but I privately disagreed.

I estimated we'd worked through the conversational topics of at least seven and a half dates by the time we were both too tired to talk. That happened as we were driving through Colorado Springs, so only the last hour of our trip passed in silence. It was a comfortable, companionable silence at that.

Mikel was driving, and he guided us through the downtown cluster and into Lakewood, stopping in front of a two-story, red brick McMansion. We both checked the address, twice.

"Annika's friends live *here?*" I asked.

He made a wordless noise of confusion. "The neighbors are gonna take one look at this mystery-mobile and call the cops."

"Maybe we should paint 'Ice Cream' on the side," I suggested.

He chuckled. We were stalling. I didn't want to knock on the door, and neither did he. Fortunately, our waffling was ended by the front door opening and a massive, grey-and-white cat dashing out onto the dark lawn. Right on its fluffy heels, body language betraying clear distress, came a short, round woman in a pink bathrobe. I couldn't stop myself—I burst out laughing.

I instantly felt bad for laughing, and I jumped out of the van and intercepted the cat before he could duck under it. Annika's analogy about "being the cat" was on my mind as the ponderous creature struggled and squirmed for freedom, but this specimen was clearly not the apex predator variety. He gave up after a few moments, went limp with a sorrowful meow of surrender, and allowed me to pass him into the woman's outstretched arms.

"Och, thank yeh," she cried, some kind of accent coloring her words. I needed to hear her speak again to place it, and she was quick to oblige. "Ye'll be Ani's friends, I take't?"

She was Scottish. Very Scottish. I nodded, then added in case it was too dark for her to see me, "Yes, are you Victoria?"

"That'd be me. I cricked the dar tay see who't was, and this awful creature had t'make his escape. As thoo he's got hard life. Well, ye've already seen me housecoat, so we're's good as friends. Come inside, come inside."

Inside, I could see that Victoria had taken the same decorating cues as my mother. No matter which direction I looked, I saw mismatched furniture crammed into every available space. Every surface was covered in random objects; paintings, posters, and mirrors covered the walls; and even the floors were a layered tapestry of far too many rugs for the available surface area. Everything was very clean, though, and the house smelled of rosemary and baking bread. The chaos made my heart want to race, but the underlying order wouldn't let it. I took my moment, while Mikel and Victoria were exchanging pleasantries, to come to grips with reality.

I had to sleep here. Just one night. I could do it. She was opening her home to a couple of strangers, and I was going to be a good houseguest, gosh darn it.

Annika had told us her friends' names—Victoria and Walter—so I waited for a lull in the conversation to ask, "Where's Walter?"

Victoria held up the cat, who'd gone completely boneless in her arms. "This'n he. Wretch. He'll warm up to ye in a mo' and try't drive ye stark raving mad. Ye're not allergic, I tek't?"

I shook my head. Mikel reached out and gave one of the cat's back paws a gentle tug, saying, "I love cats. This is… three cats."

"Aye, he's a fat thing, but he's m' Walter."

Mikel left me in Victoria's hands while he unloaded the luggage we'd need to get through the night. I regretfully turned down her offer of a late dinner, since it was nearly midnight, but I was happy to accept a nightcap in its place.

It turned out Victoria knew Annika from college, specifically an online course in cybersecurity they'd both taken last winter. Annika had signed up for kicks and giggles (per Victoria), while she herself had been sent there by her employer. They'd hit it off in the online chatroom, and Annika had cemented their friendship by turning Victoria's unsuitable C-average into a B+. It was clear from the way Victoria talked about Annika that she had no idea her online friend was a teenager.

"Ah've noo idea how she did't, but I told her if she needed anythin', she better ask. And here ye are. Ah'm told not t'ask questions, but I can't help't. What brings ye two to Denvair?"

I took a drink of my scotch, leaving it to Mikel to supply some nonsense answer about sightseeing and travel blogs. There was simply no way I could have drummed up the audacity to lie to this adorable woman.

We said our goodbyes before turning in, knowing it would be an early start tomorrow morning. We planned to push through all the way to Eureka tomorrow, a sixteen-hour drive without counting pitstops. We always had the option of stopping along the way if we got too tired, but our cash reserves were limited, and neither of us wanted to shell out fifty or sixty dollars for a crappy motel room if we didn't have to.

True to Victoria's warning, Walter followed us into the guestroom she'd made up for us. He hopped up onto the bed, planted himself on my chest, and began to purr so loudly that I had no chance of falling asleep. He was twenty pounds if he was ten, and he seemed to be emitting energy in the form of unbearable heat. To cap off the experience, he began making biscuits on my chest. My thin t-shirt was no match for his razor-sharp claws.

Mikel, who'd been consigned to the floor, watched all of this with an air of quiet indignation. At length he complained,

"Why won't he snuggle me? I'm the one who likes cats."

"I like cats," I argued. "Generally."

In the end, Mikel had to eject the beast from the guest room and shut the door. Though he meowed and scratched for nearly fifteen minutes, Walter gave up around 1:00 a.m. and finally allowed me to fall asleep.

*

Four lovely and insufficient hours of sleep later, we were on the road again. Victoria had left us a parting gift by the front door: two enormous, blueberry scones wrapped in parchment paper. They came with a note that read, "Eat up, you skinnies. Enjoy your trip."

Mikel ate both scones, with my blessing. We stopped just across the border in Cheyenne, Wyoming for coffee and more food, and that defined our experience in Wyoming. I don't know how the hours managed to pass, but they did, and we crossed into Montana as the clock struck noon. We still had nearly nine hours to go.

Something about being in the same state as our quarry made me feel skittish and paranoid, even though hundreds of miles still stretched between us. We began to see pockets of snow lingering in shady spots and blanketing mountain passes, and the temperature on the dash read thirty-nine degrees Fahrenheit when we stopped in Helena for dinner. I shivered my way into and back out of a local diner, where we added an hour to our journey and subtracted almost forty dollars from our cash reserves in exchange for the best steak and eggs I'd ever tasted. Four and a half more hours to go.

Night fell, and still we were driving. When we passed Kalispell and continued north, fat snowflakes began to strike the windshield. I turned up the heater, distracting Mikel from a story about stealing a Renoir from a private collection. I'd already guessed the ending anyway: It was a fake.

"Cold, Red?" he asked.

"This is inhuman," I grumbled.

"Don't worry. We'll be back in the warm, cozy swamp in time for summer."

"Oh yeah? Then what?"

I said it so quietly, maybe he hadn't heard me; but something about the set of his jaw told me he had. He turned on the radio, the snow kept falling, and we kept driving.

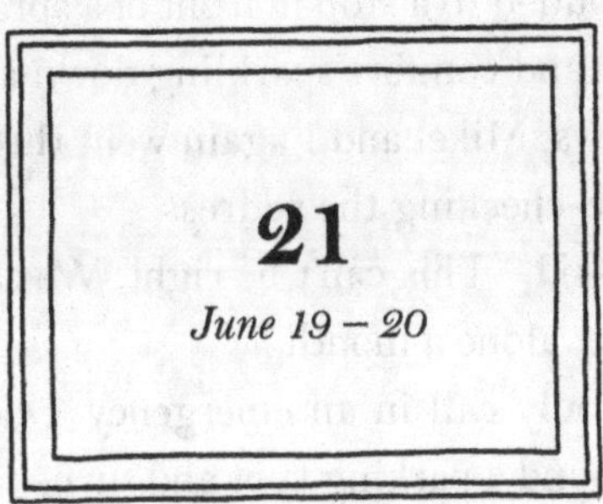


BETWEEN ALL THE STOPS, the weather, and a wrong turn that took us on a fun but unnecessary tour of an adorable town called Whitefish, we arrived in Eureka a few minutes after midnight Thursday morning. Our accommodations had been arranged by Annika, who'd been rather secretive about what we'd find at the address she'd given us. All she would tell us was that we'd be comfortable, we could stay there for a month before needing to find a new place, and we'd have a great view.

Eureka occupied about one mile of Highway 93, and it was in the rearview mirror before I could wonder aloud, "Where is this place?"

"A few miles northwest of town. I think it's a vacation rental."

"Oh, boy."

I pictured a single-room log cabin, inch-wide gaps in the walls, a wood stove its only source of heat, a hole-in-the-ground bathroom several yards away from the front door. There would be one bed, piled high with blankets, barely wide enough for Mikel and me to spoon up like hamsters trying to survive off each other's body heat at night. It was a cuddly scene, but not one in which I wanted to pass any real time.

So when we pulled to a stop in front of a sprawling lakeside lodge, glamour and comfort sparkling down at us from hundreds of windows, Mikel and I again went through the act of checking and re-checking the address.

"Call her," I said. "This can't be right. We can't afford this for one night, let alone a month."

"She said to only call in an emergency. I don't think this qualifies." He found a parking spot and turned off the van. "If Mr. and Mrs. Carter don't have a reservation, then we'll call her. You want to do the honors?"

I wasn't chomping at the bit to start flashing around my fake ID, but I agreed anyway. The lobby was warm and not as luxurious as I'd expected, the mounted heads of various antlered animals staring down at me from every wall. A crowd of men and women in flannel shirts and boots—with one younger man in shorts and Crocs—occupied the hotel bar across from the front doors. To my right, a long check-in desk was empty but for one woman staring at me with a patient smile on her face.

"Help you?" she invited, when I was close enough.

"Yes, I'm checking in."

I withdrew my Annette Carter driver's license and a prepaid Visa gift card, the closest thing I had to the credit card she'd inevitably request to cover incidentals. After a brief back-and-forth, she agreed to use the gift card in lieu of anything else and made a copy of it and my driver's license. In exchange, I received two key cards in a little paper envelope with the number 402 written on the inside.

"Enjoy your stay," the woman said. "And congratulations, dear."

"Oh—um—thank you?"

Mikel and I carried our luggage up to our room on the top floor, with a view of the lake. At this hour, there wasn't much to see, at least not outside. Inside was another story. The front desk woman's words made more sense now that I found myself in what was clearly the honeymoon suite. We paced around, individually checking out the comforts: a king-sized bed with a silky white duvet and twelve pillows, a sitting area with a fold-out sofa, a balcony with a little table and chairs for sipping martinis whilst watching the sun set over the lake, a huge flatscreen TV over a bureau with a hidden minibar, a walk-in shower and a jetted tub in the bathroom, even a gas fireplace.

When we turned to face each other, Mikel was smiling as though he'd just caught on to a joke. I didn't see what was funny.

He asked me, "Did you bring up that smaller bag—the one she told you not to open until we got here?" I found it in the pile and tossed it to him. He unzipped it and pulled out a couple more cell phones, two chargers, a wad of cash, and a folded piece of notebook paper. Opening it, he smiled, laughed, and read to me, "Claire, you're paying for this, so you might as well enjoy it. I did get you a good deal. You can see the back of Pearson's house from your window, if they put you in the right room. The phones don't have service, but you can connect them to Wi-Fi or use Bluetooth to communicate privately. Have fun being adults or whatever."

"*I'm* paying for it?"

"A harmless plot between her and your financial manager, perhaps?" Mikel guessed.

"Well this isn't..." I stalked over to him, took the paper, and read it. "This isn't some romantic getaway! We're here to commit crimes. Dangerous ones. I can't believe Ren went along with this..."

"There's a chance she pulled it off without his help. Who cares? Are you mad she spent the money?"

"No, not really. I'll be sure once I see a bill..."

"So enjoy it. Or would you rather find a nice tent to stay in? I bet we could get even closer to Pearson's house that way. Maybe even onto his property."

"Oh, wipe that grin off your face," I said, lessening the impact of my words by grinning broadly.

I gazed around the room again, seeing its finery in a new light. I was paying for this, and I could afford it thanks to Aunt Eva and Ren's father. I was here because of Ren and Mikel, and of course Annika. Across the lake was the painting that set all this in motion and the man who'd taken what was rightfully mine. When this was all over, I'd either have the Wyeth or be in jail. Wasn't it fitting to spend my last trip—lucky number eighty-three—in a deluxe room worthy of a momentous occasion?

"You know what? Fine. Let's live like kings. I'm going to take a shower."

*

I didn't set an alarm for Friday morning. We had work to do, but I was so sick of darkness that all I wanted was to open my eyes on a bright, new day.

I got my wish, but it didn't come with a full night's sleep. Sunlight pushed through my dreams and forced my eyes open well before I was fully rested, and I had to blink at the bedside clock for a long time before accepting what it said.

It was 6:11 a.m., and the day was already passing me by. I sat up to take in the view through the west-facing window. Sunlight lanced over the still surface of the lake, broken here and there by shifting clouds. Pleasure crafts and fishing boats dotted the water, and a short stretch of beach next to the boat launch was alive with adults and children. I shook my head in disbelief at the early-morning sunbathers, some people even swimming in what had to be nearly freezing water. These people, who I assumed were native to these far northern latitudes if not Eureka itself, were biologically distinct from me, possibly a different subspecies of *homo sapiens*.

Across the room, Mikel was asleep on the fold-out couch. I smiled at him, still impressed by what a gentleman he'd been last night. When I'd emerged from the shower, he had already made up the fold-out bed and didn't have a word to say about the sleeping arrangements. He hadn't complained about sleeping on the floor at Victoria's house, either. Maybe Ren had assumed a fatherly role to have a talk with him before we left, but I preferred to believe Mikel was just a good guy. Either that, or he'd lost interest and given up on me, which I couldn't really blame him for. Even so, still a good guy.

A good guy who was also an art thief. I didn't try to balance that equation. Somehow he made it work, but that was easy for me to say. He'd never stolen anything from me. He *had* lied to me, and I wasn't over that so much as ignoring it. I knew there would come a time when it felt right to confront him, and all I had to do was go about business as usual and wait for that time. I also halfway hoped he'd volunteer the information, though that seemed unlikely.

Suddenly I remembered the line in Annika's note about being able to see Pearson's house from our room, and I jumped out of bed to dig through our luggage for a pair of binoculars. Though I found them and took up a position at the window, I wasn't sure in which direction to look if not straight west. I'd wanted to print out and bring a satellite image of the area that included Pearson's house, but my compatriots had insisted that was too on the nose. What if someone found it, and turned it over to the cops after we stole the Wyeth? They had a point.

So, though I panned back and forth over the opposite shore for about five minutes and spotted half a dozen structures, I gave up trying to figure out which one was Pearson's house and went in search of coffee instead. That was much easier to find, and more rewarding. Rather than the standard pod coffee brewer, the room came equipped with a pod *espresso* brewer. I whipped up a doppio espresso, wrapped myself in a blanket, and sat on the patio to wait for Mikel to wake up.

As the sun rose over my right shoulder, activity on the beach below picked up. The clouds broke, and all at once the sky and the lake were so bright I felt like putting on sunglasses. Something across the lake, straight northwest, caught the sunlight and threw it back at me so blindingly bright I had to turn away for moment. When I looked again, whatever it was still glittered but wasn't too bright to look at anymore.

I ducked inside to grab the binoculars, ignoring Mikel's half-asleep, "Watime is it?"

I found the spot again through the binoculars. Magnified twenty times by Ren's stupidly expensive Nikon Monarchs, the point of reflected light made more sense. It was the south-facing portion of a towering bay window, at least two stories tall, that overlooked the lake. Like the prow of some huge ship, the window jutted out toward the water, a spacious deck wrapping around it. I could see two people sitting side-by-side in Adirondak chairs, either asleep or simply not moving. Though I couldn't make out their features, not even their genders, somehow I knew one of the people I was looking at was Paul Pearson. The man who had my aunt's painting was sitting *right there*, enjoying the view and probably talking about how swell it was that he'd gotten away with the theft. At least that was how I imagined it.

Under my breath, I said, "Enjoy it while it lasts, you old turd."

"Turd?"

Mikel's voice startled me so much, I dropped the binoculars. Thankfully, he caught them.

"You must be pretty mad to use language like that," he mocked.

I pointed at the house, the bay window's sheen still visible even without the binoculars. "I think that's his house. I think that's *him*."

He cooperatively spied through the binoculars. "Ah, yeah. I see someone. Can't tell if it's Pearson, though. But that's got to be his house. Look at the size of it."

"Annika picked a good room," I said.

"Hope she didn't ask for 'the one where you can see Paul Pearson's house.'"

"No way she'd be that careless." As I said it, I glanced down at the beach-goers. They were quite close enough to look up and see Mikel with a pair of binoculars pressed to his face. "But we probably shouldn't be so obvious with the stargazing. People here must know who lives across the lake."

In response, Mikel angled the binoculars down at the beach.

He got his fill of that right away, setting the binoculars down on the table and complaining, "Some little kid just flipped me off!"

"I guess that means we're done with these," I said.

I strapped the expensive binoculars back into their carrying case and buried it deep in one of our larger suitcases. Standing back to observe the mess we'd made of the room in a few short hours, I decided it was high time to get organized. If we were going to be here as long as a month, we weren't going to live out of luggage thrown all over the floor. While I worked on that, Mikel got dressed and left to find breakfast.

He returned to find me on the patio again, gazing steadily northwest and ignoring a second cup of espresso cooling on the table in front of me. Shuffling all our things into the room's drawers and closets hadn't taken as long as I'd hoped, and there wasn't much to clean after only one night. I'd had plenty of time to sink into a listless, despondent contemplation of the impossible task ahead.

Annika had sent us here with a few half-formed ideas, Mikel claimed to be working on something, and Ren had been all smiles and encouragement that we'd be able to get it done; but the fact was, we had no clear plan for getting inside Pearson's house, finding the Wyeth, and getting out again. As much faith as I had in Annika's cyber sleuthing, we also didn't know beyond the shadow of a doubt that the unattributed painting listed on Pearson's insurance forms was the Wyeth, or that he still had it. He could have sold it, given it away, lost it. There were so many question marks.

A month had seemed like a long time. Now....

I sighed, coming out of it enough to see the offering Mikel placed on the table.

"Sorry it took so long," he said. "I had to go into town, but I found a coffee shop that had—get this—a maple *bacon* latte." When I didn't react, he picked up one of the cardboard-jacketed paper cups and pressed it into my hand. "Bacon, Claire. Are you in there?"

"Yes. I… thank you. This smells really good." I took a sip, perked up, and said, "This is delicious."

"Not too sweet? I told them to skip the maple syrup."

"It's perfect. Thank you."

He'd also secured a pile of pastries and bagels, plus a couple of mini frittatas with my name on them. He looked so pleased with himself, I didn't have the heart to ask how much he'd spent.

"Why are you so nice to me?" I asked.

"That's a weird thing to ask," he said around a mouthful of cheese danish. "Why wouldn't I be nice to you?"

"I don't know. I'm just feeling doomy and gloomy."

I explained my pessimistic outlook, and he didn't waste my time with empty encouragement. He said, "I'm glad you're being realistic. This isn't gonna be easy. I don't like jobs in rural areas like this—everyone knows everyone, and people's homes and properties are sacrosanct. Not to mention guarded by more guns than people."

A playful, wordless shout floated up to us from the beach, and I said, "Maybe we should move this felonious discussion inside."

ONCE MIKEL AND I HAD relocated to the couch, which I'd folded back together, he continued as though there had been no pause.

"But rural does have its advantages. Public access to public lands is a big deal here. Pearson's property has easements through it that he can't legally shut down, and the southern rim of it juts up against forest service land. The northern boundary is so near the border with British Columbia, law enforcement crosses into his land all the time on regular patrols, and they don't need his permission to do it. He can't monitor every square foot of his property, and why would he? After all this time, I doubt he's that worried about someone breaking in."

I assumed he meant the law enforcement records Annika had unearthed—or the lack thereof. She'd checked records at the Eureka Police Department, Lincoln County Sheriff's Office, Montana Highway Patrol, and even the RCMP and U.S. Fish and Wildlife Office of Law Enforcement. Only two calls for service to Pearson's address had been recorded since he moved in: a call about a prowler six years ago where the prowler turned out to be a bobcat, and an unspecified medical emergency a year and a half ago. The only records she hadn't been able to search were U.S. Customs and Border Protection, because, according to her, "I'm not trying to get sent to Guantanamo Bay for this."

It seemed Pearson was safe and sound in his 6,300-square-foot "cabin" on his 103-acre ranch. The property wasn't actually a ranch, of course. The land had supported some farming, cattle, and other agriculture before Pearson bought it, but now it served only one purpose: his private enjoyment. We'd ascertained as much from a handful of newspaper articles written around the time Pearson arrived, most of them by indignant fifth- and sixth-generation Montanans who didn't take too kindly to the Hollywood money bomb changing their landscape and hiking up their property values for the tax assessor. Things seemed to have cooled down since then, likely due to Pearson's generosity to state and local charities and his support of seven different businesses in Eureka and nearby Rexford that would have shut their doors without his injection of much-needed funds. One of the seven was the very lodge in which we were lodged.

Whether intentionally or not, Mikel was reminding me that we had done a lot of research. That was the foundation of any good plan. I cheered up enough to scarf down both frittatas, finish my latte, and clean up everything the moment the last bite of muffin disappeared into Mikel's mouth.

Now all we had to do was build the plan. On the foundation of research, Annika had framed out a basic formula for the heist: Get into the house, get eyes on the Wyeth, get the

Wyeth out, and hightail it back home. All of this could be done either fast or slow, overtly or covertly, depending on how we wanted to play it. That was the part Mikel claimed to have been working on.

Since his plans always lived exclusively in his brain, where people like Annika couldn't gain access to them, I was accepting the existence of this one on pure faith.

All finished with the cleanup, I sat down on the couch with him and asked, "So. What are you thinking?"

"All right, tell me how this strikes you: We've got two big advantages that we need to play on. One, Pearson was very close to Eva Riordan at one point, and you're Eva's niece. Two, he knows he stole the painting. Maybe he doesn't know the whole story, maybe he does, but the easiest thing in the world to steal is something that's already stolen. Well actually, it's the second easiest thing—the easiest is something that's in transit.

"So anyway, we—meaning you—come at him in broad daylight. No tricks, no lies. You spot him in the wild, strike up a conversation, let him figure out who you are, and work on him until you get an invite to the land yacht."

"Bother a celebrity while he's trying to enjoy a day out?" I asked. "Yeah, that sounds like something I could easily do without hating it and being bad at it."

"What's the problem?"

"Well… won't he be kind of annoyed when I interrupt his lunch or shopping trip or whatever?"

"Annoyed? Are you kidding? This guy hasn't been relevant since the Cowboys won a super bowl."

"You shut your mouth!" I protested. "They're looking great this season, no way they don't get into the final—"

"Okay, focus. We're on Pearson, not the Cowgirls."

"They're America's football team, Mikel. What are you, a Patriots fan? If you are you can tell me, you don't have to be embarrassed."

Neither of us could keep the discussion from taking a detour, so we got it all out and settled into an uneasy truce before getting back to Pearson. We'd only lost half an hour.

Mikel explained, "All you'd have to do is—Look. Just picture it. He's eating at a restaurant. Let's just assume for the sake of argument that's a thing he does. You walk in, looking like you do, do a little double take, and ask for his autograph."

I groaned. He ignored me.

"Who does he make it out to? Claire Riordan. Any relation to Eva Riordan? Well yes, that's my great aunt. You've heard of her? *Heard* of her? Young lady, she and I were very close friends back when the Cowboys still had a shot at the super bowl—"

"I thought we agreed to a cease fire."

"But you see where I'm going with this. All you have to do is recognize him, and he'll do the rest."

"So before I steal the Wyeth, I make sure to tell him my real name?"

"Why not? You'd rather take the time to construct and memorize an elaborate alias before you steal the Wyeth? No fake person is gonna be more interesting to him than Eva's niece."

"You're making this sound way too simple," I complained.

"Simpler is always better. Which one of us is an art thief?"

"Ask me again in a couple days."

The way he smiled at me made my cheeks feel warm. He asked, "Didn't I tell you? You're loving this, aren't you?"

"Keep going with your brilliant plan."

"Okay. So you break the ice with Pearson, casually slip in that your degree is in Art History and you just *love* the Pre-Raphaelites—"

"They're okay."

"But he's got a Waterhouse, a Rosetti, and *two* Collinsons. And that's just what he had when he moved. There may be more. No way he hears that and doesn't want to show off his collection to his former lover's cute little niece all grown up and paying attention to him."

"Mikel. He's eighty-one years old and married. If you're suggesting he's going to conveniently develop some kind of romantic interest in me…"

"Not necessarily a romantic interest, no. But don't fight me on this, Claire. You're interesting."

"Fine. Then what happens?"

"I see three possibilities. First, he shows you his gallery, sans the Wyeth, and that's that. Second, he shows you his gallery, then lets you in on the secret and shows you the Wyeth, too. Third, he gets you to his house on the pretense of showing you his gallery, but he just makes a pass at you, and you flee for your life."

"You've seen too many movies."

"Irrelevant. All three options will move us forward, because what we need is to see the inside of the house. I need to know who else lives there, what kind of security is visible, if there are dogs or especially vicious house cats, that sort of thing. Because once you get Pearson's attention, he can focus on you while I get in there and grab the painting."

"Assuming I have his attention at all."

"Right."

"Then what?" I asked.

"Then I steal it, we go back to Texas, and he eats worms."

*

As incredulous as I remained, I liked having a place to start. Annika had supplied us with a list of vehicles registered to Pearson, his wife, and the three holding companies he owned, so we went into town to walk around and see if we spotted any.

We split up, for reasons Mikel refused to share. I sensed he was enjoying his role as mastermind and wanted me to be impressed later when this decision proved prescient. He'd grabbed a couple maps of Eureka from the coffee shop, and before we left he highlighted different and mutually exclusive routes on each one. Even on foot, it wouldn't take us long to cover the entire town.

We parked the van in the most crowded lot we could find, the hardware store, and split up immediately. Mikel headed south, and I crossed the street headed east.

Four hours later, footsore and delirious with hunger, I arrived back at the van to find Mikel nowhere in sight. He had given himself the longer route, so I decided to kill a few minutes inside the hardware store. I hadn't seen any of Pearson's vehicles, but that didn't mean much after just one search of half the town on a weekday.

As I wandered up and down the aisles inside the hardware store, a couple hundred dollars burning a hole in my pocket, I tried to imagine what sorts of seemingly innocuous things I could buy that stood any chance of being helpful later. The answer came to me after I saw four different people, two men and two women, wearing the exact same red-and-black flannel shirt, then passed a rack of the same shirts on clearance at the back of the store. If that wasn't a sign, I wasn't Catholic.

I bought one for me and one for Mikel, threw in a box knife and a roll of electrical tape, and decided to stop there; we needed to stretch our cash as far as possible. When I returned to the van, Mikel was sitting in the driver's seat.

I climbed in and asked, "No luck?"

"Not really. I saw one of the fleet vehicles at the gas station, but I didn't recognize the driver. That's it. You?"

"Nothing. I bought us some Eureka uniforms, though." I showed him the flannel shirts, which smelled strongly of automotive grease and fertilizer. "Think these might come in handy?"

He nodded approvingly. "I saw at least a dozen people wearing this shirt. Good move, Red."

"Thanks." I noticed several plastic shopping bags that hadn't been there before and asked, "What did you find?"

"Booze."

"Good, we're both contributing. Try again tomorrow?"

He nodded. "Let's find something to eat. I'm not liking that feral look in your eyes."

I talked him into stocking up at the grocery store, the better to continue pinching pennies, and went inside alone to buy enough food to get us through a few days. The prices were astonishing, and I left a couple hundred bucks lighter despite being able to carry everything in two hands without breaking a sweat.

Disgruntled, I got back in the van and said, "They sure think a lot of their food up here."

"Blame Pearson. To hear the locals tell it, prices have doubled since he showed up."

"I know. I almost cried when the cashier read the total, and he told me the rent on the building increased forty percent last year. They had to jack up prices. But I like that he told me that. I don't think he pegged me as a tourist."

Mikel fished around in one sack until he found a bag of chips. He opened it, ate a handful, and asked, "Figured out why yet?"

"Why I don't look like a tourist? No."

"You haven't noticed the proliferation of a certain recessive gene in these parts?" he asked. He didn't wait for my answer before starting up the van and getting on the road.

I thought for several minutes, but nothing occurred to me. I said, "I don't want to play a guessing game. Just tell me."

In answer, he tugged on one of the braids I'd twisted my hair into this morning. "You're part of the gene pool, Ginger. You blend in."

"Oh." I *had* noticed a lot of other redheads, plus one woman who looked like she could've been a cousin. "Another advantage for us?"

"No. I need you to stand out, not blend in." He glanced at me and added, "Don't look so discouraged. There are other ways to stand out."

"Like what?"

"Several ways I'll tell you after you've eaten, because you're gonna hate them."

He was right. I hated everything he said, but at least I hated it on a full stomach. I agreed to cooperate when Mikel reminded me of the terms of our deal: I was going to help in whatever way he said, no arguments.

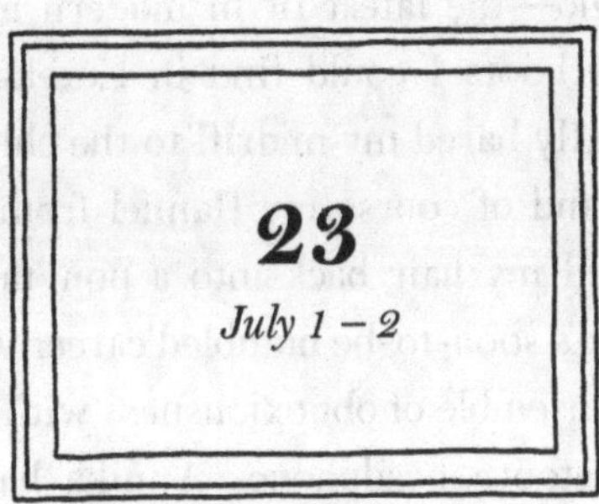


AFTER NEARLY TWO WEEKS in Eureka, Mikel and I had enjoyed enough dumb luck to figure a couple things out:

First, Paul Pearson and I shared a soft spot for the creative coffee creations at Tea Bag End, the unlicensed Tolkien-themed café where Mikel had bought me a maple bacon latte. Pearson could in fact be found there most mornings, left in peace by a combination of long-disinterested locals and tourists who were simply too young to recognize him. He usually came with his wife, but not on Tuesdays. We had no idea why.

Second, native Montanans didn't simply dislike and distrust out-of-staters in general. They shared a specific animosity for Californians, for whose ungodly riches they blamed the rising costs of everything from land to Lucky Charms. As a native and life-long Texan, I shared their sweeping aversion in a theoretical way, though I'd never met a single Californian I didn't like.

So, though I hated Mikel's plan with every fiber of my being, I couldn't argue with him that it was probably going to work. On Tuesday morning, I arrived at Tea Bag End dressed like everyone's worst idea of an Angelino trying not to look like an Angelino—the latest fit in modern mom jeans, the most expensive boots I could find in Eureka, a loose crop top that idiotically bared my midriff to the chill I still wasn't acclimated to, and of course my flannel from the hardware store. I'd slicked my hair back into a ponytail worthy of a Hallmark movie's soon-to-be humbled career woman, and I'd completed my ensemble of obnoxiousness with the expensive, minimalist Bluetooth headphones Annika had temporarily donated to our cause.

After all that work, I couldn't bring myself to pretend to chat on my headphones as Mikel had ordered. It was just too much. I waited silently through the long line, requested a large "Nice, Crispy Bacon" maple latte and paid in cash.

I could hardly blame the smiling young barista for asking, "Where are you visiting from?"

"Visiting? I wish. Pacific Palisades looks like Mordor right now," I said, laying on the drama as thick as I dared. Given the café's theme, I assumed her blank look was a response to my mention of Pacific Palisades, not Mordor. I prompted, "Pacific Palisades? Los Angeles? … California?"

"Oh! Is that where all those fires were? I'm sorry. I hope your house is okay."

I wanted to return her sweet smile so badly my face actually started to hurt. I couldn't convince it to form a frown, so my expression was neutral as I answered, "Thanks, Babe. It's fine for now, but I had to evacuate, and those fascists won't let me come back yet. Still…" I looked around contentedly, internally screaming as customers behind me waited patiently for me to finish my chat and move on. "There are worse places to be, aren't there?"

Though her smile had become somewhat fixed, she said kindly enough, "Totally."

I dropped a tip in the jar and moved on, hating myself. Pearson was sitting with his back to me, posted up at his favored spot in front of the shop's large picture window. If he'd positioned himself to make it difficult for people to catch his eye, he'd done a great job; but he had to get up sometime. I sat facing him and the door through which he'd have to exit, crossed my legs, and waited.

The old man was in no hurry, that much was clear. He'd been reading a newspaper when I arrived, but once he finished that, he just sat and stared out the window, watching passersby. I could only see his profile, but I thought he was weathering old age pretty darn well. His white hair was still thick and sleek, styled exactly as it had been from 1993 on, and the deep lines on his face were in all the right places. Age had weighed him down very little, if his excellent posture and trim frame were any clue. He'd done a much better job of not dressing like an Angelino, sporting a loose pair of work pants, boots, a worn denim shirt, and a fleece-lined canvas vest.

If I fell a tiny bit in love with the old actor, who could blame me? I'd seen enough of his films enough times to know the man was a heartthrob for a reason. Sure, his suave lines had been written for him, but it was his delivery that made women swoon—women like Aunt Eva, who had been twelve years his senior. Based on what I'd seen of his former supermodel wife, he no longer went in for older women.

Finally, when the clock was edging toward noon, he stood

up. Leaving his newspaper and empty dishes behind, he turned toward the door. I met his eyes, prepared to strike up a conversation, but he simply turned away and left the café.

I had half a second to decide whether to follow him, or try again another day. I chose the former and unabashedly pursued him outside and down the sidewalk. I was much faster.

"Excuse me," I called. "Aren't you Paul Pearson?"

Though he stopped, he didn't say anything or turn around. I stepped in front of him.

"I'm so sorry. I hate to bother you, but I just—I can't believe I'm running into Paul Pearson. *Here!* Would you hate it *too* too much if I asked you for your autograph?"

"No harm in it," he said gruffly. "Got a pen?"

"Actually, yeah. Can you sign my receipt? That way I can prove I ran into you in Nowhere, Montana. What a crazy coincidence."

The words 'Nowhere, Montana,' seemed to deeply annoy him. Though he accepted my pen and my receipt and dutifully signed his name, he didn't follow Mikel's imaginary script by asking me for mine. I took the autograph back and said "Thank you," my mind spinning. I did not have a backup plan.

Knowing I'd be pressing my luck by prolonging this encounter, especially when he unlocked the car we were standing right next to, I followed a wild impulse and turned away. I took two steps, tapped one of my headphones, and said, "Hey, Teal. What's up? What can I do for you?"

Why the name Teal had popped into my head, I couldn't say. Maybe it was divine intervention. Teal was well-known in the art world as an elusive and reclusive art dealer. Teal was neither his first name, nor his last time. Just Teal. He'd helped the Kimbell acquire a portrait by John Everett Millais less than a year ago. According to my former boss, Joe, he'd driven everyone involved half mad with effected eccentricities and increasingly absurd demands. Teal was, in short, exactly the sort of art dealer I'd been grappling with for decades.

But John Everett Millais was a member of the Pre-Raphaelite Brotherhood whose paintings so fascinated the man standing behind me, who was hopefully listening in.

I forced myself to finish the fake conversation without checking to see whether Pearson was still there. Once I'd signed off with a cheerful "Caio!" and turned back around, I was surprised and pleased to see Pearson standing by his car, making no attempt to hide the fact that he'd been eavesdropping.

Smiling my most beguiling smile, I asked, "Were you listening to my phone call? I didn't mean to blow you off—I thought I'd just about worn out my welcome."

"Apologies," he said, still gruff but now returning my smile. "I heard the name 'Teal' and couldn't help myself. That couldn't have been the Teal I think it is?"

"Oh, that was nothing," I said with a dismissive wave. "He's an old friend of my aunt. You—oh, do you know Teal?"

My own ditzy act was beginning to gnaw at my nerves, but Pearson gave me no hint whether it was having the same effect on him.

He said, "I haven't had the pleasure. He's a hard man to get a meeting with. But where are my manners?" He stepped toward me and held out his hand. I finally noticed how tall he was. Even in my substantial boots, he towered over me. I shook his hand, starstruck to a totally unfeigned degree. He said, "This is the part where you say your name."

"Claire," I breathed. "Um. Claire Riordan. It's nice to meet you."

The surprise on his face got us right back onto Mikel's script. He smiled warmly, asking, "You can't be little Claire. Eva Riordan's niece?"

"Yes! You knew my aunt?"

"Very well. I miss that fine woman every day. Now why don't you tell me how in the world you and I came to be in the same coffee shop in—What did you call it? Nowhere, Montana?"

A perfectly-timed shiver shook my whole body. "Oh. That. It's just awful, Mr. Pearson. The fires, you know? Aunt Eva's old house is okay, thank God, and I think mine is, too, but... The devastation is just mind-blowing. They're not even letting people come back yet."

"You're not a refugee?" he asked, appalled. Good grief, he was a good actor.

"I am. And just between you and me, it's beautiful up here, but I haven't been warm in *days*."

His bright blue eyes raked over me, but the twinkle in them seemed more fatherly than anything else. "It helps to cover up properly. What brought you here, specifically?"

He wasn't going to accept my vague answers, that much was clear—not if I wanted to keep him on the hook. I rolled my eyes. "Call it stupidity, if you want. I figured if I was going to get kicked out of Los Angeles, I might as well have some fun with it. Glacier National Park has been on my list for a while. And I was like, 'It's spring! It'll be great!' Ha."

"You're shaking like a leaf. I better let you go. How long are you in town for?"

"A couple more weeks, probably. You?"

He frowned, confused. "I live here. So... maybe another decade, Lord willing."

I held my breath as he reached into his back pocket, pulled out his wallet, and extracted what sure looked like a business card. He handed it to me.

"Give me a call if you want. I hate to take advantage, but if you can get me a meeting with Teal, I'll buy you a pony, young lady."

My laugh was genuine—genuine shock. I couldn't believe the ad-libbed mishmash of Mikel's plan and my impulse had actually worked. I pocketed the card and said, "Anything for a pony."

I waved goodbye to Pearson as he drove away, then returned to the café. After a fifteen-minute wait to make sure he was gone, I set out on the long walk back to where I'd parked the van. I then broke every speed limit between there and the lodge, not even caring if I got pulled over. I was so excited to tell Mikel the good news.

To my chagrin, he reacted to my tale with dismay. I had to ask, "What? That meet-cute with Pearson was an improvement on my wildest dreams. How are you disappointed?"

"You can't introduce him to Teal. That's what he wants. Without Teal, we're screwed."

I wasn't surprised Mikel knew the name, considering his line of work. I smiled smugly, taunting, "I know something you don't. How fun."

"Why don't you enlighten me?"

I invited, "Google him. I dare you."

Throwing me a confused glance, he complied and said, "Okay. Art dealer. Wunderkind. Recluse. Yadda, yadda. What am I looking for?"

"Click on images."

I watched as his eyes tracked back and forth over his phone's screen, wiggling with delight as his eyebrows popped up.

He breathed, "No way. No. Claire… you're a genius."

"Yep. No one knows what he looks like. You ready to dive into one of those elaborate aliases you mentioned earlier?"

*

The time had come to place an emergency call to Annika. Mikel and I agreed it couldn't be avoided, but we weren't happy about it.

Teal was not only a ninja at avoiding people's cameras, he was also an avowed hermit. He lived in New York and conducted all of his business over the phone or through video chat, if his clients insisted—though his camera never came on. If Pearson knew this and suspected Mikel, who I'd be introducing him to as Teal on Friday, wasn't really Teal, he may have a way of confirming whether or not the real Teal had left his NYC high-rise apartment.

So, feeling like we were about to get chewed out, we called Annika on speakerphone Wednesday afternoon. In my two phone calls with Pearson since he'd given me his card, I hadn't come right out and promised that I'd introduce him to Teal; but he believed the famous art dealer could help him acquire a new Pre-Raphaelite, and the last thing I wanted to do was disappoint him.

Annika answered after several rings, hissing, "What?"

"Nice to hear your voice too, sis," Mikel said. "Why are you whispering?"

"Because I'm in the bathroom at school. What's the big emergency?"

I explained our plan-slash-predicament, and Annika's response made me feel like an idiot. She said, "Um. Have the meeting over video?"

"Oh," I said. I fell silent, chastised.

"But I'm here," Mikel argued.

"So what? Teal never leaves New York. You were gonna have him magically transport to Montana at Claire's beck and call? Pearson's not gonna suspend disbelief just because you ask him to."

"Is there a way to make it look like the video is coming from New York?" I asked, not because that seemed important, but because I wanted to justify our phone call somehow.

I was relieved when Annika whispered, "Oooh, good point. He may have a way of checking that. Yeah, you better let me set everything up. Turn on your laptop and plug it in, but don't log in. I'll set it up when I get back from class, okay? And I'll see if I can get a bead on Teal's schedule."

We tried to catch up a little, but Annika hung up on us. Shrugging, Mikel said, "Change of plans, I guess. I wanted to get in that house, but now it looks like neither of us will."

"I can still go. I'll tell him Teal wants me to be there. He's a capricious guy, it'll sell."

"Capricious. Right. I guess it's my turn to put on an act, huh?"

I was already dialing Pearson's number. "You'll do fine. Hi, Paul? Guess what? He's in. Yep. Friday night, eight thirty, at your house. It's okay if I come, right? Teal is kinda shy, but I told him what you're looking for and he seemed really excited. Great. See you then!"

I hung up. My hands were shaking, whether from cold or excitement or nerves, I didn't know. Mikel sandwiched them between his, planting a quick kiss on my temple.

"We've got about a day and a half to plan this thing," he said. "That might be enough."

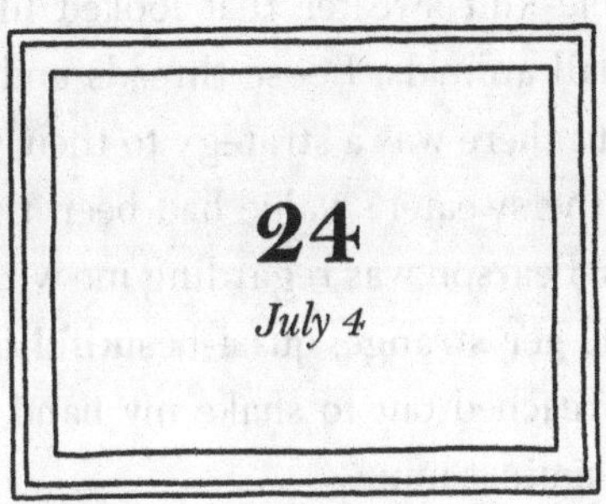



IN MY RENTED VOLKSWAGEN Tiguan, for which I'd had to drive all the way to Whitefish and back, I arrived at Paul Pearson's house a few minutes before eight Friday night. I was early by design, hoping to squeeze in some schmoozing under the guise of giving us time to set up the video call. We wouldn't want to keep Teal waiting, would we?

In black leggings, a t-shirt, my tourist boots, and of course my trusty flannel, I hoped Paul's wife wouldn't consider me a wannabe homewrecker. I didn't think I looked like a woman on the prowl, but Mikel had refused to weigh in before I left the lodge. He claimed to be in character as Teal, who would not be answering stupid questions.

Speaking of his wife, it was she who answered the door at my nervous knock. I hadn't heard a single bark, so I was surprised to see a huge, black dog sitting by her leg when she opened the door. It looked like an outsized German Shepherd, except for the pair of ice blue eyes staring intelligently up at me. I'd never seen a more breathtaking animal.

If the dog was striking, he was nothing compared to the woman standing in front of me. At six feet tall, she was slender as a willow branch, barefoot, wearing skin-hugging jeans and a gray cable-knit sweater that looked like it had been attacked by small animals. Loose threads and holes covered the garment, but there was a strategy to their placement that made me sure the sweater's value had been tripled by its ill treatment. Mrs. Pearson was regarding me with an indulgent smile that made her strange, quasi-beautiful face look nearly human. She reached out to shake my hand, and hers was warm and soft against mine.

"You must be Claire. Please come in. You're a bit early, so you caught me by surprise. Can I get you something to drink?"

Her voice was deep and heavily accented, from what country I couldn't guess. It was intoxicating.

"I wouldn't say no to a gin and tonic," I answered. "Sorry for the mix up—I meant to tell Mr. Pearson I'd be here at eight."

The dog shadowed us on silent paws through the foyer and into a sitting room. Mrs. Pearson bid me make myself comfortable while she mixed our drinks, and I really tried to; but the dog's icy gaze was still fixed on me, making me squirm. I felt like I was in one of those Roger Moore 007 movies Mikel and I had just watched.

"What's his name?" I asked.

"Her," Mrs. Pearson corrected. "Her name is Hilda." Half turning, she saw the dog sitting in front of me, staring motionlessly at me, and chided, "Hilda, komm. You silly beast. I'm sorry, she can be unnerving. She's just curious about you."

"She's *so* beautiful. What—sorry, what is she?"

"A shepsky. German Shepherd and husky. Paul got her and her brother from a breeder in Calgary early last year. I don't know where Otto has hidden himself, but he'll put in an appearance before long. Ah, Paul, there you are. Our guest has arrived."

Paul was standing in the doorway, dressed so much like his wife that I wondered whether they'd coordinated outfits. His sweater was fully intact, though, and he was wearing loafers. "Early, good. Claire, it occurred to me you might like to see my collection. Since we have time?"

"Your collection?" I echoed cluelessly, as though it had never crossed my mind that there might be art in the house. "I'd love to. But hadn't we better get this set up?" I asked, demonstratively raising the messenger bag in which I'd brought my laptop. "I think he's expecting the call to start right at eight thirty."

He agreed, and I managed to draw out the process long enough that we decided to save the art gallery tour for after our chat with Teal. Paul and I sat side-by-side on one sofa, the laptop open on a coffee table between us and Mrs. Pearson, who'd stretched out her long legs on a matching sofa. For the few unoccupied minutes before 8:30, I chatted comfortably with the Pearsons and tried to make my gin and tonic last.

Mikel initiated the video call at 8:30 on the dot, and I motioned to Paul that he could answer it. The old man looked so excited, I almost felt bad about lying to him—until I remembered why I was there.

The video flared to life, revealing a version of Mikel that would have made me fall apart laughing, if I hadn't already seen it. He was wearing a pair of tiny, non-prescription glasses which perched on his nose with no attempt to appear functional. His hair, which normally fell in a thoughtless tangle around his shoulders, had been pulled up into a miniscule bun on top of his head. His clean-shaven face and plain white t-shirt blended well with the empty, featureless wall behind him. I'd strong-armed him into allowing me to apply eyeliner, which I'd assured him was necessary to sell the disguise. It wasn't; I just wanted to push him around. It didn't hurt, though.

Wearing a deadpan expression, Mikel let his gaze settle first on me, then on Paul. Mrs. Pearson was out of frame, sipping her cocktail and playing with Hilda's massive paws.

"Mr. Teal, thank you so much for agreeing to meet with me. Can you hear me okay?"

"Yes, I can hear you, but it's just Teal. You can thank Claire. I can't say no to her."

I was glad to hear he'd decided against doing an accent. Teal would have a New York accent if anything, but Mikel had tried his out on me with a lukewarm reception. He sounded just fine using his own, natural voice.

"He said he would buy me a pony," I interjected. "Just getting that on the record."

I saw Mrs. Pearson laugh soundlessly to herself at this; then, behind her in the open doorway, I watched an absolute unit of a dog stalk into the study without making a sound. Otto was nearly twice the size of his sister, blacker than midnight, and dripping with apex predator energy. There was no way some timber wolf DNA hadn't gotten mixed in at some point.

Mikel must have seen my expression, because he asked, "Claire. Darling. What in the world are you looking at?"

I blinked, shook my head, and tore my eyes away from Otto

to refocus on Mikel. "Oh, sorry. The Hound of the Baskervilles just walked in."

That got me an audible laugh from Mrs. Pearson, who turned languidly to beckon the animal toward her. Paul said, "That's my dog, Otto. People usually react that way to him."

Mikel said, "I don't mean to get off topic, but may I see him? Anything that makes Claire speechless must be a real sight."

Paul said something in German, and both dogs sprang to their feet to sit between us and the laptop. Since she was sitting on my feet, I judged Hilda to weigh upward of ninety pounds. Otto... I couldn't even begin to guess. Otto was going to be a *big* problem.

"Magnificent," Mikel breathed. "Thank you for letting me see them, Mr. Pearson. It's good to know your collection is well-guarded. I assume you mean to display your acquisition at home?"

Mrs. Pearson called the dogs back to her, smiling adoringly at them. I had to give her credit—I loved dogs too, but seeing that pair coming at me would make me want to run, not smile.

Paul was saying, "Yes, I have a gallery on the second floor. I was about to give Claire the tour, but we ran out of time. She told you what I'm looking for?"

"She told me you are interested in purchasing a Stillman, but you'd be happy with something by one of her male contemporaries. Is that accurate?"

Paul nodded eagerly. "My wife, Iliana, loves her work. *Mariana* is her favorite. I don't suppose...?"

Having done my homework, I racked my brain for details about *Mariana*. I was so nervous, I drew a blank. I couldn't even picture it. Thankfully, Mikel had cheat sheets.

"Ah, yes. I've met several times with the owner, but she remains uninterested in selling. There are only ten verified Stillmans in private collections. As much as I'd like to help you, I must be clear that it may be impossible. Especially if you have your heart set on a portrait."

"We're flexible," Paul said.

"How much were you planning to invest?"

"I could go as high as eight million. If that limits our options, I understand, but it's a firm ceiling."

I tuned out of their conversation. I couldn't keep my eyes off Otto and Hilda, who had left Iliana to her cocktail and were now play-fighting with each other in front of the fireplace. Big as they were, they hardly made a sound as they clashed, broke apart, clashed again, and rolled back and forth over the carpet. There was something otherworldly about them, as though they weren't wholly a part of this reality. I hoped they made regular trips to the groomers, because their presence took surviving a burglary entirely off the table.

"Claire? Yoohoo. Are you staring at those dogs again?"

Mikel sounded irritated. Was he in character? I said, "Sorry, can you repeat that?"

"I wanted to know what you thought of Mr. Pearson's collection."

"I haven't seen it yet," I reminded him, knowing he couldn't have forgotten.

Paul said, "I'll give her the tour tonight. But we don't want to keep you, if you have other appointments."

"Yes. Claire, I'll talk to you tomorrow. Mr. Pearson, it was a pleasure meeting you, and I hope we can reach an agreement you and your wife are thrilled with."

"Me, too. Thank you for your time, Teal."

They exchanged phone numbers, the call ended, the screen went dark, and for some reason the wrestling dogs left off their game and sat up as though commanded by an unheard voice.

I saw no reason to disguise my true feelings about the dogs. Laughing shakily, I said, "Okay, they are really starting to freak me out. They are... like... *real*, aren't they?"

Iliana peered at them, giving my question serious thought, and said, "I'm not sure."

"Oh, you're both being silly," Paul said. "Well, Claire is. You, my dear, are simply drunk."

His wife nodded. Paul rose to his feet.

"It seems Teal requires your assessment of my art collection, Claire," he said. "Shall we?"

I stood and followed Paul from the study. Sensing we had a pair of silent shadows, I turned and saw Otto and Hilda plodding smoothly along behind us. Paul turned too, saw them, and ordered them back into the study with Iliana.

"Sometimes they get fixated on people," he said. "I can't make any sense of it. There must be something about you, though."

"Maybe they can tell I don't have a soul," I suggested.

"What?"

As we mounted the staircase, I said, "Oh, it's just a joke about redheads. Maybe a little low-brow for you."

"I'm a bit behind the times, I'm afraid," he sighed. "How old are you, if you don't mind me asking? It seems like you were just a little girl not so long ago."

"I'm thirty-eight. It's been thirty years since Aunt Eva died. Almost exactly, actually."

"Yes, thirty years ago this month. She was much, much too

young. Even with our age difference, I always thought she'd outlive me."

"Tomorrow isn't on the schedule," I quipped.

Paul, who was a few stairs ahead of me, stopped and turned around.

"What did you say?"

I repeated the phrase, making it a question. To my alarm, his eyes began to look a little misty. With a sad smile, he muttered, "Eva used to say that. Those exact words. I'm…" He gave a gusty sigh. "I'm so sorry, Claire, but I have to admit… I wasn't really sure it was you. It seemed like too much of a coincidence, running into you. Forgive me?"

"Of course. I'd be a little dubious, too. And I didn't mean any offense, calling it Nowhere, Montana, but that's really how it feels to me. Maybe Aunt Eva called me here, so we could reconnect."

Aunt Eva had been the spiritual type, and I was gambling that the words wouldn't sound too trite coming from me. Paul nodded sagely, then laughed.

"That sounds like her, too." He continued up the stairs. "I have eight of her paintings. They're the best of my collection, no matter what those pompous art appraisers have to say."

As we continued to the second floor and through the winding hallways, I told myself I was taking stock of the place for Mikel's sake. The truth was, I expected those phantom wolf dogs to reappear without warning at any moment, and I didn't want them to get the drop on me. Paul led me to the back of the house, which faced the lake, and into a windowless room behind a pair of locked doors.

Paul's art collection made mine look like a joke. The room he revealed was easily fifty feet to a side, and all four walls were lined with a single row of paintings spaced three to five feet apart at eye level. A perfect grid of sixteen pedestals sat in the center of the room, displaying sculptures, some jewelry, and a dagger. Even the light fixture was a masterpiece: a Louis Comfort Tiffany, or a skilled reproduction.

Paul saw me staring and read my thoughts, "A genuine Tiffany. Iliana almost fainted when I told her I wanted to hang it up. She lives in terror that it will fall. Would you like to explore in private, or take the guided tour? I'm sure I can trust you alone with the artwork."

"Guided, please. I'm not crazy about getting caught in your house without an escort."

"By Otto and Hilda, you mean?" He chuckled. "Really, you're making too much of them. They're actually very playful, silly things. I meant for them to be guard dogs, but they look more intimidating than they are."

"I'll take your word for it."

Despite my flimsy reasoning, Paul agreed to give me the tour himself. He possessed some really high-dollar items, including a small Rembrandt, but he clearly favored the paintings by artists he'd known personally. I only had a couple seconds to study the Rembrandt before he rushed me along to one of my aunt's paintings.

"This one is among her best work, in my humble opinion. A nude self-portrait. She painted it in Santa Fe in 1962. I always liked it, so she gave it to me right before she died."

His words sank in slowly, while my eyes were still on the dark surface of the Dutch master's interpretation of the Ides of March.

A nude *self*-portrait? Pearson was trying to pass off Wyeth's painting as a Riordan. He wasn't even hiding it! I moved slowly toward him; he was standing in front of a small canvas painted in a subdued palette of sunset reds and pinks. If he noticed me forcing air in and out of my nose, struggling with myself to stay composed, he didn't mention it.

After all these years, I was almost afraid to look at it. I forced my eyes to rise to the canvas, and there she was, recumbent on the sand, attended by cacti and sagebrush, bald hills rising to mesas behind her while the sun set over all. Her dark hair tumbled over her chest, hiding her breasts, while her left hand covered her pubic area. Her hand right was outstretched and open, as though inviting me to join her in the sand, and her eyes stared straight ahead, meeting my gaze.

I had the strangest feeling that Pearson could hear my heartbeat thundering in my chest, then screeching to a halt that just about killed me.

This wasn't right. The outstretched hand, the gaze, the hair covering her breasts, the provocative placement of her left hand. None of it matched my memory of the Wyeth. And there, painted like a faded tattoo on her own right foot, was my aunt's hieroglyph-like signature.

Heart sinking, I heard myself say, "Well, crap."

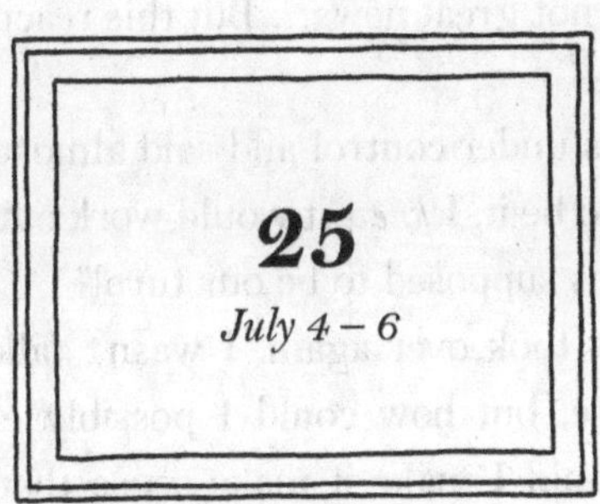


PURSUED ALL THE WHILE by defeating explosions that I eventually understood were Independence Day fireworks, I got back to the lodge after 10:00 p.m. I hoped Mikel had given up on waiting for me and had fallen asleep. No such luck.

I'd barely walked through the door when he asked, "Did you see it?"

I sat down to take off my boots. "Yes. It wasn't the Wyeth."

"So, you didn't see it."

"No, you don't understand."

I stopped talking to grapple with my shoelaces, which I'd double knotted. My nails hadn't grown back much after the attack at Marty's house, and I couldn't get a grip on the compact little knots. The more I tried, the more upset I got, until with a sob of defeat I gave up and started trying to pull my boots off without untying them. Mikel watched this unfold, stepping in when I went back to the knots. I was weeping like a baby, too overwhelmed to be embarrassed about it.

He pulled my hands away from my boots and asked, "Can

you tell me what's going on? Please?"

"It—wasn't—a—Wyeth," I choked out. "We—came—all this—way—for nothing!"

"Okay, that's not great news… But this reaction still seems a little extreme."

I got the sobs under control and said almost calmly, "This was supposed to be it. I *knew* it would work out this time. We got so far. It was supposed to be our turn!"

And the sobs took over again. I wasn't talking about the Wyeth anymore, but how could I possibly explain that to Mikel? How could I make it make sense that this last in a long line of failures, days before the thirtieth anniversary of my quest, capped off by remembering the attack at Marty's house and every horrid thing that came bundled with it, here in this weird lonely place with a man who wanted me to do one thing, *just one simple thing* for him, was making me relive every worst, lowest moment of my life all at once?

"Our turn?" he asked softly. He was staring at me, but I couldn't meet his eyes.

"I can't—you don't—I just want to sleep, Mikel, just let me sleep…"

"Are you talking about… Are you talking about your…?"

He didn't finish the question. Wrapping his arms around me, he held me for a long time until I was able to rein in the sobs once more. Then he helped me to bed, took off my boots, and turned off all the lights. I didn't protest when he climbed into bed next to me. I let the weight of his arm over my chest hold everything in, and I fell asleep the same way I'd fallen asleep so many times before: begging God to let me go to them.

*

Once again, my request was denied. I woke up on earth, under Mikel's arm, my head pounding and my throat screaming for water. Hot shame washed over me at the memory of the previous night's nuclear meltdown. I hadn't fallen apart that hard in a long time, and I hated that I'd forced Mikel to bear witness to it.

Since we hadn't found the Wyeth, and Mikel would likely not be able to arrange the sale of a Stillman to Paul Pearson, there was no reason for us to stay in Eureka any longer. I started to ease out from under Mikel's arm, my mind on packing; but he caught me and held me down.

"Oh. You're awake."

"I need you to talk to me, and I'm prepared to make it an order if that's what it takes."

"I'm really sorry about last night," I said. "That was over the top. Way over the top."

"Tell me about the painting. You said it wasn't a Wyeth."

"It was a nude in the desert, the right size, just like the insurance list said. My aunt painted it. I'd know her signature anywhere."

"The insurance list said it was unsigned and unattributed," Mikel reminded me.

I wanted to hope, but I refused to allow it, asking, "So? He could have lied. Did you see any nudes or self-portraits by my aunt on that list?" I gave him time to respond, then went on, "Besides, I remember certain things about the painting she showed me, and that wasn't the same painting. Pearson's is… sexualized, intimate. But at the same time, you can't actually see anything. And in the Wyeth, her eyes are closed. Like she was sleeping. I distinctly remember that."

"I don't buy it. What if he bought the Riordan later, or even had it forged, so he could claim it was the painting listed on the forms? Maybe he realized that little paper trail wasn't such a smart idea."

"I really want to believe you. I do. But you're reaching."

"You're spiraling." His arm tightened, pulling me against him, and he whispered, "You can talk to me. I know trauma when I hear it, and you can't keep that stuff bottled up."

I thought about what he'd tried to ask me last night, the way his voice had sounded like he was in pain. He'd been near tears too, and I'd done that to him. I shook my head.

All business, he said, "All right. As dictator, I say we run out the month. I'm happy to lock you away again, if you want to be difficult."

I forced a laugh and asked, "What can we do? He showed me his collection, the house is a fortress guarded by mythical beasts, and he was only interested in me to get to Teal."

"I know this is your first heist, so there's no way for you to know this, but these things rarely fall together on the first attempt. You have to be patient."

"What do you call trying for thirty straight years?"
"Stubborn."

I rolled my eyes. "Let me up. I'm thirsty."

"Tell me you're not giving up, and I'll let you g——"
"I'm not giving up."

He sighed. "Darn. I thought you'd argue more."

Once freed, I got up and drank several glasses of water straight from the tap. I took some Tylenol, then made my-self another espresso. I then flipped through the room service menu, searching for something to treat myself with. Recalling the steak and eggs in Helena, I found the same item on the menu and ordered myself one, throwing in an order of biscuits and gravy for Mikel. With food on the way and caffeine pumping through me, I felt a little better—and a little worse.

The food arrived and we sat on the patio to eat, savoring a much warmer morning than we'd enjoyed so far. I wanted to get a few things straight about the steaming pile of trauma I'd dumped on Mikel last night, but he was ready to get down to brass tacks.

"I'm going to need you to walk me through exactly what you saw, did, and said last night. Then you need to draw me a map of the inside of the house and anything you can remember from the outside. Was there a security guard at the front gate?"

"There wasn't a front gate," I answered. "The only security measures I saw were Otto and Hilda."

"Did you notice any cameras?" I shook my head, and he said, "Weird. What about his art collection? Anything good?"

"If I had to ballpark it, the whole collection is worth tens of millions of dollars. He's roughly doubled its size in the last ten years. There was the Waterhouse and the other Pre-Raphaelites, those we already knew about. There was a Rembrandt, a Cezanne, a Stubbs… He had some choice stuff. Plus a lot of relatively unknown painters whose works could increase in value in the future. He's got a good eye."

"What did you think of the wife?"

"Iliana? She was divine. A little weird, but she might be a lush. The whole thing felt like a scene from a movie, honestly." I foresaw his next question and said, "I didn't see anyone else in the house, but it was a big place."

"Walk me through it."

I did, but I refused to let the act of talking stop me from eating my steak and eggs while they were still warm. Mikel was forced to endure several long pauses while I chewed.

When I was finished, he asked, "So you got a pretty bad vibe from those hellhounds?"

"Not bad, just… You know what it was? It was like they were people trapped in dog's bodies, and they could see into my soul."

He picked up my coffee cup and sniffed it suspiciously. I grabbed it out of his hands.

"I don't really think that! I'm just trying to paint you a picture."

"Picture painted. I don't want to try anything with those two in the house, no matter what Pearson says. Want to make me a sketch while you're feeling artistic?"

I did my best, but I was an organizer, not an artist. The layout of Pearson's home—at least the two stories I'd partially seen—turned out a bit boxy and rudimentary, but Mikel seemed to approve. He studied my drawing, along with the notes he'd taken during my monologue, for a long time. Every now and then he'd ask me a question, but otherwise I was left to my own devices while he lost himself in thought. I found a channel of true crime reruns on TV and divided my attention between that and reorganizing my half of the dresser.

I was starting to think about lunch, and still Mikel was pouring over his notes. My phone rang while I was studying the room service menu again, and that got his attention.

"Who is it?" he asked.

"Pearson, who else? Shush." I took the call, slipping back into my Angelino persona. "Hi, Mr. Pearson! Paul, sorry. No,

I haven't talked to him yet. He's kind of a late riser. Yeah. Well, I was. I'm not sure if that's important to him, but I'll be sure to tell him. Yeah, I'd love to. Want me to bring anything? Sure, no problem. Okay, see you then. Bye!"

I hung up, then stared at the phone in my hand for several seconds, processing the conversation. Mikel left me to it.

"He asked me if I'd told you—meaning Teal—what I thought of his collection. And he wants me to come to dinner tomorrow night. Did you do that on purpose?"

With the ghost of a smile, Mikel asked, "Do what?"

"You know what I mean. You made him think he has to keep sucking up to me to get Teal's help finding a Stillman."

"He already thought that. I just encouraged it."

"Well, Mister Mastermind, you've got until tomorrow night to come up with a way to make this dinner invite work to our advantage. If you're so sure the Wyeth is there, that's going to be my chance—or yours—to look for it."

Mikel looked invigorated by my challenge. "Oh, I'll think of something, but we're not gonna have time to argue about it. So even if you think my plan is crazy or 'too simple,' you gotta go along with it. Got it?"

"Yes, sir."

"All right. Call the rental place and let them know you need the car for a couple more days. Then I need you to pick some things up for me."

He passed me a handwritten list on hotel stationary. I read aloud, "A used book from the sixties or seventies with blank pages, graphite pencil set including two-H to five-B? One-inch paint brush, size twelve mud boots, and dog treats?" I lowered the list and asked wearily, "Is this some kind of test?"

"Yeah, if you can find pencils like that in Eureka, I'll promote you to field marshal. Don't ask anyone for help, and don't lose that list. Hop to it!"

*

The rest of Saturday and most of Sunday were exhausting. I roved all over Eureka for hours looking for the items on Mikel's list, and I earned my promotion to field marshal. I also earned more work for myself, from memorizing a long list of German dog commands to taking a crash course from Annika on RFID signal detection and the use of a handheld infrared scope. Come Sunday afternoon, I was so dog tired I could barely stand, and Mikel ordered me to take a nap so I'd be fresh and alert for dinner at 8:00.

MIKEL, WHO HAD MORE than earned himself the semi-affectionate nickname Generalissimo over the weekend, wouldn't even let me choose my own outfit for Sunday night. I'd woken up from my nap to find my carefully organized clothes spilled all over the dresser, bed, and floor, with one particularly baggy and well-worn set laid out on the bed for me. He made me wear my hair in a sloppy, low ponytail, nixed the idea of makeup—which I hadn't been planning to wear, anyway—and even presented me with an enormous pair of fake reading glasses to wear all night. Worst of all, I was compelled to carry a purse. I hated carrying a purse.

It wasn't as though he'd kept me in the dark about the plan, or why I needed to look like I considered a dinner date with Paul Pearson less important than doing my laundry, but I still didn't like it. I hadn't carefully curated an ever-changing collection of stylish and expensive clothes all these years to walk around looking like a frump-a-saurus. Still, it was a good plan, and I'd long ago agreed to go along with whatever

Generalissimo said.

I kissed him goodbye and jumped in the rented Volkswagen, then found my way once more to Pearson's house on the other side of the lake. Though his house was less than a mile from our hotel room, getting down to a bridge across Lake Koocanusa and back up to the house took nearly half an hour. I was late, per my orders but in violation of my own personal code of punctuality.

Hilda was waiting on the front porch for me, and her tail began to wag as I mounted the steps. If I'd had a tail, it would have been tucked firmly between my legs. Where was her big brother? I didn't have to wonder for long. Once I was close enough to Hilda to reach out my second-favorite hand for a sniff-and-greet, Otto materialized from the shadows and flanked me.

I stood between the two dogs, looking from one to the other. Again, not a single bark had signaled my arrival. One of the German commands Mikel had me memorize was gib-laut—make noise. I tested it out on Hilda, who immediately pantomimed a single bark, her tail wagging madly. I said it again, and she "barked" again, still without a sound. I did the same to Otto, whose bark was terrifying but as silent as his sister's.

Understanding dawned on me, making my heart hurt: Their vocal chords had been cut.

Since I was ignored for the moment by humans, I tested out more commands on the two dogs. They obeyed all the core commands, and they truly seemed to enjoy doing it.

On the one hand, it seemed Pearson had told it true that these were no vicious hellhound guard dogs. On the other hand, if he'd had their vocal chords cut, he was a monster.

There was a chance they'd come that way from the breeder, but I doubted it. My softer side offered another explanation: What if it was a genetic thing? That would let Pearson off the hook for being a dog-abusing piece of dog-turd. I needed to know the answer so I could decide how much to hate the man.

I remembered the treats in my purse and gave a few each to Hilda and Otto, and they took that as a signal to resume their former positions. Hilda lay down next to the front doormat with a self-satisfied gust of air, and Otto vanished into the shadows around the side of the porch.

I rang the doorbell, expecting to see Iliana again. I was excited to see how she'd styled herself this evening, not to mention anxious for the contrast I'd present in my baggy jeans and too-big sweater. It wasn't Iliana or Pearson who opened the door, but a man about my age. He looked so much like both Pearson and his wife that my brain said 'son' before he could.

Stepping back to let me inside, he said, "Welcome. You must be Claire. I'm Bell, Paul's son."

I shook his outstretched hand like a normal person, but I couldn't stop my face from reacting to the name.

"Like the thing that rings, not the Disney princess," he said with a self-deprecating smile.

"You've had to explain that hundreds of times, haven't you?"

"Oh, yeah."

I followed him through the foyer, passing the study where I'd been Friday night and continuing into an open-concept, kitchen-living room-dining room area bigger than my parents' entire house.

The sight of Paul and Iliana sitting in matching armchairs next to the fireplace, obligatory cocktails in hand, was a relief. Trying not to look at Bell was making me twitchy and nervous. The man had taken the best features from both his parents—Paul's height, jawline, and thick head of hair and Illiana's eyes, voice, and baby-soft skin—and was so ridiculously attractive that I felt like punching Mikel for making me dress up like a librarian protesting the male gaze.

Paul hadn't warned me Bell would be here, and I was struck by worry that Mikel's meticulously thought-out plan might not work with a fourth person in the house.

Iliana greeted me warmly and then told her son, "Can you make her a gin and tonic, please? Claire, dinner isn't quite ready, I'm afraid. It's my fault—I forgot to take the steaks out of the freezer this morning."

The thought of this goddess doing something as banal as defrosting meat was too much for me to process. I searched my brain for something to say and landed on, "You must be a mind-reader. I've been craving steak all day. Must be something in the air up here."

"There is," she said, too seriously. "I was a vegetarian when we moved here."

Bell brought me my cocktail and accepted my thanks with a polite nod. He dismissed himself with, "I'm going to check on those steaks. You three just relax."

I found a seat on a leather ottoman between Paul and Iliana. Seeing Iliana's gaze rake over me, probably wondering how anyone could contrive to look so slovenly, I forced, "Sorry I was late. I went on a hike—alone, like an idiot. Got lost, of course. I didn't even make it back to my hotel in time to wash my hair. That's what I get for trying to get out and enjoy nature, I guess. Oh!" I reached into my giant purse and pulled out a bottle of wine. "I did at least think to buy this before my hike. I know you said I didn't need to bring anything," I told Paul. "But I just wanted to say thank you for inviting me over."

Iliana accepted the bottle with automatic, somewhat insincere gratitude. She studied the label for a moment and said, "Oh. My goodness, Claire. You shouldn't have. Thank you."

I knew I shouldn't have, but Generalissimo had disagreed. That bottle set us back nearly $300.

"I couldn't believe they had it in town," I said. "I had to grab what I could before they vanished in a puff of smoke. Since I cleaned them out, I figured it was only fair to share one."

That said, I checked an item off my mental list: Make them think you're loaded.

We chatted about nothing in particular until Bell returned to tell us dinner was ready. Mikel's prediction that Pearson would take his time getting down to the real reason he invited me to dinner seemed to be coming true. That meant, unfortunately, I'd have plenty of time to drink too much, embarrass myself, and wangle an invite to sleep it off in lieu of dying in a fiery car crash.

Rather than moving to the Olympic-sized dining table, we carried our refreshed cocktails outside to eat on the back patio. I was worried about surviving long enough to eat a steak in the frigid, sixty-ish degree weather, but they'd set up a pair of standing propane heaters on either side of the patio table. Add in whimsical string lights, the nearly full moon setting over the glasslike lake, and both gin and wine in abundance, and I couldn't help but enjoy myself.

I didn't actually get drunk, but pretending to wasn't all that hard. All three Pearsons clearly knew how have a good time, and all I had to do was keep up with Iliana drink-for-drink.

More than half of mine ended up dripping through the deck below my seat, which had to be some kind of misdemeanor once we'd tapped the wine I brought with me.

Dinner ended, Iliana drifted away to bed, and Bell excused himself with some mumbled nonsense about stock options and the Asian markets being open. Left alone with Pearson, I took a real-life sip of my wine and waited for him to say something. Anything.

Finally, when I was seconds away from remarking on the weather, he asked, "Get a chance to talk to Teal?"

Though he'd enjoyed the lion's share of the bottle of bourbon he and his son had been working on, he didn't sound drunk at all. I was supposed to be, so I gave an exaggerated shrug and said, "Yeah, we chatted last night. I dunno… Oh, you're talking about your thing, aren't you?"

"Well, sure. What else?"

"It's just this sketch he's been pushing me to buy. I mean on an aesthetic level, it's lovely, but I'm really kind of a Philistine and I just don't think it's worth what he's asking. Especially after you showed me… But, we're talking about you," I said quickly, before he could ask about the sketch. "I did tell him your collection was immaculate and balanced—trust me, he loves those words—and he seemed happy. I'm surprised you haven't heard from him. Or… have you? Sorry, if you already said, I must have missed it."

"I haven't talked to him since Friday night. Did you want me to top you off? This bottle is just about gone."

"Sure, thank you." I watched, blinking slowly, as he emptied the latest bottle of wine into my glass. "That hike today… This stuff is hitting me pretty hard. I hope I'm not making a fool of myself."

"Don't worry about that. We're all dedicated winos here. I'm curious about the sketch you mentioned, though. If you don't mind me asking…?"

I reached into my purse, which was sitting next to me on the bench, and pulled out my phone. Making him wait in answerless silence while I found the right photo seemed like a drunken thing to do. I got to the right photo and showed him my screen.

"This is it. Look familiar?"

"Oh. Wow. Is that a study for the nude your aunt painted?"

"*I* think it is. And look, Teal is a stand-up guy. He'd *never* try to pull one over me. But I just… It doesn't look like a Wyeth to me. And after you showed me the one my aunt painted, I'm like… this is a Riordan. I don't *like* that a Riordan is worth less than a Wyeth—obviously, I'm super biased—but Teal's price tag just doesn't make sense."

"He told you it was a Wyeth?" Paul asked.

"Mhm. I believe *he* thinks it is. I believed it was. When he called me on Tuesday, I was ready to fork over the cash just to say I owned a graphite-and-coffee study by Andrew Wyeth. I mean, coffee. Isn't that cute? But what do you think? Should I ask him to lower the price? He'd be so offended if I told him it was misattributed."

"May I see that?" he asked, reaching for my phone. I handed it over without hesitation.

I fell silent while Paul studied Mikel's sketch. By the movement of his long fingers, I guessed he was zooming in and panning over the photo. Maybe he was comparing the same details I had in my memory against the Riordan in his gallery. Mikel had drawn it from my memory, and he'd done a fantastic job of blurring the lines between my aunt's style and known sketches by Andrew Wyeth. The man really was a talented artist, not to mention a mastermind.

Paul handed me back my phone with an odd look on his face. Since he didn't seem inclined to say anything, I savored my wine and stared out over the lake. The night was getting on, and no one was dropping hints about me getting home at a reasonable hour. For the first time since Mikel had shared his plan with me, I let myself believe it really would work.

Even if it did work, though, it would all be for naught if Pearson didn't really have the Wyeth. I allowed myself two more sips, then asked, "What are you thinking about so hard?"

"This sketch… Teal says it's a Wyeth for sure?"

"Yep."

"But you think your aunt drew it as a study for her own self-portrait? The one I showed you?"

"I do now," I answered flippantly. I returned to my study of the lake, my sips of wine becoming mechanical as my body tensed up. If Mikel was wrong… Well, it wouldn't be the end of the world. Pearson would be exonerated, we'd go home, and we'd keep trying. No big deal.

I was mid-sip when he asked, "Can you keep a secret, Claire?"

*Holy train-sized cannoli, Batman.*

I nearly choked on my wine, coughing through the question, "What was that?"

"Can you keep a secret?"

"Oh." I gave him an evasive laugh. I'd done some math in my head earlier, and now seemed like the perfectly inappropriate time to throw out, "I already figured it out, about Bell. It's not like it's a big deal. I've long-since figured out why my parents wouldn't let me go to Aunt Eva's parties."

"Uh… what? No, it's not about Bell." He scratched at something on the table, half-smiling. "Eva and I hadn't been together for—You know what, let's not get into that. I want to show you something."

"Lead the way."

We left the dinner mess for the birds and went inside, and Pearson again led me up to the second floor and through a maze of hallways. We passed a closed door under which light and sound was leaking out into the hallway, and Pearson said offhandedly, "Bell's room, when he's here. I meant to apologize for not telling you he'd be joining us. He didn't tell us, either."

"I didn't mind looking at him all night," I said, grinning.

"He certainly takes after his mother," Pearson agreed. "Ah, here. I can count on one hand how many people have seen this, so I want you to promise me you'll keep it to yourself. Can you do that?"

We'd stopped in front of a door that I assumed was locked, because he had one hand on the doorknob while the other gripped a key he'd pulled from his pocket.

"Sure, I promise. Jeez, this is exciting. Is it an even bigger dog?"

Laughing, he said, "No, it's something I'm hoping will convince you to buy that sketch."

He unlocked the door and opened it, ushering me inside ahead of him before shutting us both in. I couldn't help but remember doing this with my aunt. Inside the tiny room, rather than a freestanding safe, was a medium-sized painting hanging on the wall opposite the door. The elaborate, gilded wooden frame nearly doubled its size. I stared at it, not understanding.

"It's not real," Paul said quickly, releasing the vise that had gripped my heart.

"Oh, thank *God*," I breathed. The reproduction of Vermeer's *The Concert* was beautifully done, right down to the hairline cracks in the yellowing varnish. Since the original was, by most accounts, the most valuable stolen painting in the world, I had to ask, "Why hide it in here?"

"Well, you devote an entire room to one painting, then put it under lock and key, and people are bound to wonder why. That reproduction cost me nearly as much as this house, so I figured it was the right painting to hang in here."

"It's really beautiful. Thank you for showing me."

I failed to keep the disappointment out of my voice, then squeaked an involuntary squeak when he swung the painting forward on a hinge to reveal a wall safe behind it. I watched him enter the combination on the keypad lock. He made no attempt to hide it from me.

Déjà vu washed over me like a warm, summer rain as he pulled another painting from inside the otherwise empty safe. When Pearson turned the canvas to face me, and I saw her again, my body betrayed me. I broke down in tears.

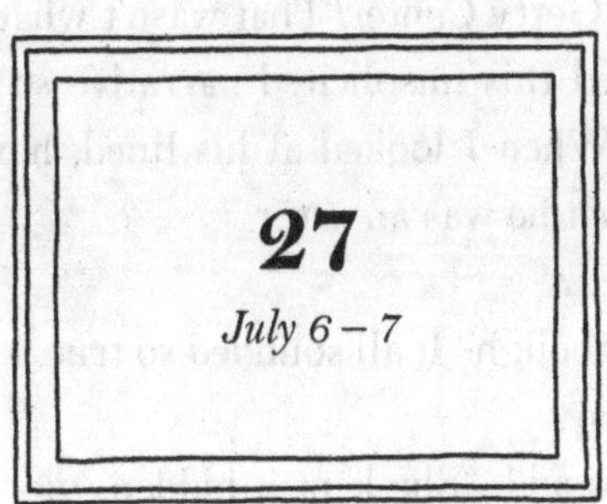



"CLAIRE, MY GOODNESS," Pearson said, laughing awkwardly. "That's not the reaction I expected at all."

"I'm sorry." I was able to pull myself together pretty quickly, but no reasonable explanation for my tears came to mind. "It's something about seeing her again, I think. I just really miss her."

"Me, too."

I checked her right foot, verifying my aunt's signature was absent. I knew I was looking at a Wyeth, *the* Wyeth, but I had to be sure. And I had to make him say it. I asked, "Why did you hide this one? I think it's even better than the one in your gallery."

"Because your aunt didn't paint this one, Claire. Andrew Wyeth did."

"You're kidding me."

"I'm not. Your aunt showed it to me shortly before she passed away. She told me she wanted me to have it, but she never got a chance to update her will. After I attended the reading and realized it wasn't mentioned, I—well, to be honest, I decided to take it. Since it wasn't specifically mentioned, it would've been thrown in with the rest of her collection and donated to the Getty Center. That wasn't what she wanted."

He'd delivered this unsolicited narrative so well, I almost believed him. When I looked at his lined, handsome face, I remembered that he was an actor.

*He's lying to you.*

Which part, though? It all sounded so true. I floundered for something to say.

He hurried to add, "She kept it hidden, too. She didn't tell me why, but I've always thought she didn't want people to know she was with Wyeth that week in Santa Fe. They'd had a brief affair, and Wyeth's wife didn't know. She was protecting him."

I breathed, "It's so sad, to keep it hidden like this."

"It is. But I have to, for her. That's why you have to buy that sketch from Teal."

"Why?"

"Because it really is a Wyeth. Show me the photo again." I complied, and he held my phone up to the painting to say, "Look at her eyes. And her breasts—sorry, I don't mean to be so blunt. But you can tell it's a study for this portrait, not the version Eva painted." He passed me back my phone with a gusty sigh and said, "If you don't buy that sketch, someone else will. Eventually someone is going to wonder—if they haven't already—why he drew a study for a painting that doesn't exist."

"And that might make people ask questions you don't want answered," I said. He nodded. I asked, "Why don't you buy it, then?"

"I will, if you don't, but Teal offered it to you."

"But you could have—Paul, you could have just called him and birddogged it right out from under me. You didn't have to show me this."

"I know, but I wanted to. She was my dear friend, but she was your aunt. It didn't feel right, not telling you. Maybe I just needed an excuse."

I was beginning to pick up on subtle tells, or at least I thought I was. The timbre of his voice changing ever so slightly, his hands trying to ball up and his conscious effort to relax them, the excessive, even aggressive eye contact. A human lie detector I was not, but I still had intuition, and intuition was telling me that last line was weapons-grade baloney.

*You're not safe just because you're not scared.*

I twitched in surprise. Why had Ren's voice popped into my head? Pearson's body language was anything but alarming, and my gut was calling him a liar, not a threat. Still, I nodded in acceptance of both Pearson's and Ren's words.

I whispered, "That's very—that's really nice of you. I guess I will buy that sketch. I mean… I wanted it before, and now… wow."

"And you won't tell anyone about this?"

"Are you kidding? This is the best secret I ever knew. No *way* I'm sharing."

That theatrical non-answer did not set his mind at ease, if his expression told it true. He said, "I don't think I want you driving home like this."

"Like what? All emotional?"

"Claire, you're drunk."

"Oh. Yeah, I am. But I don't want to impose—"

"Nonsense. We've got plenty of extra rooms, and you're not going to find any Uber drivers up here. Please stay."

I let him convince me, then asked to spend a few more minutes with the painting before he locked it back inside the safe. Even though I was sober, I was so tired I might as well have been drunk as Pearson led me to a guest room on the third floor.

"It'll be quiet up here," he explained. "And in the morning, it's the best view in the house."

"Thanks, Paul. Good night." After he'd passed out of sight down the hall toward the stairs, I added under my breath, "You've sure squirreled me away up here, haven't you?"

I checked my watch. Somehow it was nearly midnight, which did explain the sleepiness. It also meant I had just over one hour before Mikel abandoned his position and returned to the lodge. That would be plenty of time, unless Paul decided to stay up. Tiptoeing to the east-facing window, I looked down onto the back patio and saw that the string lights and propane heaters were still on. As I watched, either Paul or Bell came outside and turned everything off. A few seconds later, the glow of interior light over the deck was shuttered, and the scene below was thrown into total darkness.

Somewhere down there, I hoped, Mikel was hunched in his temporarily stolen row boat, wearing the brand new mud boots I'd bought him, waiting to hear from me.

I dug around inside my purse for the RFID scanner, verified it was still on and actively scanning, and then found my second phone. This was one of the duds Annika sent, which didn't have cell service but came equipped with an app that allowed me to exchange text messages via Bluetooth with Mikel's phone. The sight of his number on the list of available contacts made me weak-kneed with relief. He was nearby, close enough to make a connection.

I texted, "Getting anything from the scanner? It's been on this whole time."

In seconds he replied, "Nothing that looks like a camera. Where are you? IR scan yet?"

"Third floor, back of the house. I think everyone else went to bed. I'm gonna do the scan after the dogs."

"Everyone?" he asked.

"Paul's son is here."

"Great. I love surprises. Get moving. I'm still bailing at 1:00 if I haven't heard from you."

Now came my least favorite part of the plan. I checked the time again: 12:03. No time to think about it, just do it.

Slipping off my shoes, I left my room on socked feet and descended all the way to the ground floor. A lie about being thirsty was ready on my lips for anyone whose path I happened to cross, but the house was dark and silent. Since I'd last seen Hilda and Otto on the front porch, that was where I headed.

I opened the front door, bracing myself for an alarm to go off. When ten seconds passed in silence, I let out the breath I'd been holding and stepped outside. The temperature had fallen precipitously, and I was shivering in seconds.

"Otto? Hilda?" I called in a stage whisper. I jumped halfway out of my skin when a big, warm snout nuzzled into my left palm. I turned to see Otto literally inches behind me, already inside. How could something so big be so quiet? Hilda was behind Otto, regarding me with questioning eyes. I whispered, "You two are trying to give me a heart attack, aren't you?"

Neither answered. I led them into the study, plied them both with pets and treats, and shut them inside with promises of a quick release. After I'd closed the door on them, I waited outside the study to see what they'd do. For all the sounds I heard, the study might as well have been empty.

Even though Mikel hadn't identified any cameras on Annika's RFID scanner, I still had to walk around the outside of the house with the infrared scanner. No fibs about being thirsty would explain my actions anymore, especially not with the dogs chilling in the study. If I got caught now, I was on my own. I slipped on a pair of muddy, rubber boots someone had left on the porch and got to it.

Freezing to death was also an option. The temperature was in the low fifties by my guess, but in my Texas skin it felt arctic. I focused on scanning, walking, scanning, walking, repeat until I'd circled the entire house. The check went smoothly, except for a heart-stopping moment when one second-floor window glowed bright in the shape of a human being standing in front of the window. I lowered the scanner to see what I could, and I could just make out a man standing with his back to the window. I thought it looked like Bell, but it could easily have been Paul.

I got back inside minutes before one o'clock and hacked out a text to Mikel.

"No cameras, but someone awake on the second floor. South side of house."

"Ok. Dogs?"

"Locked in the study and ok with it." I described the location of the Wyeth's private room, told Mikel how to get inside, and started to let myself into the study. That was the plan, for me to hang out with the dogs while Mikel took the

Wyeth. If anyone woke up and noticed the dogs weren't roaming free, I would say I couldn't sleep, went to the study to read, and wanted their company.

Mikel arrested my progress by texting, "Who on 2nd floor? Can you get them to study too?"

"Probably Bell. I can try."

I could practically sense Mikel's elevated stress levels. Bell wasn't supposed to be here, and now we were improvising. I climbed to the second floor, not knowing whether Mikel would wait for some kind of signal from me before he came in through the sliding back door I'd unlocked.

I got lost twice, but finally I found Bell's bedroom door. I knocked on it and was gripped by panic when I realized I had no idea what to say. He answered the door before I could think of anything.

He smiled when I saw me, and I blurted, "I am just *dying* to talk to you."

"Oh?" He glanced down the hall to the left and right. "Did my parents leave you all alone?"

"Your dad convinced me to stay the night. Apparently the Montana Highway Patrol comes down pretty hard on drunk drivers. Good for them."

"What did you want to talk about? You want to come in?"

"Study," I said, adding in response to his confusion, "I locked the dogs in the study. I mean… I invited them in there, and then I came up here to grab you, and I didn't want them to be gone when I got back. They're like little will-o-the-wisps. I never know where they're going to pop up."

I was hoping for, at worst, a polite dismissal. He clearly wanted to be in his room, and I couldn't blame him. It was like a whole apartment, and I had obviously interrupted him in the middle of doing something on his computer. Three huge monitors were lined up on the desk, showing something that looked quite technical and serious, and the chair he'd vacated was still slowly revolving.

He leaned against the doorframe, crossed his arms, and asked, "So you want to hang out with me, or the dogs?"

"Hah… uh… both?"

"You're accustomed to getting what you want, aren't you?"

If he hadn't been so daggum handsome, I might have taken that as an insult. But, as with his dad, it was all in the delivery. I couldn't help but smile.

"I'm sorry. I'm keeping you from something important, aren't I?"

He looked me over from head to toe and back, concluding, "I guess it depends on what you're just *dying* to talk to me about."

Still smiling, I shook my head and turned away, calling over my shoulder, "I'm sorry for bothering you, Belle of the Ball." I heard his door close, then footsteps behind me, and I added silently, "And I'm sorry I had to play it this way, Mikel."

Bell caught up to me quickly and had the audacity to pinch me in the side, saying, "I haven't been called that since middle school."

"That's funny. I haven't called someone that since middle school."

"Did you really lock the dogs in the study?"

"Of course. I wanted to read a book, and I wanted to be attended by the two most magnificent dogs I've ever seen. What's so hard to believe about that?"

"You're something else."

Being called that by a specimen like Bell was intoxicating

enough, so I tried to turn down the gin and tonic he offered me after we'd enclosed ourselves in the study. Not to be dissuaded, he started mixing a drink for each of us anyway. While he was busy with that, I sent another message to Mikel.

"Ok, dogs and son in study with me. Make it fast."

Before I could see his answer, Bell finished up and turned toward me, and I had to tuck my phone away. He noticed the movement.

"Who are you talking to?"

"No one. I was Googling you."

"How rude." He sat down on the sofa next to me and sipped his drink, eyes dancing.

"Is it? Sorry, I've never had a night cap with the progeny of a movie star and a supermodel before."

"With an audience, no less."

I followed his glance to Hilda and Otto, who were sitting side-by-side in front of the dark fireplace, watching us.

"Platz," I ordered without even thinking.

They obeyed, and Bell asked, "You speak German?"

"Oh heck no. I heard your dad use that one Friday night. I've also heard my Jewish girlfriend say that, and given the context, I'm pretty confused about what it means."

"Girlfriend?" he echoed.

"Oh, would you like clarification of my usage?" I taunted.

"Actually, no. I prefer to use my imagination. What did you want to talk to me about?"

"My aunt," I said at once. I'd had enough time to think about it, and that answer felt like it made sense. "Her and your dad, specifically."

"Ah, yes. Hence the Googling."

"I didn't see how old you are, but your mom told me she's

been married to your dad for twenty-eight years. You are certainly older than that, no offense."

"It's the twenty-first century, isn't it?"

"It wasn't," I argued.

"Ah." He waved his drinkless hand at me. "Things weren't so different back then. Are you really worried he cheated on your aunt with my mom?"

"Not worried, just curious. Also… Any chance you remember her? My aunt?"

"I never met her," he answered carelessly around a drink, glancing at me and adding, "Sorry."

"It's okay. I've been thinking about her a lot. She seemed old to me when I was eight, but now… She died so young. It's not fair."

Bell knocked back the rest of his drink, set his glass on the coffee table, and turned his whole body toward me. Stretching his arm along the back of the sofa, he sighed contentedly and said, "Well, my dad killed her. Obviously nothing fair about that."

Paul Pearson killed Aunt Eva? He took my painting *and* murdered my great aunt?

Bell dropped this nuclear warhead on me mid-drink, and my brain interpreted it three different ways at the same time. I misheard him. He was joking. He thought I already knew.

I slowly lowered my glass and said, "What."

His eyes were round for half a second, but he regained his cool façade and said, "Oh, I just assumed you knew. You're pulling some scam on him, right? It's no skin off my nose either way."

"She died of a heart attack," I said tonelessly. "It was natural causes."

"Sure it was. Sit down, relax."

I didn't realize I'd risen to my feet until he said that. I looked down at the sofa, where my phone's screen was glowing with the receipt of a message from Mikel. Annika'd had the foresight to turn off message previews when the phone was locked, so Bell's automatic glance at the light garnered him no information. I inferred Mikel had the Wyeth and was back in the boat he'd docked under the Pearson's deck. He wanted me to know it was done, and I could release the beasts if I needed to. The man worked fast—assuming I'd interpreted the message correctly.

Belatedly, I resumed my seat. I stuffed the phone in my back pocket and retrieved my drink from the coffee table, where I'd apparently set it down.

"Drink up," Bell ordered. "I'm sorry for upsetting you. I really thought you knew."

"No," I breathed. I held onto the glass but didn't take another drink. "I didn't."

"That's not drugged, you know," he said, trying to make it a joke.

"Then you drink it."

He rose to his feet. "Whatever. I'm going to bed. You can forget what I told you or not, it doesn't matter. You can't prove it anyway."

Bell let himself out of the study, and Hilda and Otto followed him. With forced calm, I checked the message from Mikel and confirmed it said what I'd assumed. He was safely on his way back across the lake, so I could take my leave anytime. The sooner the better, now that Pearson's collection was light one Wyeth. I had to go all the way back to the third floor for my purse and shoes, so I headed for the stairs.

I got to my room and sat down on the bed, facing the window with my back to the door, to pull on my shoes. My head was telling me to pick up the pace, but my heart wasn't having it. I couldn't just walk out of the house forever without confronting Pearson. I'd been willing to let him off the hook for the theft of the painting, once I'd righted that wrong, but now things were different. If he'd really done what Bell claimed… but that was ridiculous. Bell was just trying to impress me. He was a jerk. What reason could Pearson possibly have had for murdering Aunt Eva?

By his own admission, Pearson hadn't known what was in her will. If he had expected a windfall, why kill her? Why not just wait?

I needed more information, which meant I needed to talk to either Paul or Bell again. So I needed to stay, at least through the night. I reached behind me for my purse, which I'd left on the bed, and my hand closed repeatedly over thin air. Twisting around, I saw my purse.

It was clutched in Pearson's hand. The old man stood in the doorway of my room, Bell hovering behind him with a look of mingled worry and remorse that made my blood run cold.

Standing slowly, I heard Ren's voice in my head again.

*Play dumb, Claire. It's your only move right now, and you better sell it.*

Oh, God, Ren. I missed him so much I felt like crying. I hoped Annika was taking good care of him, and vice versa.

"Why are you two looking at me like that?" I asked, smiling nervously.

Bell said, "I had to tell him, Claire. I'm sorry."

"Tell him what?" I asked. It was no use. Bell knew exactly what he'd told me, and he'd clearly confessed his loose-lipped mistake to his father. Judging by the cold look in Paul's eyes, it was in fact a big deal.

"Tell me why you came here," Paul said quietly.

Fear gripped my heart and squeezed, and I nearly choked on the words, "You invited me."

"You expect me to believe that Eva Riordan's niece just happens to evacuate to Eureka, Montana, right as one of the most reclusive art dealers in the world is trying to sell her a study for the Wyeth no one else knew existed? The one that's now missing from my safe? Does that about sum it up?"

Knowing that he'd already discovered the theft gave me a shot of courage, and I snapped back, "She wanted *me* to have it. Now I do. Deal with it."

"No, what you have is nothing. Just the clothes on your back."

"And a phone in her back pocket," Bell added. That little worm.

"See what else she's got," Pearson ordered, passing my purse back to his son. Pearson stepped into the room, came around the bed, and reached for my back pocket. I skipped away, which was pointless. There was nowhere to go but through the wall, and I was way too solid to manage that.

He grabbed me by the arm with surprising strength and turned me around, pushing me against the wall with one hand while he fished in my back pockets. Once he had the phone, he let up, but I kept my nose to the wall. Staring at mint green wainscoting made it easier to think than looking at either of the two men.

"What's the code?" Paul asked.

"Three, zero, zero, one," I recited, giving him the PIN in reverse.

I turned around, eager to see the outcome of my lie. Paul entered the PIN as given, and the phone issued one strident, angry beep before turning off. He had, as Annika had promised, "Bricked it."

Paul took the defeat in stride, tossing the phone on the bed with a bitter laugh. "Clever."

"She's got another phone in here, plus some stuff… I don't know what this is." Bell dropped the IR scanner, the RFID scanner, and my normal cell phone on the bed next to the brick. Paul picked up my cell phone.

"Unlock it," he ordered, trying to hand me the phone. I shook my head, and he said to Bell, "Hold her still."

Looking a little green, Bell nevertheless stepped into the little room and edged around the bed toward us. Before I could second-guess myself, I scrambled on all fours over the bed, made it through the door, and sprinted toward the stairs. Footsteps pounded down the stairs behind me, sending up an unholy racket that was sure to interest Hilda and Otto, wherever they were. I'd slipped the rented Volkswagen's key into my pocket out of habit, and as I ran I felt around my hip to reassure myself it was still there. The hard lump of the key fob was reassuring, but the sound of at least one pair of feet closing the distance behind me was not.

Wherever the dogs were, they chose not to participate in the chase. Paul was miles behind when I threw myself out the front door, leaving only Bell to stop me from escaping. Though I reached the driver's side door of the Volkswagen and heard the beep of the door unlocking at my touch, Bell slammed into me from behind before I could open it.

I twisted around, pleading, "Let me go, please, please let me go!"

But he was determined to drag me back inside, and he was much bigger than me. He grabbed my upper arms to peel me away from the car, leaving my hands and legs completely free. I sent the heel of my right hand into his nose and threw my knee into his groin at the same time. Though my blows felt weak, I surprised him enough to let me go. I set my back against the car, put my hands on his shoulders, and shoved him with all my might.

He didn't go far, but far enough that I was locked inside the car by the time he recovered. I threw it in gear and slammed on the gas, automatically checking my rearview mirror to make sure I wasn't dragging Bell to his death.

I saw Bell fading into the distance, his father framed in the open doorway, and two massive dogs sitting on the front walk between them, silently observing.

*

The drive back to the lodge was hell. I got lost several times, and when I pulled into a parking space at the lodge nearly an hour after my escape, my brain was pulsating with all kinds of alarms. The drink Bell had made me was drugged, of that I was certain. I'd already forgotten big chunks of what happened at the Pearsons' house. After I turned off the car, I stared at the clock until the display went dark, trying to figure out how it took me so long to get there.

I moved like a zombie through the parking lot, inside the lodge, to the elevator, up to the fourth floor, and down the hall. All I wanted was to prepare myself for what I'd say when I saw Mikel. With only a half-mile of lake between him and the room, I knew he'd beaten me there. He'd be so happy, probably greeting me at the door with the painting on full display and a bottle of champagne waiting to be popped. But that didn't make any sense. Where would he have gotten champagne?

I reached for my purse and the room key within, only to remember that I'd left my purse at Pearson's house. I knocked on the door, heart rate climbing. There was no answer. I knocked for a long time, then returned to the lobby to talk my way into a new keycard.

The woman at the front desk was the same person who'd checked me in, and she remembered me. Neither ID nor charisma was required to convince her to program a replacement key.

She ran a blank key through her machine, handed it to me, and asked, "Are you all right?"

"No. Thank you." I started to walk away, then snapped back to her, asking, "You didn't see my—uh—Mr. Carter come in, did you?"

"Sure didn't."

"Crum. Okay. Thanks again."

Worry gnawed at me, intensifying to painful levels when I entered the room to find it dark and devoid of life. I turned on the lights and paced around, trying to make my brain work. *What* had Bell given me? And why? What would've happened if I'd finished the drink he'd made me, instead of bailing one-third of the way through it? Was he trying to kill me, or... I couldn't articulate any other possibility. I expended the last of my energy by talking myself out of standing on the balcony and screaming Mikel's name, then fell backward on the bed and shut my eyes.

Sleep closed over me, time passed, and I woke up to the sound of the door opening. I sat up, dizzy and confused, and watched Mikel walk through the door. He was carrying something flat and rectangular wrapped in one of the flannel shirts I'd bought at the hardware store. His smile faltered at the sight of me.

"Is this real?" I asked.

"Uh... pretty sure?" His voice was music to my ears.

"Is that it?"

He unwrapped the rectangle and held it up for my inspection. "In the flesh. I was gonna leave it in the van, but I figured you'd want to see it. Looks like Pearson took good care of her. How long have you been here? I thought I wouldn't see you until tomorrow morning."

"There was a slight hiccup where Pearson's son told me he killed Aunt Eva and then I think they tried to maybe kill me?"

In Mikel's defense, there was no good way to respond to that. He carefully set the priceless oil painting down next to the espresso machine, then dragged our suitcases out of the closet and started packing. I watched him for two seconds, then joined in.

"I'm sorry. I should have done this already," I said.

"We can talk on the road, just pack. Where's the case you brought for the Wyeth?"

I found the hard-sided, leather case in question and began packing the painting in the layers of protective material we'd prepared for it, then I laid the case in the bottom of my largest piece of luggage and began packing my clothes around it. Mikel did the same with the gadgets and other incriminating things we'd brought along—laptop, binoculars, etc.

We'd been working in feverish silence for a few minutes when he asked, "Where are the scanners you took? And your phone?"

"They took everything. I bricked the one phone, though."

He swore and kept packing. In ten minutes we were done, but I was out of breath, lightheaded, and aching for more sleep. Mikel started carrying everything down to the van, ordering me to search the room thoroughly for forgotten items. It was a good thing he did. I found my drawing of Pearson's house, covered in Mikel's notes, stuffed between the sofa cushions, and the fake glasses which had somehow made it back to the lodge with me had fallen between the bed and the nightstand. Add in a pair of socks stuffed deep between the covers at the foot of the bed and the used, coffee-stained paintbrush in the sink, and I had such a haul to show Mikel that he decided to go over the room himself, too.

Once he'd collected a couple more items and made one full sweep of the room without finding anything, ten more minutes had passed. I was getting too nervous to stay tired. He dumped everything we'd found in a laundry bag and found two clean washcloths, handing me one.

"We won't get everything, but we don't have to make it too easy for them," he explained.

Then we went over the whole room wiping down every hard surface, obliterating fingerprints, palm prints, and footprints as best as we could. The chore was calming in a sense—I did love a clean, shiny surface—but set my mind racing at the same time.

Mikel had said stolen objects were the easiest things to steal, and I believed him; but we had no guarantee Pearson wouldn't call the police to report the Wyeth stolen. Neither I nor anyone else alive could prove he had no right to it, so we'd just have to wait and see what he did. In the event of an investigation, our false names and hard-to-find fingerprints might slow the police down a little; but they'd eventually figure out we were here, and they'd clearly see Mikel carrying the stolen painting into the hotel. Unless he'd done something to the security cameras without telling me.

But Bell's confession on behalf of his father changed everything. Pearson was not only a thief but a murderer, and what cold case detective in the world wouldn't love to solve the thirty-year-old murder of a famous artist at the hands of her movie star lover? I couldn't help but fantasize about a scenario in which Pearson was convicted of murder, I proved somehow that Aunt Eva had willed the Wyeth to me, and everyone involved just decided to be really cool about all the crimes Mikel and I had committed to get it back.

Though it was an exercise in futility, that fantasy got me through the wiping-down chore, into the van, and onto the long road south to Texas. This time, I was the one who fell asleep the moment we hit the highway.

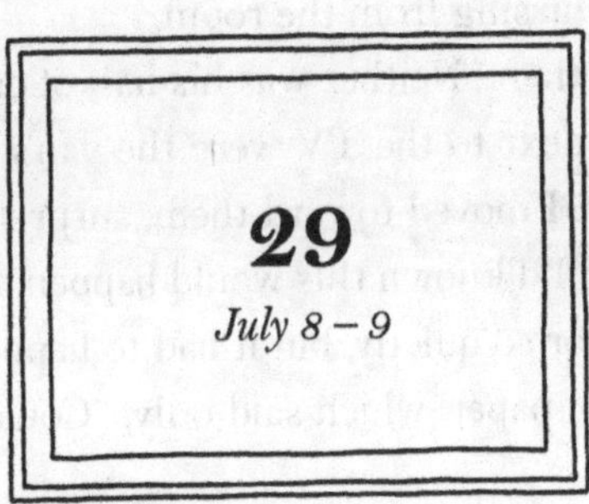



WE STAYED IN CHEYENNE, WYOMING Monday night, then tried to make it all the way back to Ren's house on Tuesday. This turned out to be impossible, when after only eight hours on the road we were both so tired we couldn't safely drive. I blamed the scenery, or rather the lack of it. We made it to Amarillo, Texas, got the cheapest motel room we could find, and fell asleep on a pair of rock-hard, double beds at two o'clock in the afternoon.

I woke up in darkness so absolute, I couldn't even tell if my eyes were really open. I lay still, breathing, replaying my most recent memories to figure out where I was. The sound of cars and big rigs rushing past on the interstate yards away settled it: I was in a crappy motel room in Amarillo, and I'd slept the day away.

Well rested and bursting with pee, I sat up and fumbled around for a lamp or a light switch. I found something on the wall between the two beds and scrabbled around until light flared to life way too close to my face. Recoiling, I endured a moment of blindness before I was able to stagger to the bath-room and take care of business.

When I came out, a discussion of dinner on my lips, I real-ized what was missing from the room.

Mikel wasn't there. Neither was his half of our luggage.

On the table next to the TV were the van's keys on top of a scrap of paper. I moved toward them, surprised by how un-surprised I was. I'd known this would happen, hadn't I? May-be not so soon, or so quietly, but it had to happen. I picked up the torn piece of paper, which said only, "Couldn't have done it without you."

I breathed, "You didn't…"

I dragged my biggest suitcase onto the bed and threw it open, tossing things left and right in my haste to get to the bottom, where the hard-sided case lay with the Wyeth safely inside. I hoped. The case was still there, but I unzipped it and peeled back a corner of wrappings to get down to the wax-pa-per layer protecting the painting's surface. Through the hazy, translucent layer, I saw enough to calm my racing heart.

Mikel had slipped away, but he'd left me the Wyeth. Why? Tucked into the case outside the top layer of protective wrap-pings was most of a sheet of notebook paper. I pulled it out, saw the missing corner that matched the scrap on the table, and turned it over to reveal a much longer, hastily scrawled note in Mikel's handwriting.

*Claire,*
*It's later.*
*I have to go, but I want you to know how all*
*this happened. Ren's father hired me to find the*
*Wyeth 15 years ago. All he told me was that*

Eva Riordan hadn't had a chance to include it in her will, and it was stolen shortly after her death. He didn't tell me it belonged to you, or that you were looking for it. He told me he and Eva were close, and he wanted the painting for himself. Now I think he meant to give it to you, for what it's worth.

I don't think he knew Pearson killed her, because he would've had me start there if he had. Without your clue about the guestbook, we wouldn't have found it, so I didn't feel right taking it with me.

I don't know if Ren will come clean about this, so I'm doing it for him. He found out his father hired me, and we met to talk about my progress. That was almost a year ago. He didn't tell me you were looking for it. He never mentioned you by name. But he did put me in touch with a certain wealthy donor at the Kimbell who needed an art thief.

Lastly, about the Caillebotte. Remember our deal—keep it to yourself. I know it's your favorite, but my version is pretty good too, right?

Tell your folks thanks for the van.
MC

I read the note three times, then folded it up and put it in my pocket. Half of me wanted to keep it, and the other half knew I needed to destroy it. I wasn't ready to decide yet.

*

Driving through the night, I got back to Ren's house around 3:00 a.m. Wednesday morning. I'd taken the long way, through Lubbock, out of vague paranoia about being followed. By whom, I couldn't say. I was less than shocked when Ren let me inside with the unhappy news that Annika had vanished about twelve hours ago.

"I'm sure she's fine," I assured him. After he'd heard my news about Mikel's abscondment in Amarillo, he seemed to relax.

He looked tired, ten years older, as he sighed, "So they're probably together. Good. I've been worried sick about that kid."

"Ren." I gripped his arm, preparing myself to ask him about what I'd read in Mikel's note. I chickened out and asked, "Do you want to see it?"

"Heck yeah."

He helped me bring all my luggage inside, then poured us each a glass of champagne while I found the hard-sided case and set it down on the kitchen island. Our mutual sadness about Mikel and Annika took a back seat for the moment; I was practically vibrating with excitement as I unzipped the case and started stripping away all the coverings. A layer of waterproofing, three layers of wool padding, more waterproofing, and then I was down to the painting itself, wrapped in wax paper that had been taped over it like Christmas wrapping. I carefully set the painting face down on the discarded wool to rip off the wax paper, and to Ren's and my mutual surprise, we found a cream-colored envelope tucked into the bundle.

"You have to read the card first," Ren said, grinning.

"Oh, fine. I don't even know what this is..."

The envelope was made of expensive-feeling vellum and unsealed, and on the front was an elaborate, embossed 'P' that quickly turned my smile upside down.

"I think this is from Pearson's house," I whispered. "How…?"

Inside was a tri-folded, single sheet of plain paper. One side was blank, and the other was a photocopied Bill of Sale. My eyes slid over the words again and again, seeing nothing.

I passed it to Ren and said, "You read it, my brain is shutting down."

He took the paper, studied it for a moment, and said, "This is a bill of sale for a painting. It says you paid Paul Pearson twenty-six thousand dollars for a nude self-portrait by Eva Riordan. That sure looks like your signature, Claire."

He showed me the paper, his finger helpfully directing my gaze to my signature. Next to it was what appeared to be Pearson's signature. Since the original had been run through a copier to produce this sheet of paper, only the shape of the signatures was probative. I was willing to bet the original had been destroyed.

Ren dropped the paper and pulled out his phone. I finished unwrapping the painting and turned it over, groaning. It wasn't the Wyeth. It was the Riordan.

"You transferred twenty-six thousand dollars via EFT on Sunday to a numbered bank account. The memo just says 'painting'. Claire… What is going on?"

"How did I have that much cash on hand?" I argued.

"Looks like I gave you a payout of the same amount earlier that day. Which I absolutely did not." He slammed his phone down on the counter, growling, "That wretched demon child…"

I wanted to scream and laugh at the same time, but laughter

won out. "So I drove all the way up to Montana to personally buy this painting from Paul Pearson. Wow. That is… exactly something I would do." I mulled everything over and forced myself to say, "Ren, I have to tell you something."

He moaned, "Do you? Do you really?"

"Art and Fart told me you and Mikel talked the day before I introduced him to you. They've got most of a case against all of us, even Annika. They told me to get them enough evidence to nail Mikel and you if I could, or they'd prosecute me for accessory after the fact. I don't think they're interested in prosecuting Annika, at least."

Ren stared at the ceiling, thinking. He sighed. "I think you better give them what they want. You can't go to jail, Claire. I can't let that happen."

"Were you involved? With the Kimbell?"

I held my breath, silently begging Ren not to lie to me again. He shook his head, and my heart sank, but he said, "Barely. Leonard Money had been hounding me for months to find him an art thief. I wasn't planning to help him, but last year my dad decided to spring the surprise of the century on me. You may not believe this, but Dad hired Mikel years ago to find that painting. He hated to see you getting disappointed over and over, but he didn't have the heart to tell you to stop. He knew you needed a mission, a purpose, especially after… Anyway. I found some payments to Mikel and asked Dad about them, and he spilled the beans. I met with Mikel, he agreed to let me pass his contact info to Money, and we got to talking. I knew right away you'd like him. And I was right, wasn't I?"

"You were playing *matchmaker?*" I cried.

"I didn't think you'd try to blackmail the guy!" He almost

laughed, pulled himself together with the aid of a swift drink of champagne, and said, "How else was I going to get you to cut the cord with Marty?"

"You meddling, unbelievable... I can't... I'm speechless. Actually speechless."

"And yet, you speak."

"Since we're being honest, finally, I did already know some of that." I found Mikel's note in my pocket and passed it to Ren. "I'm glad you decided to tell me the truth." I watched Ren read Mikel's note and sipped my champagne. As soon as he finished, I asked, "Is it true? You never mentioned me by name?"

He gave me a cagey, tight-lipped. "Mhm."

"Because I've been wondering how Mikel knew about the gin and Topo. He ordered me one, when we went out. Said it was a wild guess. It's not that important now, but still."

"It's true that I never mentioned you by name... until after I set him up with Money."

"Oh, boy."

"He was casing the Kimbell for a long time. He noticed you, asked me if I knew you. What was I going to do, lie?"

I barked a laugh. "Imagine that."

"I told him I used to date you. Gave him the tip about your drink. Amongst other things."

"I hate you," I said, unable to keep from smiling. "I don't think Mikel needed any leg-ups from you."

"I thought he might."

"You know, I never would have called him if I hadn't noticed that the Caillebotte was a fake. That was what gave me the idea to blackmail him."

"Did it?" Ren asked, not caring.

"I went straight to it the day after the break-in and noticed Mikel's signature immediately. Of all the paintings in the Kimbell, some worth a heck of a lot more than the Caillebotte, why steal that one? Was he trying to get my attention? Did he know it was my favorite? If so, who told him?"

Ren shrugged. "Who knew?"

I soaked in his self-satisfied smile, wanting to slap him. "No. Huh-uh. He told me himself, if he'd known I'd pick up on the fake that quickly, he wouldn't have signed it. He was telling the truth about that, I'd bet every last penny on it."

"Maybe I didn't mention that it was your favorite. Maybe I just threw out, in casual conversation, that it was worth fifty million dollars and would soon be going back to France. Whatever he did with that information was his choice."

"Horse manure."

"I swear on my mother's grave, I did *not* think you'd blackmail the guy."

"Well..." I finished my champagne, declining a refill. "Whatever you did or didn't do or say or lie your butt off about, you were right. I really liked him."

"He liked you too, Claire Bear. I'm sorry it turned out like this."

# 30

*July 28*

TWO MONTHS TO THE DAY AFTER the break-in, I found myself back at the Kimbell for the first time since spotting Mikel's forgery hanging in the Caillebotte's frame.

The beloved Impressionist masterwork was returning home to France the next day, and it had been gracing the Kimbell's collection for so long that most people didn't know it was on loan from the Musée d'Orsay. Loyal fans of the painting had been dismayed to hear it was time to say goodbye, and that had translated into big-time bucks for the Kimbell.

For a cool $650 donation, anyone could have the pleasure of wishing the Caillebotte farewell at a black-tie, after-hours exhibition at the museum. The Kimbell's staff were welcome to attend for free, but my attempts to get my security guard job back had failed. My name was Mudd, at least in the art museum world, but no one stopped me from laying down $1,300 to secure tickets for Ren and me.

We both needed the forced pause of a black-tie affair, even if it was on a Monday night. Ren had been pulling unspeakably long hours trying to purge his physical and digital records of any trace of contact with Mikel, going back fifteen years to when Ren's father had hired the art thief. The more he looked, the more he found. He was beginning to fear the whole exercise was pointless.

Meanwhile, the Fort Worth detectives were losing patience with my unhelpfulness and had begun alluding to their deal having an expiration date. I privately believed that was unsportsmanlike and had publicly hired a lawyer on Ren's recommendation. My lawyer had scared the cops into giving Lucius back after they'd impounded the Hellcat as evidence, but he had yet to persuade them to leave me alone.

We were exhausted, worried, and—though we didn't talk about it—we missed Mikel and Annika. They had vanished so quickly and completely that I knew we'd never see them again unless and until they wanted to be seen. When I'd heard about the farewell exhibit, I'd jumped at the chance to regain some meager form of connection with Mikel by viewing his incredible forgery one more time.

Arm-in-arm with Ren, I led him through the dense crowd to the Caillebotte. It hadn't yet been moved from its long-standing location. All that fuss was slated for tomorrow, after which it would be loaded into a specialized, climate controlled truck, driven to the airport, and entrusted to the cargo hold of a commercial flight bound for Paris.

When we stopped in front of the painting, or as close as we could get within the milling crowd, I let the colors wash over me for the last time ever. Maybe it wasn't really a Caillebotte, but it was close enough. I even allowed myself the simple enjoyment of counting the rivets one last time.

Much too loudly for the fine-looking crowd around us, I

blurted, "Twenty-*six?*"

Ren gave my arm a tug, whispering, "Keep it to a dull roar, please."

I put my lips to his ear to hiss, "That sneaky little show-off broke in here again and covered up the extra rivet. Look, count them."

He did, and I waited with bated breath for him to react in some way. He just laughed.

"You think this is funny?" I asked. "He was here… He was *right here.*"

I felt moisture queuing up in my eyes and blinked furiously, trying to keep this from happening. I was *not* going to cry at the Kimbell, in front of Ren, in a five hundred dollar dress. Ren pulled his arm out from mine and wound it around my shoulders, gently guiding me away from the Caillebotte.

"None of that. Come on, let's get you a drink."

"I don't want a drink, I want him." Ren stopped, giving me time to rethink that, and I sighed, "But if a drink is all I can have, lead the way."

Over cocktails in a sheltered, quiet corner, Ren and I enjoyed several minutes of reminiscing about Mikel and his one-of-a-kind little sister. This devolved into an argument that we'd already had six or seven times: Do we tell the Kimbell about the fake Caillebotte, or not? I was against it, but Ren insisted my deal with Mikel was already moot. Mikel had taken the Wyeth, and it didn't look like he intended to give it back to me.

"He didn't say he'd give it to me, he said he'd help me find it," I said.

"The intent was perfectly clear," Ren shot back.

"Well what good would it do to tell them now? We'd only

end up in worse shape legally than we already are."

"That's awfully mercenary, don't you think? Telling them is the right thing to do."

"Oh don't try that," I scoffed. "If I can live with it, I know you can."

For a moment I thought I had him, that the argument was over once and for all. He fell silent and gazed into abstraction behind me. I turned around to follow his eyeline and was forced to reassess. He was actually eyeballing a stunning woman who seemed to be returning his attention.

"Do you know her?" I asked.

"Actually, yes. Do you mind if I…?"

"Go for it. I'm heading home, anyway. This shindig seems to have lost its pizzazz."

Ren gave me a swift, very chaste hug goodbye and made a beeline for the woman. I carried my empty cocktail over to the bar, exchanged it for a full one, and returned to the centerpiece of tonight's to-do. The crowd had thinned somewhat, allowing me to get closer to the painting. I searched for visual evidence of Mikel covering up his signature, but he'd done too good a job. The painting was now indistinguishable from the Caillebotte to my eye, and I wondered how long it would take someone to notice the switch. Probably a while, unless the Musée d'Orsay made a habit of checking recently-returned paintings for authenticity.

I stood in front of the painting until my drink ran dry again, then found my way into the gift shop to buy an exhibition catalog to commemorate the night. The usual paving-stone sized catalog assembled for an exhibition had been pared down to the size of a small paperback, since there was only one artist and one painting to gush over tonight. I bought a copy and flipped through it, searching for a photograph of the Caillebotte.

There were dozens, of course. The booklet included photos of the painting dating back decades to when the masterwork first arrived at the Kimbell, paired with various art world heavies, celebrities, and politicians who'd come to see it over the years. The last photo featured the museum curator and some other staff assembled around the Caillebotte. Though they were much harder to see, I counted the rivets again. Twenty-seven. I slammed the book shut.

At least I had physical evidence that I hadn't imagined the whole darn thing. Happy with my purchase, I hailed a cab and headed back to my apartment.

In the lobby, I glanced toward Mr. Miller at the front desk, but he wasn't there. Trying not to be worried by his absence—he was probably just in the bathroom—I continued up to my apartment. Inside I slipped off my shoes, hung my keys on the hook by the door, and hurried to the shelf by the TV to add my newest exhibition catalog to its rightful place.

I was so focused on this satisfying chore that I didn't notice the person sitting on my sofa until she said, "Dude. How are you not noticing me?"

I whirled around. How *had* I missed her? A young, blonde woman, petite in the extreme, was sitting on my sofa starting up at me from behind an oddly familiar pair of overlarge glasses. I had to stare at her for several, breathless seconds before recognition broke through her odd appearance.

"Annika?"

"Yeah. Wow, you were *so* focused on that bookshelf. I'm gonna worry about you now..."

"How did you get in here? Is... is Mikel...?"

"Sorry, just me. In disguise, even worse." She tugged at her blonde hair, which had to be a wig. "That's a really pretty dress."

"Uh. Thanks. I paid way too much for it." I stood awkwardly in the middle of the living room, waiting for her to explain her sudden appearance. "Do you want a… oh, not a drink. Some water?"

"No, thanks. I just came to give you some gifts from Mikel. He would have come himself, but, um… He didn't."

The lame excuse made me angry, which I didn't want to be. I was happy to see Annika, to know she was alive and well. I swallowed my anger but still said, "One of those gifts had better be an explanation."

"Several, actually," she said happily. "Who's first, Wyeth or Caillebotte?"

"What? Uh… Wyeth, I guess."

"Okay. Well. He's keeping it. I assume you've figured that out already." I nodded. She went on, "He does feel bad about it, but I couldn't convince him to give it to you. He thought if I told you exactly what he did, you'd be less mad, which isn't making a lot of sense now that I'm saying it out loud…"

I sat down next to her. "Give it a try anyway."

"He was always gonna keep it. Apparently he made sure the deal was for him to help you find it, but not *get* it? I had nothing to do with that, by the way. When you told him about the similar painting by your aunt, he decided to take both and switch them. He put the Riordan in the van, then brought the Wyeth up to the room so you could put it in the case yourself. Then he switched them while you were busy in the room. He had me put together the bill of sale and transfer a post-dated payment to Pearson to make it look legit. The old man hasn't reported the theft, by the way. I'll get to that part in a sec."

"I have to admit," I said, pausing to get my emotions under control. "I really didn't think he'd do that to me. He seemed like a good guy."

"He is, but… Claire… he's a thief."

"Where is he?"

"Laying low, which I'm supposed to be, but this had to be done in person. You were at the Caillebotte farewell tonight, right? Did you notice anything about the painting?"

I refused to give her the answer she wanted, responding with nothing but a blank look.

"Here, maybe this will jog your memory."

She reached over to grab a long, cardboard tube that had been leaning on the arm of the sofa next to her. I hadn't noticed that, either. She opened it, pulled out a bundle of canvas that was bigger than she was, and passed it to me. I couldn't help but set it on the floor and unroll it, but my eyes wouldn't accept what I was seeing. By size alone—it was nearly four feet tall—I had a sneaking suspicion what it was even before I registered the blues, the train, the curve of the bridge. I unrolled it far enough to see the rivets in the center of the bridge.

"This is the fake?" I breathed.

"The work of Mikel's own hands. Good, isn't it? He wanted you to have it, so you can rest easy that the one going back to France tomorrow is the real thing."

"When did you… When did he…?"

"Well, taking it down was a lot faster than putting it up," she said.

"Putting it up where?"

"At the Kimbell. He put it in the frame over the real one."

I sat back on my heels, the large roll of canvas curling back onto itself as soon as I let go. I didn't understand any of this. "He never took the Caillebotte out of the Kimbell?"

Shaking her head, she said, "I wish I could take credit for this one, but it was all Mikel. He always meant to take it in transit—meaning tomorrow. That's *much* easier. But he wanted to give it some time, to let people get used to it and let photos of it get into circulation. And if someone noticed the fake, they'd take it down and find the original behind it, and they'd have a weird mystery on their hands, but not really a crime." She studied the look on my face and said, "I know, I know. There was still no reason to add the extra rivet. My theory is, he wanted someone to notice, so he wouldn't have to take the real one. He's very self-sabotaging. Won't admit it to save this life. Anyway, he knew you'd think he fixed the forgery and let it go to France, so he told me to give you that."

"Why give up on the theft at all, though? His stupid plan was like ninety percent done."

"Well obviously the fact that Money figured it out was a huge liability. Especially since we still don't know *how* he found out. Plus, he wanted to let you off the hook. It was the least he could do. Now you don't have to worry about the real painting. And he claims he saw a stolen painting in Pearson's house that gave him a 'come to Jesus' moment, whatever that means."

I wondered whether she meant the reproduction of Vermeer's *The Concert*, which had been stolen from a museum in Boston years ago and never recovered. I didn't ask. I wasn't sure my brain could handle anymore explanation.

Almost afraid of the answer, I asked, "Is there anything else?"

"Oh, yeah." She'd hidden a thick, manilla envelope between herself at the arm of the couch. She handed it to me with a sigh of deep regret. "I found out about your deal with the police while you and Mikel were in Montana. I really wanted to clear Mikel's name, but that's beyond even my skills. He's cooked, hence the laying low. So, you can give that to the cops. It's all the evidence they need to lock him up for a long time, and we kept Ren's name out of it."

I gripped the envelope, asking, "What about you?"

"Also cooked, but a minor, so maybe they'll go easy on me if they ever catch me. Either way, your deal was for evidence, not a conviction or jail time. If they don't honor it, I'll fire-bomb the entire Fort Worth Police Department."

"Literally?"

"We'll see. Now, just a few more things, then I have to get out of here. That night we hung out in the hot tub, I was mad at Mikel because he knew the police would have our phone records, because he was an idiot and gave you his phone number. Instead of telling you that, he risked everything to keep you in the dark. He *claimed* he told you about his deal with Ren's father?"

"He did."

"Okay, good. On the off chance you ever want to see Mikel again, I'm supposed to tell you that's very unlikely. At least not for a while. Either he'll have to run out the clock on the statute of limitations for what he did, or we'll find some proof that Pearson killed your aunt, and we'll try to leverage that for leniency. It's all really uncertain. Okay."

She stood up, unusually short even for her thanks to the flat-soled shoes she wore. I stood too, sensing the imminent end of her visit.

"This one is from me."

I accepted the piece of paper she held out. "Phone numbers?"

"Top one is Iliana Pearson, bottom is Teal. The real Teal. That was *not* easy to find, even for me. I've been reading correspondence between Pearson and his wife that they definitely think is private. Get her that painting she wants, the one by the Stillman lady, and I think you might find she's got loose lips. I think she knows what happened when your aunt died, and she's about to find out her husband is a murderer."

I raised my eyebrows, not sure how to respond to that. Her smile was so serene and self-satisfied. I said, "Annika, I'm going to miss the heck out of you. I'm seriously never going to see you again?"

"Let's not talk about never," she argued. "Anyway, I think that's everything. I better go. Mikel told me to say, 'I love you, and I'm sorry, and you can keep looking for the Wyeth if you want.'"

She gave me a quick, tight hug and darted away, across the apartment and out the door before I could say a word.

# Epilogue
## *Later*

I WAS NEVER A BIG FAN of life getting back to normal. Normal meant forgetting things. Memories and feelings faded to the point where they couldn't hurt or thrill me anymore, and that the last time I saw someone would be the last time I'd see them in this life. Inevitably that day would come where I'd wake up and go about my business without a second thought, as though my life hadn't been changed at all by events and people that should have changed it forever.

Something that should hurt, should knock the wind right out of me, didn't cause pain or joy or anything. The first normal day came and went without fanfare, and life was back to normal whether I wanted it to be or not.

A normal weekend meant catching up on the latest organizing influencers, exchanging messages with new clients, decluttering my apartment, drinking wine, and deep-conditioning my hair. I was doing all five at the same time one Saturday afternoon when a text chirped from my phone. It was Mr. Miller. He'd finally agreed to text instead of calling, which I thought was very kind. It was my problem that phone calls still made my heart race and were therefore reserved exclusively for Pam Larson.

He'd texted, "Visitor here to see you. Mrs. Pearson. Ok to let her up?"

I said "Sure" right away, not really believing it was the Mrs. Pearson I thought it was. In one minute I'd wrapped my gooey hair in a towel, thrown on some clothes, brushed my teeth, and come to grips. Of course it was *that* Mrs. Pearson. How many other people could it be?

I'd called Teal the very next morning after Annika gave me his number, and the call had rung once before going to voicemail. He'd screened me out. I'd left a voicemail I hoped would be tantalizing enough to get his attention, dropping Iliana Pearson's maiden name from her days of supermodel glory and telling him an unnamed mutual friend had given me his number. All Iliana wanted was a phone call, I'd claimed, because he was the only person who could help her acquire a Stillman she had her eye on. I'd recited Iliana's number, hung up, and never heard back.

If they'd made a deal, I expected at most a thank you note. A personal visit was a bit much.

When her knock came, I was more or less ready to answer the door. It wasn't like I could prevent Iliana's appearance from making me feel like a stray cat that had wandered inside. I opened the door and there she stood, a woman of sixty-eight ready and waiting to be mistaken for my younger sister. Iliana was thirty-eight when Aunt Eva died. I was thirty-eight now. Why that was significant, I didn't know. I also had no idea what to say to her, so I just stood there looking dumb.

"Hello, Claire. I'm sorry to come unannounced." Her eyes

flicked upward to the towel around my head. "Is this a bad time?"

"No. Come in. Can I get you something to drink?"

"Water, please. Thank you."

I grabbed her a bottle of water and added one for myself, thinking maybe staying hydrated was her secret. I'd try anything. She followed me from the kitchen to the living room and sat down on my sofa, facing the front door and perching on the very edge of her seat. Her body language was almost fearful. She definitely did not want to be in my apartment. In black slacks, a black silk shirt, and violently red heels, she struck such a pretty picture I actually looked around for a hidden cameraman.

"What brings you all the way to Texas?" I asked, leaving the "and my apartment" part unsaid. When she didn't answer right away, I sat down at the opposite end of the sofa and decided to wait her out. I was in no rush.

Finally she said, "I left Paul. I live in Manhattan now. Bell decided to come with me, and he's doing well in the city. I think he missed it."

"Iliana, I'm happy to see you, but why the heck are you here?"

She took in a deep breath, but it seemed dissatisfying. She opened her water bottle, took a tiny sip, and then another deep breath. "I know you gave my number to Teal. I don't know how you did that. He was able to sell me *Mariana*. I can't tell you what that means to me. The man we talked to, that night... that wasn't really Teal, was it?"

I shook my head silently.

"However you did it, thank you. This arrived shortly after the sale was finalized and I was still waiting for the painting to be delivered."

She found a folded sheet of paper in her purse and handed it to me. I hardly glanced at it before bursting out laughing. She frowned, annoyed.

"I'm sorry," I pressed my hand to my mouth to stem further laughter. The photocopied message, assembled from cut out magazine and newspaper letters, looked like a movie prop. "Is this real?"

"I didn't think it was. I was ready to throw it in the trash. But when Paul saw it, the way he reacted… It must be real, to him. A bit sensational, but effective."

In ragged lines of mismatched letters, it read, "You killed Eva Riorden. I have proof. You will be hearing from me." I scanned it several times, unconsciously searching for a clue about who made it. I suspected Annika, but at length I realized who Iliana must suspect.

"Iliana, I didn't send you this. I know how to spell my own last name."

"I don't care who sent it. It's Paul's problem. I want nothing more to do with it."

"So… why are you here?" I asked again.

"To tell you what happened thirty years ago. I know what I saw and what Paul told me, but none of it made sense until I saw the way Paul looked at that ridiculous message. When I understood what it meant, that he murdered her, I left. He's not going to tell you any of this, so I am. I owe you that."

"Wow." I looked down at the note again and said, "I'm going to pour myself a glass of wine. Do you want one?"

"Yes, I do."

I poured the wine, we each finished our water, and then I sat back to sip and listen while Iliana Pearson launched into her story.

"Paul and Eva were lovers for a long time. They were very close, practically married. I know he loved her. She must have felt the same way, because at one time she was going to leave most of her fortune and her home in Pasadena to him. She told him, and then he told me. We had been carrying on an affair on and off since I was twenty-nine. I got pregnant with Bell, and he thought if Eva found out, she'd change her mind about remembering him in her will. He was right.

"She didn't find out until Bell was nine. We were all so close, and by then I thought everything would be okay. Paul was being faithful to Eva, and I had Bell, and I considered Eva a very good friend. But I brought Bell over for a visit one day, and I think she looked at him and realized—Well, you met him. He's obviously Paul's son. It's always been obvious.

"Three days before Eva died, she had a party at her house. That was nothing unusual. She and Paul disappeared for a while, and when he reappeared he left immediately. He looked angry. He called me the next morning and told me he wanted to be a better father to Bell and wanted me to give him another chance. As though *I'd* ended our relationship.

"He told me much later, after we'd left Hollywood, what he and Eva talked about that night. She was drunk. She showed him a very valuable painting by Andrew Wyeth and told him she was leaving it, and the money she'd been going to leave him, to you instead. But she said she hadn't had a chance to change her will yet. Paul didn't realize until the reading that she only meant the painting, not the money. When he learned you were getting the money and another friend of ours was getting the house, he went back to the safe and took the painting. He told me he wanted something to remember her by. And she'd been so drunk she'd said the combination out loud while she was entering it.

"He knew he'd stolen it, but he didn't think anyone would care. He thought no one else knew about the Wyeth. When he showed it to you, he wanted to see your reaction, to see if you knew Eva meant you to have it. Now I know he killed her, because he thought he could stop her from changing her will. It was just about money, all along. He tried so hard to get in touch with Teal—the man you introduced to us as Teal—to buy that sketch, but he didn't care about *Mariana* at all.

"This note, about proof. I don't believe it. I don't think any-one can prove he killed her. But as long as he believes they can, the Wyeth and the Riordan are safely yours. That's the way it should be."

She pulled more paperwork from her purse, this time tucked into a file folder.

"Here is the provenance paperwork for the desert nude your aunt painted. It was worth a lot more than twenty-six grand, but he kept the money, so that belongs to you."

Iliana left her unfinished wine on a side table and rose gracefully to her feet. I was so overwhelmed by everything I'd just heard that I watched her walk all the way to the front door before I realized she was leaving. I hurried after her.

She paused at the door and turned back to me. "Thank you for letting me get that off my chest. I'm sorry for what Paul did. I miss her, too."

I couldn't think of anything to say but, "What about Hilda and Otto? Did you take them, too?"

She smiled warmly. "They love Manhattan. Silly beasts."

We said our goodbyes and she left, and I tried to return to my previous tasks. I needed to rinse the goo out of my hair, nail down appointments for next week, and get some food into my stomach. The paperwork from Iliana had to be filed away with the rest of my provenance documents, and I had to decide what to do with the note she'd left lying on the sofa.

Forgetting all of that, I walked into my guest room-office-art gallery and got to work on a project I'd been putting off for far too long.

Mikel's fake Caillebotte was so large, especially after I'd had it framed, that it wanted to take up an entire wall all by itself. I'd given up on rearranging everything to make it all fit, with the result that my spare room looked like a torna-do-ravaged war zone. Pictures leaning against the wall, ham-mer and stud finder sitting right out in the open like decora-tions, drywall filler solidifying on a putty knife I'd left out. It was disgusting.

Several hours and a lot of expended patience later, I had it all sorted out. Paintings were level, old holes in the wall were patched and painted over, and order had been reestablished. The Christenson, as I was now calling it, occupied the end of what was now Gallery One. Gallery Two, once I began assembling it, would have to spill out into the living room.

As a final touch, I found a small sticky note and wrote "Eva Riordan" on it. This I stuck over the words "Andrew Wyeth" on the plaque next to Aunt Eva's self-portrait.

I had no plans to give up my search for the Wyeth, but with no empty frames in my gallery, I finally felt like I could take my time and enjoy the chase.

Thanks for reading! If you enjoyed *The Lost Portrait*, please take a couple minutes to leave a review or rating wherever you found it. Reviews help readers decide whether to buy my books, and every single review helps so much—even the bad ones!

Want to be the first to know when new stories come out? You can sign up for my mailing list on my website, akweller.com. You'll get my occasional newsletter, and you'll receive a link to download a free short story.

▼

## About the Author

AK Weller was born and raised in Texas, moved to New Mexico, and now lives in Montana with her husband, four cats, and three dogs. She mostly enjoyed brief careers as a technical writer, private investigator, social worker, and pet sitter before finding her calling as a semi-employed writer. AK writes mysteries and thrillers while running her own graphic design business. Her favorite books to read over and over again were written by JRR Tolkien, Stieg Larsson, Sue Grafton, Michael Crichton, and JK Rowling.

<u>Book 3: Bigger Fish</u>
Home from her unlikely triumph in Argentina, Anna thinks her life is getting back to normal until a surprise visit from David Marchand sets her on a collision course with Luke Jackson once again. With a little help from two people straight out of Anna's past, they'll unravel a mystery that takes them out of the frying pan and into the fire.

<u>Book 4: No Port in a Storm</u>
After unraveling a murderous family feud, FBI castoffs Anna and Jim travel to Italy to deliver a final peace offering. Amidst their fraught romance, they find no shortage of ways to make new trouble. While fostering unlikely friendships against an idyllic Mediterranean backdrop, they provoke dangerous enemies closer to home. Emily, Luke, and Dude were supposed to be safe in Texas, but suddenly they're in the crosshairs again. As tensions escalate, Jim's clever schemes are put to the test. When generations of hostility erupt into all-out war, will Jim's cunning save them, or will Anna's fighting spirit be their only way out?

▼

## Coming soon from AK Weller

<u>2.15.2020</u>
In the prequel to *Enemy Closer*, Anna Bowman escapes her boring hometown and joins the FBI. After a few years as a quiet but efficient cog in the machine, she tries to achieve her childhood dream of becoming an FBI Agent, only to be rejected and bewildered. Ensnared instead in the intrigues of Agent James Camposanto, Anna will embark on an unexpected assignment in Houston, Texas with her protégé, Thomas Holladay. What really happened on February 15, 2020, in Houston, and how in the world did a divorced art historian from Manchester, Texas end up there?

<u>Friday the 14th</u>
Anna Bowman and her older sister, Emily, just wanted a fun night out to celebrate Anna's twenty-fifth birthday. While enjoying some much-needed time away from their significant others, the sisters accidentally pick up a new friend at a casino in Oklahoma. When a tongue-in-cheek plan to burn down each other's houses and collect the insurance money falls into the wrong hands, Anna and Emily will have to band together to stop an arsonist... if they decide they want to. Find out who's left standing on *Friday the 14th.*

### A Last Time for Everything

*A Last Time for Everything* tells the tragic and unbelievable origin story of 17-year-old Anna Bowman and the events that set her on the path to joining the FBI.

## Sam Walsh, PI Mysteries

### Prequel - Tiger by the Tail

Private Investigator Samantha Walsh has been in denial about her true identity for 25 years. When a terrifying figure from her past explodes back into her life, Sam will have to decide how much she's willing to sacrifice to stop running from her father's killers in Tiger by the Tail.

### #1 - Sam vs. the Black Hat

Newly independent PI Sam Walsh needs clients, and she can't afford to be picky. When her old boss sends a prospective client her way, Sam takes the case - a classic cheating spouse - against her better judgment. Caught between a dishonest client and a dangerous, shadowy foe, Sam will either solve her first case or die trying. Sue Grafton's iconic Kinsey Millhone is catapulted into twenty-first century Texas suburbia in book one of the Sam Walsh, PI Mysteries.

<u>Underworld: A Short Suspense Thriller</u>
Underworld follows mystery woman Seffy Nix as she moves into a 140-year-old mansion that seems to be haunted by a slovenly, inconsiderate ghost bent on distracting her from the mission that brought her to small-town Helena, Montana.

<u>The Beast and the Books: A Short Monster Story</u>
All alone one night, Rodney is clearing out a storage unit. His biggest problem is his wife's massive book collection, at least until the lights go out and he realizes he's not alone. Something is living deep in the bowels of the storage facility, and it's about to make a break for freedom. Unfortunately for Rodney, he's right in the creature's path.

<u>Anywhere But Home: A Memoir</u>
A short memoir about budding author AK Weller's increasingly nonsensical attempts to fill a void in her life caused by an abusive relationship. From Oklahoma to Texas to Colorado, she hops from one distraction to another until she realizes the answer to her problem is starting over.

<u>The Institute: A Short Story</u>
High school junior Miguel thought getting an underage drinking charge would derail his life at New Mexico Military Institute in Roswell, but when his new friends draw him into their world of pranks and mischief, he'll discover there's a lot more going on at NMMI than he ever imagined. Will Miguel maintain his hard-won GPA and graduate with a diploma that will open doors for him to wherever he wants to go, all while learning how to mix a little fun into his busy life? Will his new friends have his back when things start to get spooky?